THE TWILIGHT KINGDOM

FEYLAND BOOK 3

ANTHEA SHARP

FIDDLEHEAD PRESS

Visit the author at www.antheasharp.com and sign up for her mailing list, Sharp Tales, for a free story and news of upcoming releases!

Editing by L. Temple and Editing720
Cover by Ravven

QUALITY CONTROL: This work has been professionally edited, but typos still can slip through! If you encounter any typos or formatting problems, please contact antheasharp@hotmail.com so they may be corrected.

For all the musicians in my family – but most especially for Ginger.

PROLOGUE

In the dimness where night gives way to dawn, two fey monarchs met in the center of an oak-encircled clearing. The starlit grass shimmered with magic, cold and bright, as the pair faced one another.

Deep shadows stretched behind the Dark Queen. Stars tangled, icy and brilliant, in her midnight hair, and her eyes were black as an eclipse. Things better left unseen in the bleak hours of the night crept beside her on disjointed limbs. Their feral eyes glowed as they crouched in the clouded tatters of her gown.

The Bright King carried midday in his wake, his hair shining with remembered sun, his golden armor aglow. The small fire of pixies hovered at his shoulders, wreathing him in a crown of light.

The creatures of their courts watched the fateful meeting. Fantastical forms capered in and out of the trees or perched, moon-pale, wizened, and gnarled, upon the branches.

"Greetings, brother," the Dark Queen said, her dusky voice filling the silence like smoke.

"Well met, sister." The Bright King inclined his head. "Have you an answer to our troubles? Troubles which, I recall, you worsened with your obvious meddling in the mortal world."

The queen's eyes narrowed, glittering. "You failed as well, despite your trickery. Despite your promises and enticements."

Her tone was edged with ice, and the creatures nearest her shifted away.

"The mortals are clever," the king said. "Much as it pains me to admit such a thing. Fair Jennet and Bold Tamlin—"

"Speak not those names to me!" she cried. "Your pain cannot compare to mine. It is a constant coal burning beneath my breast. Yet we must lay aside our differences and work together. The entire Realm suffers, Unseelie and Seelie both."

At her words, the watching fey folk muttered and hissed. The bright lights trailing the king dimmed, and the cold midnight of the queen faded. A bitter wind stirred the grasses at their feet, bringing with it the scent of decay.

Glancing over his shoulder, the king lowered his

honey-rich voice. "It is dangerous for us to do so. It upsets the balance. We do not want to wake *them*."

"When have *they* bothered themselves with the Realm?" Frigid anger rolled off the queen. "We are dying from lack of mortal sustenance, and they pay no heed. Perhaps, when we break through into the human world, *they* will stir. But by then, it will be too late."

From the shadows, a tall, antlered figure raised his eerie head. The red-eyed hounds at his feet howled, their spectral cries wavering through the air—the Wild Hunt, always eager to be loosed.

"Leash your hounds," the king said, his voice tight.

"I will not wreak havoc upon your court, if that is what you fear." The Dark Queen laughed, the sound like ice cracking on a winter lake. "At least, not yet. So, brother, are we in accord?"

"Little good our rivalry does us, if our entire land is imperiled." The king frowned. "It forebodes me, but I see no other course. We shall strive together to restore our kingdoms. But mark me well—when strength returns to the Realm of Faerie, I shall spare you no mercy."

"Nor I you." The Dark Queen sent him a knife-edged smile.

The watchers in the shadows stirred again, their eyes bright and menacing. Blades and teeth shone in the silvery light and a band of redcap goblins hissed, eager to battle their long-standing enemies.

"Be still!" the Dark Queen cried, her voice slashing the air.

The goblins subsided, but restive tension hummed through the clearing. Brightness clawed farther above the horizon, and the dark creatures of the Unseelie Court drew back into the dimness beneath the trees.

"A truce, until the Realm is secure," the king said. "Together we will open the gateway to the mortal world. Now seal the bargain—in blood."

The queen raised an imperious hand, and one of her willowy handmaidens approached, a pewter bowl cradled between her hands. The faerie maid knelt on the soft grass between the monarchs and held the bowl up, her pale head bowed.

From her gossamer sleeve, the Dark Queen drew out a long, black thorn, the point sharp and deadly. The king nodded and produced a shining golden needle. The monarchs extended their hands over the bowl, each one poised to prick the other's palm to the bone.

The wind ceased and the fey folk held their breath. Silence descended across the Realm. In the dark bogs, Phoukas rose, lifting their eerie horse-heads. Hobs huddled in their bracken hovels, and even the most frivolous of pixies dimmed.

"By this blood, the Realm will live," the king said.

"By this blood, the Realm might die," the queen countered. "Seal our fate, brother."

The king's golden needle plunged into the queen's

palm. She let out a sharp cry, quickly swallowed. A trickle of blood, dark as midnight, fell into the bowl, and the faerie maiden holding it trembled.

Quick as dusk descending, the queen stabbed the king's hand with her black thorn. He hissed in pain as a trickle of blood, glowing like distilled sunlight, fell into the bowl.

The instant the blood touched blood, a vortex of light swirled up, red flame and cold blue fire, heat and darkness, flooding the clearing like a visible scream. The monarch's faces lit with eldritch color as light clashed against dark. Around them, their courtiers fell to the ground, turning their gazes away from that terrible light.

The tall oaks bowed and swayed, bending like grass as the land carried the magic deep into itself.

The maiden holding the bowl cried out, high and shrill. It was the sound of a hawk descending; it was the cry of its prey as cruel talons pierced to the heart. Radiance spilled from her body, then coal-black cinders as she turned to ash. The bowl tumbled to the grass, empty.

The Realm shuddered. Stilled.

"It is done," the queen gasped. "Seelie and Unseelie are united."

The king dipped his head, his face lined with strain.

"My court will linger no more in this place." She glanced at the sky. "Already it grows too light. We shall meet again."

She lifted a pale hand and swept back into the midnight half of the Realm. Her retinue followed: banshees with hollow eyes, sharp-toothed goblins, a silent-helmed knight encased in black armor, and all the varied dark denizens of the Unseelie Court.

The king beckoned his own court into the noontime brightness of his domain. They streamed into the light, pixies and hobs, sprites and faerie maidens, the clear notes of a harp shimmering behind them. Then the clearing was empty; only a charred circle on the grass bearing testament as dawn brightened the sky to pale gold.

Something stirred between the oaks, and two figures stepped from the shadowy trees. The taller one seemed nearly human, though dressed in faerie raiment. A battered guitar was slung across his back, and regrets and secrets lined his face.

His companion was a nut-brown sprite garbed in a tatter of leaves and dreaming, his hair tangled around his sharp features.

The two exchanged somber looks, a wealth of worry in the air.

"So, Bard Thomas," the sprite said. "It is as we feared."

"Aye." The man shook his head in a weary gesture. "The way forward is almost too difficult to contemplate."

A chill breeze shivered the leaves of the trees, and he pulled his cape more tightly about himself.

The sprite floated up until he could set one long-fingered hand on the man's shoulder.

"Hold fast," he said in a high, piping voice. "The balance will be restored. It must be."

Thomas nodded, his eyes deep with sorrow. "Yes. But at what cost?"

TAM LINN STEPPED up to the reception desk in the echoing VirtuMax lobby, his heart threatening to hammer right through his ribcage.

He glanced down at his jeans—the good ones, with the ripped hem barely visible and no holes in the knees. Even though he'd taken a shower and put on his cleanest clothes, he felt grimy in the pristine white lobby, as if being from the Exe left a stain around him—an oily cloud that followed wherever he went.

"Hi," he said to the woman at the desk. She looked almost plastic in her perfection. "I'm here for the beta-testing team."

She didn't meet his eyes—just stared at his access badge, as though she couldn't believe a guy like him was permitted here, in the hallowed company compound. He half-expected her to demand his badge; maybe bite on it to make sure it was real. As if he could have gotten past the gates and scanners using a dummy pass. With the security around VirtuMax, that would be severely impossible.

Finally, she wrinkled her nose and shoved a tablet and plas-pen at him. "Sign in. Full name. Purpose of visit."

He filled out the form, then slid the tablet back to her. Before picking it up, she shot a spray of disinfectant over it. Nice.

"Wait over there." She pointed her chin toward a row of white chairs on one side of the lobby, then watched him go as if she expected him to leave black streaks on everything he touched.

A professionally dressed woman with dark hair occupied one of the chairs. Head bent to her tablet, she didn't bother glancing up at him. Tam shoved his hands in his pockets, too nervous to sit. His gaze went past the receptionist, and he studied the angular silver logo dominating the far wall. VirtuMax. The best game company in the world—the company he'd spent years daydreaming about. He couldn't believe he was actually here.

Too bad it was for all the wrong reasons.

He'd made it through the front doors, but not as an internationally celebrated gamer or top-notch developer. No, he was just a high school student from the worst part of town whose life was fraying apart. The only thing he excelled at was simming.

And even that ability wouldn't have gotten him on the game-testing roster, except for his connection with Jennet Carter, whose dad was a project manager for the company. Tam still couldn't believe Mr. Carter had recommended him for the beta team. Not after warning him to stay away from Jennet.

Jennet—who was on the beta team, too. When was she going to get here?

He let his hair fall over his eyes and covertly studied the other woman waiting in the lobby. She didn't look like a gamer. For one thing, she was older than most simmers, plus she was dressed way corporate. Maybe here for some kind of interview?

Then the doors swooshed open and Jennet came through, and nothing else mattered. Her blond hair was braided back, and she was wearing a purplish sweater that made her eyes seem even bluer than usual. She saw him and walked right over, a big smile on her face.

"Tam—you made it."

He could tell she wanted to reach for him—take his hand or give him a hug. He wanted it, too, with a yearning that twisted inside him. But here in the VirtuMax lobby, in front of the receptionist and who knew how many cameras? Bad idea. He forced himself not to lean towards her, lift his hand and touch the satiny skin of her cheek.

"Of course I'm here," he said. "Didn't you send George with the grav-car to pick me up?"

"Well, yeah." She glanced down at the floor. "I thought, for this first time, maybe you wouldn't mind."

"It would have taken me about three times as long otherwise. So thanks."

No buses ran up to the privileged compound of The View, and certainly not to the high-security headquarters beyond. VirtuMax didn't want the town riffraff coming anywhere near their pristine, well-ordered little world.

"Who else is on the team?" he asked. She'd have inside information.

"Do you want the good news first, or the bad?"

"Bad—but don't tell me. It's Lassiter, isn't it?"

She nodded, and he tasted the tang of bitterness on his tongue. Roy Lassiter was the son of VirtuMax's CEO, and a decent sim player. He was also a prime ego-head, with a huge grudge against Tam and Jennet. A grudge that wasn't entirely unwarranted, though it was Lassiter's own fault things had gone the way they had.

Being on a team with him was going to be... interesting.

"The good news is that Zeg's playing too." Jennet raised her brows at him. "That *is* good, right?"

"Yeah." He let out a breath. "That's pretty prime."

Zeg was old enough to be his dad—in fact, he was the uncle of Tam's good friend Marny, and ran the best sim café in Crestview. He was a techie and a gamer of the highest order. The tension running through Tam went down a notch. It was a huge relief to know he wouldn't be the only non-Viewer on the team.

"That's Coranne Smith over there." Jennet tipped her head toward the woman perched on the chair. "She's an employee. They pulled her in from another unit for beta testing."

So, the professional-looking woman was on the team after all. She didn't seem very intimidating—but outside appearances could be deceiving. In-game, she might turn out to be a fearsome player.

"Anyone else on the team?" he asked.

"Yes." Jennet hesitated. "Um—my dad."

Tam swallowed back a curse of surprise. Of course. It made sense, in a crazy way. Jennet's dad could keep an eye on them the whole time and make sure his daughter wasn't being contaminated.

"I couldn't believe it, when he sent that message he'd recommended me for the beta team," Tam said. "I thought he hated me."

"He doesn't hate you." Jennet let out a low sigh. "He just doesn't think you're good for me."

"Yeah, spoilage from the Exe, trashing up his place. Sullying his daughter."

Color bloomed in her cheeks, though she held his gaze. "One kiss is not 'sullying.' And you're not spoilage, so stop it. He knows we make a great team. He can't ignore that, even though he doesn't quite believe Feyland is real. At least he understands we watch out for each other."

"I've pulled you out of the fire a time or two," Tam said.

And he'd go right on doing it—anything to keep her safe. It seemed her dad cared enough about her well-being to bend some of his own rules. Tam felt a grudging spark of respect for the man. At least they could agree on this one thing.

"And vice-versa." She set one hand on her hip. "I've rescued you an equal number of times, Tam Linn. Not that I'm keeping track or anything."

Damn, he wanted to gather her into his arms and hold her tight, despite the cameras and onlookers. She'd gotten him out of the most severe trouble he'd ever known. He could never repay her for that brilliant courage, though he tried.

He let out a silent breath. Seriously, he needed to keep his distance from Jennet, at least where people could see. No sense breaking the tenuous peace between him and her father.

"Six people on the beta team," he said. "That seems sparse for a project this big."

"Trust me, I've had to listen to Dad complain about it endlessly. If he were still project manager, he'd have run things differently, but Dr. Lassiter is pretty tight about stuff. People have to get clearance, and since the prototype FullD systems are only playable on-site—well, it's not easy to find testers."

Because Crestview was a nothing town in the middle of nowhere. She didn't have to say it. Anyone with any talent got out as soon as they could. Although, since VirtuMax had moved in, that could change.

"I wish Marny liked to sim," he said.

She was the most solid person he knew, physically as well as mentally. Too bad she was claustrophobic. It was an understatement to say she and sim equip didn't get along. Donning the gloves and helm, sinking into the sim-chair—it was too much for her. The only time she'd ever simmed, she'd been under a magical persuasion that hadn't ended well.

There was a commotion at the door, and he glanced over to see a group of people enter the lobby. A couple of them were obvious security-types, surrounding a young woman with bright magenta hair. Tam blinked, astonishment rooting his feet. Only one person in the world had hair like that. Superstar gamer Spark Jaxley.

"No way," he breathed.

Jennet's eyes were wide, too. They watched as the receptionist came out from behind the desk, practically bowing to the ground as she greeted the new arrival.

"Welcome to VirtuMax, Miss Jaxley. Such an honor. Please come this way. We have a private room where you can wait until the rest of the team is assembled."

The gamer nodded, and her whole entourage turned and followed the secretary down the wide hall.

"She said *team…* do you think Spark Jaxley is going to be beta testing with us?" The question shivered through him, and he couldn't quite wrap his head around the idea.

"Dad mentioned something about the company trying to bring in big outside talent." Jennet sounded unsure. "This is huge, though. I bet VirtuMax offered her a sponsorship for the FullD. After all, she represents their Slix system."

"Right."

Tam had seen the vids advertising the company's top-end sim system. Spark Jaxley was featured prominently, her bright hair flying as she performed one amazing in-game feat after another. It would make sense to pull her in for the FullD launch, though it no doubt cost VirtuMax an astronomical sum. Enough to feed the whole city of Crestview for five years or something. His stomach hurt, thinking about what Spark was probably worth.

Half of him wanted to turn on his heel and stalk out of the VirtuMax compound, where the privileged air and knowing looks of the employees were making him sick. But he couldn't do that to Jennet, or to her dad, who'd put himself on the line by recommending Tam.

The other half of him, though, was more than ready for the challenge. That part relished the idea of pitting himself against the best gamer in the world. And winning.

"Attention." The amplified voice of the receptionist echoed sharply through the lobby. "All beta-testing team members please assemble to the right of the desk. You will be escorted to the game hub momentarily."

"Roy's not here," Jennet said. She didn't look too upset about it.

"Probably having gourmet coffee with his mom in the CEO's office." Tam looked out the glass-fronted doors as they walked by, scanning the empty walkway for a bear-like figure. "I hope Zeg makes it."

"I'm sure he'll be here in just a minute." Jennet pressed her lips together in that worried way of hers.

"If they let him through the gates."

He could just see it—Zeg in his battered old gas car, smoke pouring out the back, while the Viewer security guys tried to find some reason to turn him away.

"He's got clearance," Jennet said. "Dad told me everyone was good to go."

"Then we'll see him soon."

Tam said the words firmly, like he believed them. Like saying them would make them real. He needed Zeg to show—needed some solidity from the world outside the compound's walls, to keep him grounded. Remind him of what was true.

The air was sterile and cool in the VirtuMax halls, but heat flushed just under his skin. Tension tugged his breath. There was too much at stake, too many variables and secrets to navigate: Jennet and her dad, Lassiter's enmity, the astounding fact of Spark Jaxley's presence.

Not to mention a game that held layers of deadly magic.

2

JENNET HADN'T EVER BEEN SO deep inside VirtuMax's headquarters. As the receptionist led her, Tam, and Coranne Smith down the hall, she couldn't help peeking into the rooms they passed. Mostly just people sitting in front of screens—until they got to the tech hub.

It was a huge round space, divided by partial walls that didn't reach the high ceiling. Each section featured a different type of VirtuMax's products—an array of Slix systems with five people geared up and playing, a bank of netscreens showing the games the company had developed over the years, and in the back, spotlit like star performers, the FullD sim-systems.

The receptionist marched up to a black-haired man standing in the middle of the hub. "Here are your subjects, Mr. Chon," she said. "I've alerted Miss Jaxley, Mr. Carter, and Roy Lassiter to come down."

"Thanks." The man nodded his dismissal, then turned to face the newcomers, his expression unreadable. "As soon as the others join us, I'll give you the intro speech. Meantime, sit tight."

There weren't any chairs. Jennet shot Tam a look, then turned, getting a feel for the place. The hum of running equipment underlaid the pings and occasional explosions coming from the games. It was like being in a sim café—except the gamers were oddly silent. No whoops of joy or exclamations of distress. When playing became a job, did it really take all the fun out of it? Or were the players just more self-conscious, gaming under scrutiny? She'd know soon enough.

Tam nudged her with his elbow, and she looked up to see Roy Lassiter coming toward them. His face was set in a scowl that didn't do much for his already ordinary looks.

"Jennet Carter. Dragging your trash behind you, I see. You should have left the Exie back in the slums— where he belongs."

"Shut it, Roy." She felt Tam clench with anger beside her. "He's a better gamer than you are, and you know it. Or did your forget that duel you guys fought?"

"Oh, I remember." Roy's mouth twisted, and he glared at Tam. "Just stay out of my way."

"I plan on it." Tam glared right back.

Jennet folded her arms. "If that's the thanks we get

for saving you, Roy, maybe we should have left you in the Bright King's court after all."

"Like I should *thank* you for ruining my life?"

She was opening her mouth to reply when Spark Jaxley walked into the room.

The hub suddenly buzzed with activity, as though the queen bee had arrived. Players and techs set aside what they were doing and came to cluster around the magenta-haired gamer, their voices full of praise and admiration. Her security guys stood back and let her shake hands and exchange words with her fans—which seemed to be all of VirtuMax.

"Miss Jaxley!" Mr. Chon waved for her attention. "Please join the briefing. Everyone else, get back to work."

With a smile of regret that looked real, Spark Jaxley moved away from the throng of admirers and came to join the rest of the team. Two of her entourage followed.

"Sorry," she said. Her voice was low and husky. "It won't happen again."

"I'd hope not." Mr. Chon glanced at her security guys. "These gentlemen won't be necessary. You do understand that the beta testing is under the utmost protection. They're welcome to wait with the rest of your people, in the suite."

Jennet raised her brows. Spark Jaxley got a suite. Of course. Probably she'd have a gourmet meal catered in for lunch, while the rest of them ate at the employee cafeteria.

Spark nodded, then exchanged a few low words with her men. They left, no doubt back to donuts and coffee.

"All right." The black-haired man swept his gaze over them. "We're missing—ah, there you are, Mr. Carter."

"Ready when you are, Mr. Chon."

Jennet's dad came over to her. She noticed he didn't look at Tam, standing on her other side. Awkward. She'd be simming with her dad and her off-limits boyfriend, inside a computer game that could kill them. Fun times.

"Now we just need Mr. Fanalua," Mr. Chon said.

Zeg. Jennet rubbed at the burn scar on her left palm. Would he make it? For Tam's sake, she hoped so. She glanced at Tam, noting the tightness of his shoulders, the wary look in his green eyes. Having Zeg here wouldn't fix everything, but it would help.

Mr. Chon's messager pinged. Frowning, he looked down at it, then let out an exaggerated sigh.

"Our final team member is on the way. I expect you all to be prompt in the future."

"I was here in plenty of time," Roy said. "It's those townies—unreliable."

"Hey." Tam stepped forward.

Jennet set her hand on his arm, willing him to relax. If he rose to Roy's baiting, they'd never get anywhere. Spark Jaxley watched the interchange, one bright eyebrow cocked. Clearly, she didn't miss much.

On the other hand, Coranne Smith was staring off to the side, seemingly lost in her own thoughts and paying no attention to the undercurrents swirling between Tam, Jennet, and Roy.

The receptionist marched up to the group with a slightly breathless Zeg in her wake. She delivered him without a word, then turned on her heel and clacked back down the hall.

"Sorry 'bout that," Zeg said.

He smiled, looking like a big bear, all beard and frizzy brown hair. His eyes were sharp, though—skimming over the assembled team and probably taking in way more than he'd ever let on.

Mr. Chon sniffed, then glanced at the glowing clock numerals prominently displayed on the wall above them. "I expect dedication, people. Dedication means you're here on time. Now, we're behind schedule, so listen up and hold any questions until the end."

Zeg shrugged out of his jacket, and moved to stand beside Tam. Jennet could practically hear the anxiety humming through Tam ease off.

"Welcome to the tech hub," the team leader continued. "I'm Lan Chon, and I'm in charge of this beta testing. Any problems or issues with the game or setup, let me know. We're here to iron out the bugs. I understand some of you have experience playing earlier versions of Feyland."

He paused, his gaze questioning—though surely he

already knew who had been in-game before. This was just to inform the rest of the team.

"Yeah," Roy said, crossing his arms.

Jennet and Tam simply nodded.

"Forget anything you think you know about the game. We've made a number of changes since..." Mr. Chon cleared his throat. "The content has been reconfigured."

Jennet knew the words he'd just swallowed. Since Thomas Rimer, the lead developer, had died. In his sim chair. Playing Feyland. She shivered.

"VirtuMax is looking to launch the FullD system with Feyland in three weeks, so we have a lot of work ahead of us."

Coranne Smith shifted, and Roy muttered something under his breath.

Mr. Chon held up one hand. "Yes, it's a tight deadline. That's why we need you here every weekend and most afternoons. The company has some ground to make up, since the game's... restructuring. Which is why we insist on punctuality." He glanced at Zeg, who just looked complacently back at him.

Three weeks. Jennet bit her lip, hard. Despite what Mr. Chon said, she had the cold suspicion Feyland wasn't that different. Maybe the game interface had changed but, deeper in, things were no doubt as magically treacherous as ever.

Tam's hand brushed against hers, like he knew what

she was thinking. How could they keep VirtuMax from ever releasing Feyland?

Because once the game was out, the mortal world would never be the same.

Mr. Chon led them to the back of the hub. "This is the FullD area. Each of you has been assigned a sim system."

He gestured to the row of premium sim chairs, the gleaming helmets, the gloves studded with LEDs. Behind her, she heard Zeg pull in an awed breath.

"There are tablets at each of the chairs," their team leader continued. "At the end of every hour-long session, please take the time to note down any questions, concerns, or unusual events that might have occurred during that time."

Unusual events? She glanced at Roy. Had he managed to convince his CEO mom that something was severely tweaked with this game?

"Please locate and stand beside the system marked with your name. Your tablets are pre-loaded with the information you've provided, so please, make sure you're in the right place."

The endless questionnaires from VirtuMax had asked everything: age, likes and dislikes, every scrap of gaming experience she'd ever had. The company was thorough, she'd give them that. But would they be conscientious enough to actually pull Feyland from production? Provided she and Tam could prove how dangerous the game was.

"Scuse me," Roy said. "Can't I just play at home, on my system there? I mean, won't that be more like the average player's experience?"

Mr. Chon frowned. "Feyland and the FullD are configured for multiplayer immersion. These systems have been tuned to perform together. So, no, you can't go off and play at home."

"But I have three systems networked. Couldn't I take a couple others with me—one or two of the leet players?" He wiggled his eyebrows at Spark Jaxley, obviously trying to get in good with her.

"I'm aware you have equipment at home." Mr. Chon's voice was cool. "However, we need you to remain in a supervised and controlled environment. Whatever you choose to do in your spare time is your business, but if you want to be on the beta team, you play here."

Roy huffed out a breath. "Fine."

Mr. Chon set his hand on the back of the first sim chair. "You're at this end, Roy." He continued down the line. "Coranne, you're next, then Miss Jaxley. Mr. Linn, Miss Carter, Mr. Carter, and Mr. Fanalua here, at the other end. Please take your places and sign in on the provided tablets."

Roy shot Tam a venomous glare—clearly *he* wanted to be the one sitting next to Spark Jaxley. Not that it mattered. Once they were in-game, they'd all be in the same space. Or would they? Jennet already knew there were two pathways in Feyland, one leading to the Dark Court, one to the Bright. Both were full of danger.

And what about the mysterious *other* path? The one she and Tam had been told would open before them when they needed to find it? She'd caught a glimpse of it, once, an eerily luminous circle of thin-stalked purple mushrooms.

Throat dry, she settled in her chair, glad to have Tam and her dad flanking her. Maybe it didn't matter who she was next to, but she found it comforting. She picked up her tablet and signed in. As she pulled on the sim gloves, Mr. Chon continued with his briefing.

"I won't be accompanying you in-game. Your helmets are fed into a flat-screen array, which I'll be monitoring with my developers. Coranne Smith will be acting as company liaison inside Feyland. If you have an issue, let her know. She's been entrusted with the game master codes and overrides. Please take careful note of any problems you encounter, and fully log your report onto your tablet at the break."

"Do we have to all play together?" Roy asked. "I mean, won't you get more data if there are a couple different groups exploring the game?"

"Eventually," Mr. Chon replied. "For now, you're going in as a group. Your interfaces have been loaded with a few pre-selected character classes, so that we can get a feel for the playability and skills as they interact."

"You mean we won't be able to choose which class we play?" Tam asked.

"You will—in a limited sense. However, Mr. Linn, your gaming preferences have been taken into account. You'll be satisfied with the options provided."

Which wasn't much of an answer, except VirtuMax knew what character types he'd chosen in the past. The company knew where all their personal preferences lay, even if, like Spark and her Dad and Zeg, they'd never set foot in Feyland.

"Lame," Roy mumbled.

She couldn't tell if it were directed at Tam, or at VirtuMax for limiting their choices. Still, it was the company's test. They could run it how they wanted. Nothing changed the fact that she and Tam had a nearly impossible task ahead, regardless of what characters they were playing.

"Gear up," Mr. Chon said. "The point of this test is to see how players navigate the game, so I'm not going to give you any more information. Again, please pay attention to any difficulties you encounter. Good luck."

Jennet glanced at Tam. They were going to need all the luck they could find. He gave her a half-smile.

"See you in there," he said, then pulled on the gaming helmet.

She took a deep breath and did the same.

The visor screen was dark, except for white letters blinking in the lower right corner.

Feyland: A VirtuMax Production
Beta 1.1.004

Faint music began playing, mysterious and chiming. Light slowly etched across her vision, a delicate tracery like webs or tree branches.

WELCOME TO FEYLAND

The words unfurled on the screen. The letters glowed a rich gold that deepened to crimson, then faded to grey, as though they had burned down to ash. The music twisted, and the dim letters suddenly whirled up into a flurry of dark-edged leaves.

The last time she had played, Jennet had glimpsed eyes watching from the shadows—but not this time. Still, tension pulled at her shoulders. Who knew *what* was watching, waiting for them inside the game.

The screen cleared to show the familiar character-creator interface, but instead of the usual dozen types of characters and classes, Jennet had a choice of three.

Spellweaver had always been her top pick—there was something appealing about standing back from the fight and throwing blasts of magefire at her opponents. Magic was more fun than hacking at stuff with a sword, though she had no doubt Tam would end up with one of the heavy-armor melee classes.

She clicked on the next character, a fox-faced Kitsune holding a bow and dagger. Another magic user, though it was a tricky kind of magic, relying on illusion and elemental forces. The last time she'd played a

Kitsune had been with Roy Lassiter. The memory left an unpleasant taste in her mouth.

Her third option was a Healer. She rolled her eyes. Why did the game designers always think girls wanted to play that role?

All right, Spellweaver it was.

Now to choose how her character looked. In the past, Feyland had always made the in-game avatar similar to the person playing. If she chose dark hair, the game turned it blond. It was a player's first indication that something was freaky and Feyland had a mind of its own.

She deliberately selected short black hair, green eyes, and a small mouth—none of which she possessed in real life. There, that should give her something to report on when the game changed it. She gave the Spellweaver a different name, too. Xandra. No way *that* could be mistaken for Jennet.

"Finish selecting your characters." Mr. Chon's voice sounded through the helmet speakers. "Then enter game."

Okay, she was ready. Well, as ready as she'd ever be.

Jennet pressed her lips together, and sent her character into Feyland.

3

GOLDEN LIGHT FLASHED through Jennet's senses... but without the disorienting lurch she usually felt when going into Feyland. When the light cleared, she found her character standing in the center of a grassy glade. She shot a quick glance at the faerie ring of mushrooms surrounding her, trying to determine where she was in the game.

From prior experience, she knew that moon-pale mushrooms led to the Dark Court, and white-speckled red ones began a journey to the Bright Court. And that one time—a shiver scraped the back of her neck—she had seen those strange purple mushrooms, their stalks luminous and eerie.

This ring mixed the pale and the red mushrooms, with none of the weird purplish ones. She let out a breath. Did that mean that they weren't going to go to either of the courts?

Tall trees surrounded the clearing, their leaves shimmering silver in the breeze. But unlike her other times in-game, she couldn't feel the wind on her face. She sniffed, barely detecting a faint herbal scent in the air.

Feyland was an incredibly immersive world. For too long, she'd thought the FullD system was responsible, that VirtuMax had made incredible tech breakthroughs.

And they had—but the magic of the Realm of Faerie had intensified the experience far beyond the programmer's dreams. Yet this version of Feyland was strangely lacking. Had the company truly managed to partition the game off from the Realm, without even knowing about it?

Other figures were materializing in the clearing as the rest of the beta team arrived in-game.

Tam was a Knight—no surprise there—wearing gleaming silver armor with a sword at his side. Next to him, Spark Jaxley glanced around the clearing with one eyebrow up. Pointed ears pricked out from her magenta hair, and she had a bow strapped to her back. Looked like she'd chosen the Kitsune class to play. Somehow, it fit her. She'd managed to match her hair color exactly, although her features were slimmer and more feral.

Roy arrived next, in his usual character of choice—Mercenary. He swaggered over to Spark, his gold armor and arm-bands shining.

"What do you think?" he asked, his voice crystal-clear through the speakers.

The celebrity tilted her head. "I'll let you know when I have an opinion."

"Oh." Roy's smirk faded.

Clearly he'd wanted Spark to say something about how great his avatar looked. And he did look good—all muscled and sporting a huge, two-handed sword—though not as good as Tam. Jennet shared a tiny smile with her knight.

A large figure in a hooded grey robe appeared next to Tam.

"Zeg?" Tam asked.

"Yep."

The character pushed back his hood and smiled, brown eyes twinkling above a frizzy beard that covered most of his face.

"I didn't know there were beards in the character creation interface," Jennet said.

"There are, if you know where to look."

"You rolled a Priest?" Tam asked.

"I figured a group this size, somebody needed to play heals."

Zeg laced his fingers across his stomach, looking natural in the robes. A blunt mace dangled from his belt, but his character wouldn't be doing much fighting. Jennet made a note to keep an eye on him. A good team looked out for one another, and *especially* didn't let their healer get into trouble.

"Who are we missing?" Spark asked.

"My dad," Jennet said.

Of course. He was the noob in the bunch, the one with practically no gaming experience. This was going to get embarrassing real quick.

"Great." Roy folded his arms. "Team Carter for the win."

"Shut it," Tam said. "Not everyone has wasted the hours you have in this game."

"You know, I think we ought to test out the duel capabilities here," Roy said. He pulled his sword off his back. The edge glinted, sharp and dangerous. "It's a new feature—one that will help you remember your place, Exie."

Jennet drew in a breath. Would injuries carry over, even in the beta testing? She didn't want to find out quite this soon.

"Boys." Zeg held up his hands. "Save it for later. I'm sure Mr. Carter will be here any moment."

As if waiting for his cue, her dad's avatar material-ized in the center of the clearing. He was bald, wearing bright saffron robes, and carrying a quarterstaff.

"A Martial Monk?" She couldn't help the way her voice shot up at the end of the word.

Oh, this was just great. Not only was her dad a

complete beginner, he'd chosen one of the flashiest classes to try and play.

Dad grinned at her and held out his hand. A small gray rock sat on his palm.

"Snatch the pebble from my hand," he said.

Before she could say anything, Roy swooped in and grabbed the pebble. He held it up between his index finger and thumb, then shook his head.

"Gotta work on those reflexes," he said.

Quick as a flash, Zeg was standing there, holding the pebble. Roy looked down at his empty fingers and made a face.

"As do you, young Padwan," Zeg said.

Jennet smothered a laugh. It was good to have Zeg along.

"Coranne?" her dad said, turning in a circle. "I thought I was last one in. You here?"

Suddenly, Coranne Smith appeared at the edge of the circle. Her character wore all black, with a black headband holding back her dark hair. A wicked-looking dagger hung at her side, along with a spiked morning star. She'd chosen a Rogue as her character—and she had somehow arrived in-game and gone invisible without any of them noticing.

"Yes," she said, her voice dry. "Are we finally ready to begin?"

"Come on," Roy said, gesturing to the mossy path

that led away from the faerie ring. "First quest-giver is this way."

"What happens if we go into the woods?" Jennet's dad asked.

He turned and took a few steps into the forest, his robes brilliant orange against the green and silver foliage. Then, abruptly, he disappeared.

"Dad!" Jennet cried.

"Hey, hey, it's all right." He reappeared in the center of the ring. "Guess we can't go that way."

Ms. Smith nodded. "There are certain parameters built in. Even though we can see the woods, we can't go there. Not every landscape is fully accessible."

Jennet thought back to her and Tam's earlier adventures. They'd certainly gone off the path more than once —but they'd been in the Realm of Faerie then. This was the game.

But would it *stay* the game?

The party of seven started down the path, Roy in the lead. Tam hung back, taking up the rear, which didn't surprise her. The woods rang with the sound of birdsong but Jennet didn't see any birds. She glanced up into the riffling leaves overhead. Nothing moved there, no bright feathers, no silver shimmer of pixies.

It didn't take long to reach the end of the grove and emerge from the trees. Set at the edge of a flower-spangled meadow sat a classic thatched cottage. Whitewashed walls gleamed, and red geraniums spilled from the flowerboxes edging the diamond-paned windows.

An odd creature stood on the front step. It had brilliant lime-green hair that stuck straight up, a knobby nose, huge feet, and big ears that fanned out on either side of its head. It watched them approach with wide, friendly eyes.

"So," Spark said, "how do we know which Non-Player-Characters are interactive?"

"Talk to them," Jennet's dad said. "If you get no response, they're just for color, not actual characters who can advance the game."

"That could get annoying," the magenta-haired gamer said. "Isn't there some way the designers can flag the active NPCs? I don't like wasting time in-game."

"Hm." Jennet's dad nodded. "Maybe we could give them a special tabard or something, so they're recognizable. Don't forget to write that suggestion down during the response period."

"Everyone ready?" Roy asked.

He stepped up to the creature, clearly about to activate the first quest.

"One moment, Roy," Ms. Smith said. "I think it would be more useful to let someone with no experience of the game take the lead here."

"Yeah," Tam said, so quietly Jennet almost didn't catch the words. "That's sort of the point of beta testing."

She caught his eye. Of course Roy would try to run

things. She was glad Ms. Smith was along to help slap him down.

"Fine." Roy folded his arms. His mouth flattened into a petulant expression.

Jennet glanced over the party. Even though her dad was the total noob here, he at least had some knowledge of the game mechanics. Coranne Smith, too. That left Spark and Zeg as the outsiders.

"Miss Jaxley?" Zeg held his hand out, palm up. "Care to do the honors?"

She shook back her magenta hair. "Call me Spark, everybody. Last names seem so formal, and we're going to be spending a lot of time in here together."

Roy perked up at that, and Jennet could almost see the thoughts turning behind his eyes. Yeah, right. As if he and Spark Jaxley would ever hook up. Jennet suspected the gamer-girl was smarter than that. She'd probably seen more than her share of shallow, opportunistic guys.

"Greetings," Spark said to the little creature. "We are a band of travelers newly come to this land. Have you any advice for us?"

The girl had the lingo down, that was for sure.

"Hello," the creature said. "Welcome to Feyland, where many thrilling adventures await. I can assist you, but only if you gather me twenty-four Rondel Blossoms from yonder meadow. Do you agree to my task?"

"Yes," Spark said.

Ding. A chime filled the air, and Zeg looked up.

"What was that?" he asked.

"The game has indicated that we accepted the quest," Coranne Smith said.

"Flower picking." Roy gave a snort. "Weak."

"Maybe," Zeg said. "Still, you don't want to underestimate even the simplest actions. Who knows what picking flowers could lead to?"

"Come on," Jennet said, leading the way into the meadow.

The grass grew knee high, scattered with purple, bell-shaped flowers. It was strange to see the wind moving the grasses, but not feel it. She'd gotten used to Feyland's uncannily real atmosphere. Without the magic of the Realm, the game seemed flat. Did Tam think so, too? She'd have to ask him, once they got out.

"The flowers are glowing," Spark said.

Jennet's dad opened his mouth, but before he could answer, Coranne Smith spoke.

"If something glows, it's an indication that you can interact with it in the game environment."

"Glad she's not my teacher," Tam said into Jennet's ear. "She'd put me to sleep during every lecture."

Her dad stood in front of one of the purple blooms, frowning. "How do I pick it?"

"With your hands?" Roy said.

Jennet's dad waved his hands, passing them right

through the flower. Roy rolled his eyes and reached for the bloom. And missed. Tried again.

"It's obviously bugged," he said, frowning.

The other members of the party were trying to pick the flowers, with no luck. Zeg was making a game of it, as if by sneaking up on the flower, it wouldn't notice him and would let him pick it. Roy pulled out his two-handed sword and started swinging it in broad, flashing arcs, trying to behead the blooms.

Tam and Jennet watched from a safe distance. Beyond the meadow, a dark forest rose, evergreens spiking up into the sky. Clouds began to gather in the distance.

"You try," Tam said.

She reached for a nearby bloom, but didn't have any more luck than the rest of them.

"Definitely broken," she said.

"One moment." Coranne Smith held up one black-gloved hand. "I'm going to exit game and get this solved."

An instant later, her character disappeared.

Roy strode over to where Tam and Jennet stood. "Ready to duel, Exie?"

"Is Player-Versus-Player combat even enabled in here?" Jennet asked. Roy had said so, but she didn't believe everything that came out of his mouth.

"It would be good to find out." Tam gave her a serious look.

Jennet rubbed her palm. He wasn't talking about the ability to fight other players. He wanted to know if injuries would carry over into the real world—a sure sign that the magic of the Realm was in effect. And a compelling bit of evidence to show VirtuMax that their game had severe issues.

Still, she didn't want Tam to risk himself, just to see if he could.

"You're on," Roy said. "Give us some room, blondie."

He hefted his blade and gave Tam a toothy grin.

"It's all right," Tam said to her. "I'll be careful."

She knew better—he'd be his usual drastically heroic self. If he let his arm get cut off, she would never forgive him.

She stepped away, heading to where Zeg and Spark stood. Her dad, oblivious, was still trying to pick the flowers.

"Tam knows what he's doing," Zeg said. He didn't sound worried—but then, he didn't know what this game could really be like.

"I've always thought PVP was the best way to learn your character's abilities," Spark said. "Playing directly against another person, as opposed to the computer, always pushes the limits." She smiled at Jennet, an open, honest grin. "Hey, when the boys are finished, want to show them how it's done?"

Jennet glanced at her mage staff. The crystal at the end shone blue-white.

41

"I've played a Spellcaster in-game before," she warned.

Spark's eyes brightened. "I love a challenge."

"Okay then." She grinned back at the magenta-haired girl.

"Yaa!" Roy's yell cut through the air.

Jennet looked up in time to see him rush at Tam, his broadsword raised overhead. Tam had his sword drawn, his shield strapped to his left arm. He caught Roy's blade on the edge of the shield and diverted it, nimbly stepping out of the way, then thrust in with a counterattack. Metal clanged on metal as Roy swept Tam's sword out of the way.

"They're pretty well matched," Spark said.

"Both of them have seen serious combat in-game," Jennet said.

There must have been something in her voice, because Spark shot her a look, pink eyebrows raised. "All three of you have played the proto-version of Feyland?"

"Yeah."

Sort of. If getting sucked into the Realm of Faerie counted as the proto-version.

Another clash rang out as Roy and Tam connected, and Jennet turned her attention back to the duel. Spark was a smart one. Already it seemed the gamer-girl suspected there were things going on below the surface.

And, depending where the game took them, she might be in for more than she could imagine.

Roy gave a victorious shout as Tam dropped his guard, holding his shield way too low and not even pressing the attack.

"Tam," Jennet said under her breath. "What are you doing?"

Roy rushed forward, thrusting with the tip of his blade. Jennet's breath tightened. At the last second, Tam shifted to the left. Instead of Roy's sword puncturing his chest, the blade connected with Tam's upper arm. He dropped his sword, and she couldn't tell if it was because he'd truly been injured or not.

"Got you!" Roy cried.

Tam nodded. "You win. Good fight."

He didn't sound hurt, but Jennet couldn't stop herself from running to his side.

"You all right?" she asked.

"Yeah." He rubbed at his arm. "The game disarmed me when Roy got that hit in."

"Your armor looks okay."

The silver plate was unmarred—no big hole with Tam's blood seeping out. She released the breath she'd been holding, and reached for him. A flash of orange caught her attention as her dad came over. Those robes were way too bright. On the other hand, she'd always be able to keep track of him. Hastily, she dropped her arms and hoped her dad hadn't noticed the almost-hug.

"You guys were fighting?" he asked. "Is that part of the game?"

"Characters can choose to duel one another," Jennet said.

"For fun?"

Tam nodded.

"I'll have to try that some time," her dad said.

Great. "Not with Roy," she hurriedly said.

The last thing she wanted to see was her dad suffer immediate defeat at Roy's hands.

"I'd be honored to duel you, Mr. Carter," Tam said, sounding a little stiff.

The air in front of them blurred and Coranne Smith appeared, a black blot against the meadow.

"PVP can wait," she said in her usual, dry tone. "The quest should be fixed. Let's move on."

"Hey," Zeg called. He held up a purple flower. "It works."

"Good," Coranne said. "Everyone gather blossoms, please."

"How will we know when we have enough?" Zeg asked.

"They will cease being interactive," Ms. Smith said.

Seeing the puzzlement on her dad's face, Jennet added, "They'll stop glowing."

"Ah." He reached and picked a nearby bloom.

The rest of the party spread out. Soon everyone held one or two of the purple flowers. Jennet was reaching for her third when the light surrounding it faded. Another ding chimed through the air. They must have gathered enough of the blossoms.

"All right," Roy called. "We're done. Everyone meet back at the cottage."

On the heels of his words, a tremendous bellow shook the meadow. Tam thrust his flowers at Jennet, then pulled his sword and stepped to the front of the party.

Dark shadows gathered at the far edge of the meadow. Heavy thudding shook the ground, followed by the crash of breaking branches. The pine trees thrashed wildly, and a hideous ogre pushed his way out of the forest.

The ogre stood four times Tam's height, and his long, jagged teeth were filed into sharp points. He carried a spiked cudgel the size of a grav-car in his clawed hands, and his arms and legs bunched with muscle. The brown tunic he wore was covered with blotches and stains Jennet didn't even want to try to identify. His beady black eyes scanned the meadow and fastened upon their party. With another air-shuddering cry, the ogre lunged toward them.

4

TAM GRIPPED his sword tightly as the ogre hurtled forward. The monstrous creature lifted his cudgel, and Tam shifted. One good hit from that thing, and he'd be flattened. He'd have to take it down at the legs, try to even the height advantage. From the corner of his eye he saw Lassiter moving up. Coranne Smith flickered out of sight behind him. Good, the melee fighters were moving into position. He hoped Jennet could keep her dad back, although the monks were supposed to specialize in hand-to-hand combat.

As the ogre got close, Tam waved his sword. He wanted the enemy's attention firmly on him. Since his character was the tank—the one with the best armor—it was his job to take the brunt of the enemy's attack. Then the rest of the party could pour on the damage, hopefully without being pounded on themselves.

Quicker than he expected, the ogre brought his spiked weapon down in a blurring blow. Air whistled past Tam's left ear as he flung himself out of the way. The cudgel just brushed his side, then hit the dirt with a thud, spraying soil and uprooted grasses.

Yellow light flashed across his vision—the sign he'd been injured. He got to his feet, bracing himself for the pain that didn't come, and backed up a couple paces. An emerald glow surrounded him, and the flashing yellow light faded.

"Thanks for the heal," he called over to Zeg.

"Any time," the priest said. "I like keeping busy."

Lassiter moved in and swiped at the ogre's pillar-like leg. He connected, and thick green blood oozed from the cut. The ogre growled and tried to bash Lassiter, who jumped nimbly out of the way.

"First blood," he said, smirking at Tam.

An arrow sped from behind them and struck the ogre's shoulder, quickly followed by a bolt of arcane power—Spark and Jennet getting their hits in. Their enemy shook his head, searching for the source of this new aggravation, but before he attacked the less-armored members of their band, Tam surged forward. He plunged the tip of his sword into the ogre's thigh, as high as he could reach. Damn, the creature was tall.

Lassiter hit the ogre from the other side, and a flicker of black cloth behind their enemy revealed Coranne, plunging one of her daggers behind its knee.

"Raghr!" the ogre cried.

He stumbled and went down on one knee, swinging his mace in vicious sweeps. Tam leaped out of the way, but Lassiter got tagged and went down with a strangled *oof*.

A second later, healing green light covered the Mercenary, and he bounded to his feet. Good thing Zeg had rolled a healer—they'd be in rough shape now if he hadn't. Without his help, both Tam and Lassiter would be out of commission, leaving the rest of the party too vulnerable.

Arrows and spell-bolts rained down on the ogre. Coranne darted in and out, pricking at the ogre's sides and staying away from that evil cudgel. Tam narrowed his eyes, judging the distance to the creature's leg. The timing would be tricky, but if he could run up onto the ogre's bent thigh, he'd be within striking range of its heart.

"Cover me," Tam called to Lassiter. "I'm going in, left."

For once, Lassiter didn't argue. He moved to the ogre's right side, swinging his two-handed sword in big, flashy arcs. While their enemy was distracted, Tam pelted forward, blade at the ready. His momentum carried him onto the ogre's leg, the flesh rubbery and unstable beneath his boots. Before he lost his balance, Tam struck, aiming between the creature's ribs.

"Look out!" Jennet called.

No time to pull his sword free. As the ogre bellowed and thrashed, Tam jumped clear. An instant later, the cudgel whooshed through the air where he'd just been standing. The force of the ogre's swing twisted the creature and, still making a deep racket, their enemy toppled.

"Yeah!" Jennet's dad rushed over. "Look, we won!"

He kicked at the downed ogre's side.

The creature's closed eyes slitted open, black malice gleaming in its gaze.

"Mr. Carter, watch out!" Tam shouted as he lunged forward.

Too late. A last flick of the spiked weapon, and the ogre caught Jennet's dad squarely on the side. Orange robes fluttered as he flew through the air and landed in a crumpled heap.

"Dad!" Jennet rushed to his side and went to her knees. "Zeg, quick."

Silver light flared over the slumped figure of the fighting monk, but nothing happened. Mr. Carter lay unmoving.

The ogre let out a low groan, and Tam glanced over to see that Coranne had plunged a long, thin blade into its heart. No more unexpected cudgel-swipes—but the damage had been done.

"Dad—answer me." Jennet shook the monk's shoulder, a rising note of panic in her voice. "Dad?"

"I'm right here." Mr. Carter's voice came through the sim helmet.

Jennet's character sat down abruptly. "Where?"

"Uh, I'm in the mushroom circle where we entered the game—but things look strange. All washed-out and shimmery. I guess I died?"

"Yeah," Tam said. "Zeg, got a rez?"

Most healers had the capability of resurrecting a character who had died in combat. At least, they did in the normal games Tam had played. In Feyland the rules could get skewed. They were lucky there was no hint of fey magic around, or Jennet's dad would have been toast.

"How do I get un-dead?" Mr. Carter asked.

"If you were playing solo," Jennet said, "you'd have to run back to where your body was, and re-animate there. But Zeg should be able to catch you."

"Yep," Zeg said.

He raised his hands, forming a ball of light between his palms. The silvery glow floated over to the huddle of orange robes, and a moment later Jennet's dad sat up.

"Great," he said. "So, did we win?"

Tam glanced at the still form of the ogre lying on the trampled grasses, the hilt of his blade sticking out of the creature's chest. He strode over and wrenched the blade free. Slimy green blood marred the steel, and with a grimace he wiped it clean on the grass.

"Not the most elegant fight," Spark said, resettling her bow and quiver onto her back, "but we won."

"Dad, you have to be careful," Jennet said.

"How will I learn anything, if I'm careful? So—what now?"

"We turn in the quest and see what our next task is," Lassiter said.

Coranne Smith collected her own blade from the dead ogre's body. "It's time to break and fill out our reports."

"Can't we turn in the quest first?" Spark asked. "That way we can make sure this whole cycle is working, and get a feel for the game arc."

Tam smiled, inside where no one could see. Sure, Spark sounded all pro and casual, but he caught the glint in her eyes. She was hooked, and like any true gamer was longing to see where Feyland would take them next.

"Very well." Coranne said. "We can complete the quest."

"Let's go," Lassiter said, turning and heading back toward the cottage.

"What happened to the flowers we picked?" Spark asked. "Mine disappeared when the fight started."

"They probably went into our inventory," Jennet's dad said.

Spark tilted her head. "How do we access it?"

"In the lower-left corner of your interface, you'll see the letter *I*," Coranne Smith said. "Select it, and it will show you the items in your possession."

"I guess you've made some changes to the game," Jennet said.

"We are constantly refining the interface," Coranne said. "Don't assume you know how anything works, even if you're familiar with previous versions of Feyland."

"Right," Tam said, trading a glance with Jennet.

"Hey!" Roy Lassiter waved at them from the top of a nearby rise. "Are you guys coming or what?"

The others headed back through the meadow, but Tam lagged behind. As he'd hoped, so did Jennet.

"Do you think we can still summon stuff?" she asked him.

"One way to find out." He paused and held up his hand. "Cookies," he said, imagining the most delicious, mouth-watering chocolate chip cookies in the world.

Nothing happened.

"Hm," Jennet said.

She lifted her arm, her lips pressed together. Concentration made her blue eyes sparkle even more brightly, and then she shook her head.

"I guess being able to summon items had more to do with the Realm of Faerie than game mechanics."

"Makes sense," Tam said. "Remember how it would drain our energy when we summoned things in-game? That's pretty magical."

"You're right. But it changes things."

"Into a regular game, you mean." He frowned. He

didn't like the uncomfortable prickling thought that he actually *missed* the magical elements of Feyland.

"I know." Jennet's voice was a little wistful. "But that's what we want, right? A regular game, without deadly faeries trying to break through into our world."

"Yeah," he said. "Come on, let's catch up."

The rest of the party was waiting in front of the cottage, where the creature with lime-green hair stood, grinning, on the stoop.

Lassiter frowned at them. "What an honor to have you finally join us."

Tam didn't bother to respond, though he saw Jennet's dad give them the eye, too. Seriously, they hadn't lagged behind long enough to even get a kiss in.

"Everyone ready?" Spark stepped up to face the little creature, who blinked at them with its placid, wide eyes. "Greetings," she said.

"Brave adventurers," the quest-giver said. "You have completed the task I set you. I shall collect the twenty-four Roundel Blossoms now."

The same soft *ding* filled the air, accompanied by a flash of golden light. Tam made a quick check of his inventory and saw that the blue flowers were gone. In their place was a curled scroll of parchment.

"You have each been given a summons to the City of Stronghold," the creature said. "Beware the dangers along the road. Once you reach the city, you will have the opportunity to gain new skills and embark upon many more adventures. Good luck!"

"Stronghold?" Lassiter said. "Couldn't they get more creative?"

"It is a perfectly appropriate name," Coranne said stiffly.

Tam leaned closer to Jennet. "New content. Do you think this is Chon's work?"

They'd never seen a city in Feyland before, only a scattering of villages, groups of standing stones, and a few solitary huts. And once, the caverns of the Goblin King. A shiver prickled his skin. He and Jennet had barely gotten out of there without becoming the goblins' lunch.

"Probably Chon and his group added it," she said. "Standard world building."

Tam nodded. Most large multi-player games had at least one big gathering place where characters could re-supply, get new quests, meet up with others, and upgrade their skills.

"All right, everyone," Coranne said. "Please exit game and fill out your reports."

"Hold on." Lassiter held up one hand. "When we log back in, where will our characters be? 'Cause we used to have to complete an entire level before logging, or we'd be back at the beginning again."

Coranne Smith wrinkled her nose. "You'll find that a number of major bugs have been dealt with. You'll return to wherever you left your characters. In this case, the beginning of the road."

"What road?" Jennet's dad asked.

"That one," Zeg said, pointing.

Where there had been empty meadow, now a wide cobbled road led past the forest and disappeared over the rolling hills. In the distance the sky held a golden hue, and the wind riffled the tall grasses.

Tam and Jennet took a step forward, Spark and Lassiter right beside them. Something about that road called to them.

"Not yet," Zeg said in his deep voice. "The road will wait."

"Is X still the command to exit?" Mr. Carter asked.

"Yes," Coranne said.

Mr. Carter's character blinked out, leaving only air where he had been standing. Zeg followed, then Spark.

"Fine," Lassiter said. A second later, he was gone.

Tam tilted his head at Jennet. "After you."

As soon as her Spellcaster disappeared, he hit the X. It didn't escape his notice that Coranne Smith was the last to leave, her arms crossed, her expression set. Spy for the company, for sure—and he didn't trust her one bit.

5

JENNET PULLED off the sim helmet and took a deep breath. That had been... different. Encouraging, on one hand, that there had been no sign of fey magic—but also a little disturbing. She couldn't shake the feeling the faeries were just biding their time. It couldn't be this easy.

Around her, the other members of the beta team were pulling off their gear. Spark hopped out of her sim chair and stretched from side to side. She didn't seem to care that Roy couldn't take his eyes off her.

"Have to stay limber," she said. "Some day they need to invent a standing rig."

"Interesting idea," Jennet's dad said. "Write that down."

Mr. Chon hurried up, carrying his tablet. "It's about time," he said. "I expected you all forty-seven minutes ago."

"That's odd." Coranne Smith glanced down at the shiny, old-school watch strapped to her wrist. "I was keeping close tabs on the time."

"A glitch in the chronometer interface," Mr. Chon said. "Don't forget to flag it. Now please, don't talk amongst yourselves. I want your individual impressions, recorded as quickly as possible. Make note of any problems you encountered or questions you had."

The group fell silent as everyone input their experience of the new, improved Feyland. Jennet couldn't say everything she really thought. Since VirtuMax didn't believe the magic of the Realm of Faerie had ever seeped into their game, she could hardly point out how different Feyland felt without it.

"I'm done," Roy said after a few minutes. "Going to get a snack before the next session, all right?"

"We're done for the day," Mr. Chon said.

"What?" Jennet's dad stood and set his tablet down beside the sim chair. "Less than two hours of game play? What kind of test is that?"

"We have more than enough information to process for now," the lead developer said, a cold note in his voice. "And this is no longer your project, Mr. Carter."

Jennet's dad folded his arms. "We're back in tomorrow though, correct?"

"Yes," Mr. Chon said. "Two gaming sessions."

"But what about when the week starts?" Jennet asked. "Some of us have school."

She glanced at Spark. What was the celebrity simmer going to do about school? Surely not go to Crestview High. She probably had some fancy homeschool-type program going anyway, since she spent so much time on the road.

Mr. Chon looked at her. "If you'd bothered to read the schedule in full, Miss Carter, you'd see that we have a number of afternoon tests lined up. Being on the beta team shouldn't affect your studies."

His tone implied that if it did, she wasn't a very good student. Either that, or the testing was more important than anything she'd learn in school. And he was right— though not for the reasons he thought.

"Everyone—we'll see you here at 10 a.m. tomorrow," Mr. Chon continued. "Be on time."

He gave Zeg a look the big man ignored.

"I'll see you at home, Jennet," her dad said. "I'm staying here with Mr. Chon and Ms. Smith to help process the feedback."

"All right. Bye." She gave him a little wave.

Her dad worked too much, but it was important for him to get back on the Feyland project. For him, and for her. She glanced at the two other VirtuMax employees. They didn't look thrilled at having her dad stay—but they didn't seem inclined to kick him out, either. Every pair of hands was needed as the company pushed for release.

The rest of the beta team trailed out of the testing area. Roy sidled over to Spark and gave her one of his toothy smiles.

"Can I show you around Crestview?" he asked. "Not that there's much to see. Where are you staying?"

"VirtuMax is putting me up in the company guest quarters," Spark said. "Maybe I'll message you later if I feel like going out."

"Great—you do that. Here's my info." Roy held a card out to Spark.

Somehow Jennet wasn't surprised Roy had his own cards made up. What title had he given himself? Prince of Everything?

The gamer-girl took the card and put it in her pocket, with an expression Jennet recognized polite, with no intention of following through.

"Nice meeting you all," Spark said. "See you tomorrow."

She turned and went down the hallway, her magenta hair a bright slash of color against the silver-gray walls. Two of her security people were waiting. They took their places on either side of her and escorted her away.

Roy frowned and watched her go, then stuck his hands in his pockets.

"Later, Jennet," he said, ignoring Tam and Zeg

standing behind her. "I'm going to check in at the CEO's office and have a chat with my mother."

"Bye," she said, trying not to roll her eyes. As if they didn't all know that Roy's mom was the head of VirtuMax.

Tam fell into step beside Jennet as they headed for the lobby. She wished she could take his hand, or at least touch him on the arm.

"I didn't know VirtuMax had guest quarters," he said.

"They have one of the big houses set aside for visiting VIPs. I guess Spark qualifies."

Tam nodded. "For someone that famous, she's surprisingly real. Not as full of herself as some people."

He meant Roy Lassiter, of course.

"I don't think anyone can beat the Royal One when it comes to ego," she said, using the name the fey folk had called him. "But yeah, Spark seems nice."

Unfortunately. Here was this gorgeous, talented gamer, who—like Tam—came from a poor background, and she had to be a decent person into the bargain. It made Jennet uncomfortable, especially now, when she and Tam were off limits to one another. She let out a low sigh.

"I know," Tam said. "I wish I could come over."

"Why don't you?" She couldn't help the wistful note in her voice.

He shook his brown hair over his eyes. "You know that's impossible. Your housekeeper would love to blow the whistle on me. No, we have to be happy with what we can get."

Her throat tight, Jennet said, "It's not enough."

She'd finally gotten Tam to see that they should be together—just in time for the world to keep them apart.

His mouth twisted in a wry smile. "I've always had to make do, Jennet. Even this much of you is enough. For now."

Heedless of who was watching, she reached for him. He pulled her into a quick hug, and she felt the brush of his lips over her hair.

Zeg cleared his throat. "Want a ride home, Tam?"

"Sure," he said, stepping back. "It's a hike to the nearest bus stop."

They reached the gleaming lobby, where the receptionist sat at the front desk glowering at them like a black beetle.

"Care for a lift too, Jennet?" Zeg asked as they pushed out through the shiny glass doors.

"That would be great," she said. "Let me just grab my g-board."

Neither she nor Tam mentioned that she only lived a few blocks from company headquarters. Any extra time they could steal together was worth it.

She grabbed her board from the rack outside and tucked it under her arm. The day was cold and overcast, and she bent her head against the wind, glad she'd accepted Zeg's offer.

"I'm in the far lot," Zeg said. "Guess they didn't want my guzzler too near the front of the building. Give the wrong impression, you know." He winked.

Gas cars were still in use, but not by anybody who could afford the technology of grav-cars. Zeg's battered white sedan sat in the very back of the lot. Missing paint scabbed the front hood, and the rear passenger-side sported a huge dent.

"Put your board in here," Zeg said, keying open the trunk. "And the right back door won't open—crushed shut since I got hit—so go around."

Jennet stowed her board, wrinkling her nose at the combined smells of fuel and mildew, and slid into the back seat next to Tam.

"Close the door?" he said.

"Oh, right."

Embarrassment flushed through her. This wasn't a grav-car, where the doors glided open and shut at the touch of a button. She took hold of the inside handle and pulled the heavy door shut with a thud. Zeg turned the key, and the engine coughed to life.

"Is everything all right with your car?" she asked after they'd sat without moving for a few moments.

"Just letting her warm up." Zeg patted the seamed dashboard. "We'll be good to go in a minute."

"Come here," Tam said to her in a low voice, lifting his arm.

He didn't need to ask twice. Jennet slid over, tucking

herself against his side, and his arm settled around her. They were breaking the rules, but Zeg was giving them good cover. If asked, she could truthfully say he'd given her a lift home. She wouldn't mention she'd spent those five minutes soaking up as much of Tam as she possibly could.

His battered brown coat smelled faintly of smoke, and his arm felt warm and solid around her. The one safe place in the world was right there, beside him.

"Go left out of the parking lot, then right," Tam said as Zeg finally put the car in motion.

The motor vibrated through Jennet's chest. Surely she'd ridden in a gas car before, but she couldn't remember it. The vehicle bumped and bounced over the road, so different from the smooth ride of a grav-car.

"That's my house, up ahead," she said. "The one with the fountain."

They'd gotten there too soon. Zeg brought the car to a jolting stop and she reluctantly pulled away from Tam's warmth. The door squeaked as she pushed it open and climbed out. Tam followed her.

"Going to sit in front," he said, opening the passenger-side door.

Jennet leaned past him into the car, meeting Zeg's warm brown eyes.

"Thanks," she said, meaning more than just the quick ride.

He nodded, the smile lines around his eyes deepening.

"Any time," he said. "Don't forget your board."

When she straightened, Tam was right there. Close enough to brush her lips across his—a stolen kiss that would have to last for days. He gave her a crooked smile, then stepped to the back of the car and pulled her g-board out of the trunk.

"Here," he said.

"See you tomorrow." She held her board tightly, since she couldn't hold him.

He dipped his head, then climbed back into the car. Zeg pulled away from the curb in a cloud of acrid smoke that made her hold her breath.

Despite the lingering fumes, Jennet stood on the driveway, her back to the huge, empty house waiting behind her. She watched the battered guzzler carry Tam away, until it turned the corner and was gone.

6

As Zeg's car rattled and smoked through the pristine empty streets of the View, Tam tried to hold on to the warmth of Jennet pressed against him. It wasn't much, just a scrap of brightness for him to fold away and keep close to his heart.

The tall gates of the exit slid open. Zeg gave the guards a cheery wave they didn't return, and the car lurched under the silver archway marking the boundary between the compound and Crestview.

Back into the real world—the world of crazed little brothers and struggling moms. The world where nothing was simple or easy.

"What did you think of that?" Zeg asked.

Tam leaned his elbow on the dash and faced Zeg.

"Which part? It's a different reality up there."

"Certainly is. Though you've spent a little time in the View, I hear."

"Yeah."

He'd gone with Jennet a few times to her fancy, computer-controlled house—until the night Security caught him breaking in. He'd had to do it to save her, not that the cops listened to his explanation. He'd nearly been arrested, and her dad had forbidden them to see each other. Mr. Carter was deaf to their arguments that the Realm of Faerie was using the game to break into the mortal world.

Tam wished Jennet would press the issue more, but she was surprisingly timid around her dad—probably because her mom had left the family when Jennet was way young. Some residue of childhood fear kept her from pushing back too hard against the only parent she had left.

"Feyland is a fun game," Zeg said. "They've obviously worked to create an immersive environment. I think it will be a hit, despite the basic level of the battle mechanics. Or do the fights get more complex?"

"Um, they do."

And at the first sign of magic seeping into the game, Tam was going to tell Zeg everything. He tugged at the seatbelt cutting across his chest. The question was, had the Feyland he and Jennet played gradually become more challenging because of the programming, or because of the magic? He had a sinking feeling he knew the answer.

"Good," Zeg said. "I like a challenge."

He swerved the car around a deep pothole. Things got more run-down the closer they got to the Exe. Lurid graffiti etched the sides of abandoned buildings, their broken-out windows staring into the street like empty eyes.

"You can let me out here," Tam said. "The streets just get worse."

"It's only a couple more blocks, right?" The car lurched into a rut. Zeg grinned and gunned the engine, and they shot forward again. "Heh, this is better than playing Crazed Auto."

"Ok then." Tam couldn't help smiling. "Turn left at the next intersection. My place is partway down the street—the old auto shop."

It wasn't deep into the Exe, but even living on the outskirts was hazardous. Still, it was the only home he'd ever known.

"That it?" Zeg pointed to the old shop.

A rickety staircase ran up one side of the building, leading to the flat-topped roof where Tam's house was built. It looked tiny and dingy, like a shack compared to the mansions in The View. The blue tarp covering most of the roof was streaked with dirt, and the rusted metal patches on the walls gave it a bruised look.

But inside was what mattered—his mom and little

brother. His family, no matter how flawed. It wasn't like he was any kind of perfect specimen, himself.

"I'll pick you up tomorrow," Zeg said.

It wasn't a question, and Tam knew arguing would be pointless. When Zeg made up his mind, he was solid as a mountain. A lot like his niece, Marny, in fact.

"Right. See you then."

Tam climbed out of the car and closed the door, careful not to slam it. The vehicle seemed held together with wire and hope. But Zeg was good with mechanics, always fixing the consoles and interfaces at his sim café. As Zeg drove off, Tam half-expected the car to leave a trail of random parts and spewed oil behind, but it held together.

Kind of like Tam's life. Holding together.

He went up the stairs, skipping the spongiest tread, and fished his keys out of his pocket. It took a couple of jingling moments to undo all the locks and deadbolts, but the old-fashioned tech was the only way to really be secure. Electronic scan locks were laughably easy to hack—at least, the ones they could afford.

And although it didn't look like they had anything worth stealing, there was a big wad of cash hidden in his mom's bedroom. Payoff from VirtuMax, after their game had put him into a coma. Blood money.

Plus, locked in the empty auto shop downstairs sat a brand-new Zing model sim-system he still couldn't bring himself to play. He knew he'd love it, but it would be an admission that things were all right, that VirtuMax had paid off their debt.

Which they hadn't. His life was worth more than a game system.

That debt would pale to nothing, though, if the fey folk managed to break through into the mortal world. All the cash and prime sim-systems in the world wouldn't be worth a thing.

The memory of the Dark Queen shivered through him. Midnight-deep eyes, black hair tangled with stars, her voice like burnt sugar and roses. She could command anyone. She could hold the world enthralled.

"Tam!" His little brother's voice cut through his reverie. "Come in quick and look at this one."

Tam shook his head, hard, and forced himself back to the present. He pushed the door open, then made sure to do up all the locks again before turning to see what the Bug was doing.

The floor of their living room was littered with folded paper airplanes, made from torn pages of ancient magazines. His brother stood, poised on the couch. He gave Tam a huge grin, then launched a plane straight at Tam's face.

"Hey!" Tam ducked.

"Did you see it? It took me lots of tries, but I finally got it right. 'Cause it needs weight to fly, which is weird for something that's supposed to go in the air."

"Good job." Tam glanced around the room. The

kitchen alcove was empty and the bedroom door closed. His throat tightened. "Where's Mom?"

"Sleeping. She told me not to set anything on fire."

Tam let out a low breath. Mom was still home, not out roving the streets. And at least the Bug had listened to her—although the kitchen seemed messier than usual. Tam squinted.

"Peter, what did you use for ballast?"

"For which?"

His little brother plopped down and began making another plane.

"What did you weight the planes with?"

"First I tried extra paper, but that didn't work. And then I thought maybe pieces of a plate, but it was too heavy, so I kept looking for just the right stuff."

That explained the broken dish. And the tipped-over container of dry rice.

"You used rice?"

"Yeah—it's perfect. Except it spills out a little."

Tam looked at the floor—what he could see of it through the strewn and folded pages. Sure enough, little white bits were scattered all over. Still, a broken plate and some rice spread around were minimal compared to the mess the Bug usually made when unsupervised. At least the kid hadn't gone downstairs and decided to take apart the Zing system to see how it worked.

"We'll have to clean up in a minute, ok?" Tam said.

His brother made a pouty face. "I wanna show you how to make one. Please, Tam, please."

"Alright."

He sat beside the Bug, his hands busy folding paper —but he couldn't help glancing at Mom's closed door. It started this way. She'd go off her meds and sleep and sleep. And then, one morning, they'd wake up and she'd be gone. Or they'd come home from school to an empty house, the space where she should be cold and aching.

His fingers clenched hard around the plane he was making.

"Aw, Tam," his brother said. "You ruined it. Now you have to start over."

"Yeah."

Wasn't that always the way.

7

THE NEXT MORNING, Jennet wanted to wait in the VirtuMax lobby for Tam, but her dad hustled her along to the testing hub. Everyone was there—except Tam and Zeg. She glanced at the glowing numbers on the wall and bit her lip. Three minutes before the townies were unforgivably late.

Roy nudged her. "Maybe if your boyfriend had some modern tech, he'd be able to keep up with the basics. You know, like telling time."

She narrowed her eyes at him and pointedly turned away.

Spark, looking sleepy, cradled a cup between her hands. Did she stay up late at night, gaming? Jennet used to, especially last summer, when she'd first discovered the prototype version of Feyland. It was exhilarating, exploring an immersive new game while the rest of the world slept on, oblivious. Too bad the experience had nearly killed her.

Now, she and Tam had to make sure the treacherous magic of the fey stayed bottled up. But how?

The last time they had been in the Realm, their allies, Puck and Thomas, had spoken of dangerous quests and a foreboding place called the Twilight Kingdom. The memory of it made a prickle run up her spine.

Mr. Chon surveyed the assembled team and frowned. One minute left. Jennet heard the warm rumble of Zeg's laughter in the hall, and let out her breath. They'd made it.

A moment later the pair joined them, just as the clock hit the hour. She smiled at Tam, and Zeg winked at her. It wouldn't surprise her if he'd timed it so close on purpose.

"Today, we're trying something different," Mr. Chon said. "The main city of Stronghold features multiple options for adventure. Once you reach it, I'd like you to split into smaller groups so we can study the mechanics of several quest lines simultaneously."

"Great," Roy said. "I'm with Spark."

"I will accompany you as well," Coranne Smith said.

Roy made a face, and Jennet swallowed her laugh. Hard to get all romantic with the sour Ms. Smith along.

"Tam and I will quest together," Jennet said. She shot a glance at her dad, hoping he wouldn't feel the need to invite himself to join them.

"Excellent," Mr. Chon said. "Mr. Carter and Mr. Fanalua will make up the final team."

Jennet leaned back. That would be interesting. And at least Dad had a healer to pull him out of trouble.

"We'll be switching up the player configurations once you reach the end of these quest lines," Mr. Chon continued. "So don't get too comfortable."

"Good plan," her dad said.

He seemed a bit easier around the team leader today. After working with him on the data last night, the lines of tension on Dad's face had eased.

"Gear up and head in-game," Mr. Chon said. "Stronghold awaits."

A minute later, Jennet's character materialized in the meadow at the beginning of the cobblestone road. The rest of the team assembled around her, and she shared a quick glance with Tam. It was a huge improvement over the magical version of Feyland, where your character would go back to the starting faerie ring again if you didn't complete the key quests at that level.

Jennet's dad strode out onto the road, his orange robes swirling. Wind stirred the tall meadow grasses, and a soft, golden haze filled the sky.

"It's better to let the tank lead," Roy said, pushing past him. "In case of evil monsters."

"I thought *I* was the tank," Tam said in a low voice.

"You're a better one than Roy," Jennet said. "But it's

not worth arguing over. We'll reach the city and split up soon."

He set a hand on his sword. "There are supposed to be dangers along the way."

"Yeah. I hope my dad doesn't die again." She glanced ahead, to where the rest of the party had started down the road.

She and Tam caught up as the group crested a rise. The road descended to a small valley, then forked. At the junction sat two figures. One was a beautiful young woman wearing a shining silver gown, the other was a stooped old woman in a tattered grey dress.

"They don't look dangerous," Jennet's dad said.

"Appearances can be deceiving," Spark said.

"Greetings," Roy said when they reached the women.

"Welcome, travelers," the younger woman said, her voice as warm and smooth as sunlight. "Do you seek the way to the city?"

"We do. Which direction is it?"

The woman lifted her arm and pointed to the right with a graceful finger. "Your path lies that way."

"Thanks." Roy turned and started off in the direction she had indicated.

"Wait," Tam said. He nodded to the old woman dressed in rags. "We haven't heard from everyone here."

"Right." Zeg bowed to the old woman. "Greetings, goodwife."

"Ha!" Her voice was like the caw of a crow. She

nodded toward Roy. "Swayed by pretty ways and words, that one is. Tell me, travelers, what do you seek?"

"The best road to the city of Stronghold," Jennet said.

The old woman bent over, her cackling filling the air. "Now there's one who speaks well and wisely. The best road lies in that direction."

She lifted a gnarled hand and pointed to the left.

"Our thanks," Zeg said. "Come on Roy, we're going this way."

"No, we're not," Roy said. "I'm taking the first road."

"Now, Mr. Lassiter," Coranne began. "I think it's best if—"

"Hey, we're supposed to split up and explore the game, right? We can meet again once we get to the city, since apparently both these roads lead there." Roy put his hands on his hips. "Who's with me?"

"One moment," Coranne said. "Let me get authorization."

Her character wavered, then disappeared.

Roy rolled his eyes. "As if I need permission to play this game."

"It's called a beta test for a reason," Tam said.

Roy opened his mouth to retort, but was cut off by Coranne's returning figure.

"Mr. Chon has agreed," she said, a sour note in her voice. "The heavy armor classes are splitting up. Roy goes right, Tam left. Miss Jaxley and Mr. Carter, you're with Tam. Miss Carter, myself, and Mr. Fanalua will accompany Roy. Once we reach Stronghold, reconvene at the Lucky Tavern."

Jennet tightened her grip on her mage staff. Great—she was stuck with Roy, while Tam got her dad. She glanced at Tam and he shrugged, the light glinting off his silver armor. They both knew arguing would get them nowhere.

"See you in town," Roy said. "Come on, gang."

"Good luck," Jennet said to Tam. "Take care of my dad."

He gave her a level look from his green eyes. "You be careful. It's not a coincidence that your party has four players."

Jennet nodded. It was obvious to everyone but Roy that his choice of road was the more dangerous one. But if Mr. Chon decreed they were taking it, what could they do?

The road started innocently enough, meandering through the open fields, but ahead of them a dark forest lurked. Zeg fell back to walk beside her.

"Interesting that this group includes the healer," he said. "And excludes the least experienced member of the team."

Jennet nodded. "We're in for trouble."

The sense of menace intensified as the road led them into the forest. The golden light of the meadow faded behind them while shadows deepened on either side. Tall, tangled evergreen trees blocked out any view of the sky and fleshy-leaved purple bushes edged the road. Roy lost some of his swagger, and the four of them drew closer together. Ahead, the road narrowed, the cobblestones cracked and discolored.

"Nice choice, Roy," Jennet said.

He slitted his eyes at her. "Always have to be right, blondie?"

"No bickering," Coranne said. "We have a forest to get through."

Roy let out a huff and stalked ahead, Coranne at his heels. The road forced them to go single file, and Zeg gestured for Jennet to pass him. Apprehension tickled the back of her neck as the trees pressed close, filled with watching eyes.

Between one second and the next, long silken cords appeared over the roadway. Roy shouted as they wrapped around his limbs and hauled him into the air. Coranne vanished, using her rogue ability, and Jennet whirled, her mage staff at the ready. Before she could fire off a spell, or even identify where the enemy was, she, too, was wound in sticky threads.

Above her crouched a bloated spider, each hairy black limb at least five feet long. She struggled to get her staff free, but it was wrapped tightly in the webbing. The spider pulled her up with quick, jerky movements, and she caught sight of more spiders skulking in the nearby trees.

"Watch out!" she called to Zeg.

Two spiders scuttled along the branches, firing gouts of webbing at him. He dodged and darted, managing to stay clear of the strands.

Jennet pushed at the webbing. It gave a little, then sprang back. Using her fingernails she began shredding the strands, which worked somewhat better, though the sticky grey stuff stuck unpleasantly to her skin. Near her, Roy swung back and forth, his sword trapped uselessly on his back.

"Do you have another blade?" she asked.

"A dagger in my boot, but I can't get to it."

She managed to tear out more of the strands, enough to poke her mage staff through. Carefully, she extended it toward Roy until the glowing crystal at the tip hovered a few inches from his webbing.

"Hey," he said, "don't blast me."

"Don't worry."

She didn't need fierce arcane bolts of energy for this. Instead, something like a static shock to sizzle away Roy's bonds without harming him. Much.

In the earlier version of Feyland, she'd been able to focus her mind and harness the mage power in different ways. Could she do that now? She closed her eyes and imagined a quick arc of power, reaching out and burning away the webbing holding Roy captive.

He let out a yelp, and she opened her eyes. Several of the strands had charred.

"It's working," she said. "Hold still."

ANTHEA SHARP

"While you fry me?"

"Hurry," Zeg called up to them. "The mama spider is coming. And she doesn't look happy."

A huge arachnid scuttled down the road toward them. Her sharp jaws clicked together, and she was covered in a slick-looking carapace the color of old blood. The spiders in the trees drew back, though one got a lucky hit in, binding Zeg's arm to a nearby branch.

A heartbeat later, Coranne appeared, slicing him free with one of her wicked-looking daggers.

"Be quick," she hissed up at Jennet. "Zeg and I can't take her on by ourselves."

"We can," Zeg said, rubbing his arm. "But it won't be pretty."

Jennet concentrated again, imagining a bright trickle of power severing the web strands. They parted abruptly, and Roy hit the ground with a thump. Before he could get to his feet, the spider was upon them. Green goo dripped from her fangs, and she raised her forelegs, displaying razor-sharp talons.

"Keep me alive," Coranne yelled.

She dashed in front of the spider and stuck her dagger into the joint of one leg. The creature let out a high shriek and swiped at Coranne, grazing her side. Coranne stumbled. Then a flash of emerald light surrounded her, and she straightened. Still, even the best healer couldn't keep a rogue alive for long in a fight like this.

Roy scrambled to his feet and drew his sword, ready to dive into combat.

"Wait," Jennet cried, "cut me loose."

He turned and sliced through the webbing holding her, dumping her unceremoniously onto the ground.

"Thanks," she said, but he was already charging at the spider, sword raised.

She scrambled to her feet in time to see Coranne stumble and go down. Zeg waved his hands furiously through the air, preparing some heavy-duty healing. The spider poised to deliver a death bite to the rogue slumped on the ground.

"Get away!" Roy yelled, slashing at the spider's mouth with his bright sword.

The spider hissed and scuttled backwards a few paces, then hesitated, head swinging between Coranne, who was now covered in healing light, and Roy, brandishing his blade. Coranne disappeared, and the spider settled on Roy. Raising her sharp talons, she lunged forward.

Roy darted to the side, making their enemy turn, and Jennet fired off a magical bolt. Blue flame exploded against the spider's carapace, but didn't do any damage. She'd have to aim for the tender bits.

"Turn it at me," she called to Roy.

He parried the spider's attack, then danced back around, pivoting the creature toward Jennet. This time, her magical fire hit the spider square in the face.

The spider screeched and reared up, waving her forelegs.

Quick as thought, Coranne materialized under the spider's belly. She stabbed upward, a dagger in each hand, and their enemy screeched again, even louder this time.

The branches above them rustled, and hairy black spiders began dropping out of the trees. A dozen of them advanced, their eyes gleaming eerily.

"AOE!" Roy yelled, ducking under the red spider's slashing attack.

Area of Effect spells—yeah, definitely needed. Too bad Jennet only had one in her arsenal, Sheet of Flame. Raising her staff, she sent a wall of fire toward their enemies. Three of them died instantly, flipping onto their backs, legs curled in and lifeless. The others kept coming.

"Again," Coranne called.

"I can't—it's on cooldown!"

Sheet of Flame took thirty seconds to reset. And they only had about ten seconds before the wave of spiders overwhelmed them.

HEART POUNDING IN HER THROAT, Jennet targeted the closest spider and released a single bolt of magic. The spider stumbled, then flipped over dead—but she didn't have time to take them out one by one.

Coranne sprinted toward the creatures, a vial in her hand. She flung it to the ground, and noxious green smoke rose up. The first couple spiders to encounter it halted, and then started to spin around in circles, but the rest kept coming. Jennet managed another bolt, but that still left four of the spiders, advancing to where she and Zeg stood their ground on the cracked cobblestones.

Zeg lifted his hand and conjured one of the priest's rare damage spells. A flare of purple light sped toward the spiders, and two of them keeled over. Jennet used the end of her mage staff to knock one of the creatures back, but the other darted in, hissing. It sank its fangs into her leg, and she cried out at the sudden stab of pain.

Then Coranne was there, covered with green spider blood, her blades flashing. The last of the smaller spiders curled up, dead on the sticky roadway.

"Are you all right?" Coranne asked.

"Yeah."

It hurt, more than Jennet expected it to. The game interface was supposed to simulate small amounts of pain—a sensation like tingling—but the point of Feyland wasn't to inflict pain.

So why did it feel like she'd been jabbed in the leg by a poisoned fork? She rubbed the puncture wounds, smearing green blood onto her hands.

Healing light surrounded her and the pain eased, but didn't entirely fade.

"Hey," Roy called, his voice strained. "A little help here."

Zeg muttered and instantly busied himself with healing Roy, who was taking serious damage from the big spider. Coranne dashed back, pulling out her Morningstar mace, and Jennet raised her staff. Blue light sizzled out, scorching the spider. Roy sliced and Coranne bashed and Zeg healed and slowly, excruciatingly, the spider began to falter.

Jennet disliked fights that turned into grinding the enemy down. Win or lose, finish it fast was her preference—and with a full party, they would have beaten the mama spider a lot earlier.

Finally, the creature staggered. Roy let out a victory yell, cut short by the sudden gush of yellow ichor the spider spit out. Coranne leapt to the side, but Roy got the stuff full on. He fell to his knees, his sword wavering.

"Kill it," he said, "kill it *now*."

Jennet summoned up Sheet of Flame again and sent it scorching forward, just as Coranne aimed a vicious strike at the spider's eyes. With a screech that made her ears ring, their enemy collapsed. The spider rolled onto its back, its legs drawn up stiffly. Dead.

"Took long enough," Roy said, staggering up. "Can you cleanse this stuff off me?"

He grimaced and brushed at the yellow goo covering his breastplate and arms. Jennet would bet serious credits he was glad Spark wasn't there to see him covered in spider ooze.

Zeg nodded, and sent emerald light to surround Roy.

"That was rough," Jennet said, glancing at the thirteen spider corpses littering the forest floor.

"We handled it though." Roy sheathed his sword. "Come on. Let's get to the city."

The rest of them followed, giving the red spider a wide berth. The thing might be dead, but Jennet sure didn't want to touch it. Her leg still ached where the spider had bitten her.

"We *handled* it," Zeg said quietly, "but that was pretty

damn near a wipe. Coranne's quick, I have to give her that."

"And you're a prime healer," Jennet said. "I know you got us through that fight, against the odds."

He nodded, his bearded face thoughtful. "I wonder what kind of battle the others faced."

"Whatever it was, I'm sure they dealt with it just fine. Tam's a great player."

Spark was too, probably. No doubt they made a good team. Jennet shook her shoulders, trying to make the jealousy fall off.

"I see the city," Roy called from up ahead, where the trees thinned.

Jennet increased her strides, though her leg pinged with discomfort at every step. The forest ended, and the party paused at the edge of a steep hill. Below them, the road zigzagged to the city of Stronghold.

Immense stone walls surrounded the city, and she could see guards patrolling the ramparts. Brightly colored pennants flew from tall towers at the four corners of the city. From their vantage point, Jennet glimpsed whitewashed buildings with red slate roofs, a few green open spaces bounded by trees, and at one end of the city, a small lake, shining in the sun.

At the very center stood a castle built of gleaming white stone.

"Bet we end up talking to the king," Zeg said.

Roy made a strangled sound, and Jennet glanced at

him. The last time Roy had dealt with a king in Feyland, he'd gotten in severe trouble. Unwilling sympathy moved through her.

"Relax," she said, looking into his pale face. "It's just a game, remember."

He swallowed and gave a jerky nod. "Right."

Zeg raised his bushy brows, and Coranne glanced between Jennet and Roy, but neither of them could possibly guess the truth—that Roy had stumbled into the Court of the Bright King, and found himself enticed and bound by fey magic.

"Who knows," Zeg said, "maybe it's a queen instead."

Now Jennet was the one pushing back fear, as memories of her own battles with the Dark Queen washed over her. Her hands tightened on the smooth wood of her mage staff, but she forced herself to breathe normally.

They were safe. This Feyland wasn't connected to the Realm of Faerie. That castle down there didn't hold dangerous, slippery magic that would ensorcel them all. It was just a game. Just a game.

"Come on," Coranne said, starting down the hill. "We're wasting time."

Jennet made herself follow Zeg toward the huge oaken gate set in the city walls. King or queen or something else in the castle, at least Tam was in there somewhere, waiting for her.

· · ·

TAM LEANED against the stone wall outside the Lucky Tavern and watched the artificial bustle in Stronghold's streets. Eventually the city would be populated with real people's avatars running around, but for now it was just NPCs: a pie vendor wandering back and forth, a soldier on a brown horse who circled past every five minutes, a troupe of jugglers performing the same moves over and over in the square fronting the tavern.

Where were Jennet and the rest of her party? He folded his arms and tried not to acknowledge the anxiety crawling up his spine. Damn, he'd known she was heading into trouble, and it was all Lassiter's fault. The guy still hadn't learned, despite everything that had happened to him in-game.

At least Jennet had Zeg with her—but if they didn't show up soon, Tam was going out to find them.

A burst of laughter floated from the open door of the tavern, where Spark and Jennet's dad were sitting at a table. Tam was too restless to stay inside, plus the music loop was way short. If he heard that same sprightly flute tune one more time, he'd scream.

At the end of the wide cobbled street, he caught movement—more purposeful than the random wanderings of the NPCs. He jumped onto a nearby watering trough to scan the crowd. Yes, there was Jennet in her blue mage robes, Zeg's big form next to her, and Lassiter, his bronze armor gleaming and a tight expression on his face. Coranne was harder to spot, slinking along like a shadow, but she was there, too. Everybody accounted for.

Tam leaped down and strode to meet them.

"There you are," he said. "We've been waiting a while."

Since Jennet's dad wasn't there, he pulled her into a quick, relieved hug.

"Sorry," she said. "We were detained by some spiders. Did you guys come through all right?"

"Yeah. Your dad and Spark are in the tavern." He gestured. "We can catch up in there."

When they stepped through the door into the rustic main room of the Lucky Tavern, Jennet's dad jumped up.

"Is everyone here?" he asked, craning his neck.

"Yes," Coranne said in a dry voice. "Every pixel intact."

"I just wanted to make sure." Mr. Carter gave Jennet a close look.

Even though Jennet's dad hadn't directly experienced the dangers of Feyland, he'd seen the effects. Even if he still didn't believe. Tam was glad to know he wasn't the only one who'd had dire thoughts about the rest of the party lying mangled and perma-dead on the side of the road.

Roy strode over to the hearth, where a large fire burned cheerfully without giving off any heat.

"We had a fierce battle," he said. "Not one of those

simple fights. What did your party encounter?" He narrowed his eyes at Tam.

"A few bogles," Tam said. "Pretty easy to dispatch."

"I even took one on myself." Jennet's dad sounded proud.

Spark nodded, her magenta hair catching the light. "Four of them sprang up out of the ground, but it wasn't a hard fight. Five minutes, and we were on our way."

Jennet glanced at Roy. "Next time, maybe pay better attention to your options," she said.

"Whatever." He moved to the scuffed wooden bar. "Do they have ale here?"

"Yeah," Spark said. "It tastes like bananas. So do the oat cakes."

"Still?" Mr. Carter shook his head. "I thought they'd fixed that part of the interface."

"Other issues have taken priority," Coranne said. "I assure you, resolving the taste component is on the debug list. Speaking of which, it's time to log out. It's crucial that everyone note down their impressions of the journey to Stronghold."

"Great," Spark said. "I'd like some lunch that *doesn't* taste like banana."

"The company has provided sandwiches and other items," Coranne said. "We still have an afternoon session to complete."

Tam met Jennet's eyes. Another session where the two of them would be able to split off from the main group. And hopefully find the Realm and get some answers.

After lunch, the beta team assembled in-game at the Lucky Tavern. Tam stayed beside Jennet, impatience tickling his ribcage. This was their chance to get back into the Realm of Faerie, where they could *do* something. This version of Feyland seemed fine, but it was tame. Too tame, like a tiger pretending to be a domesticated kitty. He didn't trust it one bit.

"Have fun, everybody," Zeg said, then nodded at Jennet's dad. "We're going to grab our quests."

Lassiter made a face. "Pretty sweet deal, Mr. Chon just sending you upstairs at the inn."

"Age has its privileges." Zeg smiled.

"More like being noobs has its privileges," Lassiter mumbled under his breath, so the adults wouldn't hear.

Spark gave him a sharp glance. "I checked out the city map, and our quests aren't far. We pick them up just inside the castle."

Lassiter swallowed. Like Tam and Jennet, he knew any court in Feyland could be dangerous beyond imagining. Still, fear was never an excuse for acting like an ass.

Jennet set her hand on her dad's arm. "Be careful, all right?"

"You, too." His blue eyes, so much like his daughter's, went from Jennet to Tam.

"We have the rest of the afternoon to explore our questlines," Coranne said. "Mr. Chon will send a game-wide message twenty minutes before logout. That should give you time to finish up what you're doing. Good luck, everyone."

The group murmured farewells and good wishes. Once outside the tavern, Spark, Lassiter, and Coranne strode up the wide main street leading to the castle. Spark turned and gave them a wave before the buildings blocked them from sight.

Finally, Tam and Jennet were alone. He hoped their fey allies were paying attention.

"Mr. Chon said we pick up our quests at the lake," Jennet said.

"This way," Tam said, leading her down a small passageway between the tavern and the shop next door. She gave him a curious look, but didn't argue.

Spark wasn't the only one who'd taken a quick glance at the city map. Navigating the streets and alleys of Stronghold was cake compared to the routes he had to take in and out of the Exe.

A few minutes later they stood at the lake's edge. Short grass led to the wind-ruffled water, which lapped calmly at the shore. Scattered trees gave the area a park-like feeling, despite the massive stone walls of the city rising along the lake's other side.

"Over there." Jennet pointed to a cluster of NPCs gathered at the far end of the water.

As they got closer, Tam saw that they were two men and a woman, dressed in the quasi-medieval clothes most residents of Stronghold wore. Behind the trio, though, was a smaller figure—one who wasn't standing still with computer-generated patience. Tam squinted, making out tattered garments like windblown leaves, bright eyes, and a mischievous, ageless grin.

"Is that…"

"Puck!" Jennet hurried forward.

The sprite nodded up at them, then laid a long, crooked finger across his lips. With his other hand he gestured to the NPCs. Clearly Puck didn't want his presence revealed to whatever tracking devices the VirtuMax people were using to watch the game-play.

"Right." Tam cleared his throat. "Sorry you stepped in the *muck*, Jennet. But here are our quest givers."

She nodded, and turned to the quest givers. "Greetings."

"Greetings, travelers," the woman said. "Do you yearn for adventure, and to serve the crown?"

Jennet glanced at Tam.

"We do," he said, hoping they hadn't just made a promise to the fey folk.

Surely Puck would keep them out of that kind of trouble.

"The princess lies ill in the castle," the shorter of the

two men said. "To save her, the healers require special herbs not found near our city."

"Rue, Sweetmeadow, and Briarblossom," the woman said. "They can be found only in the meadows of Tir. We require adventurers who will go forth and collect these herbs, braving the dangers that lie beyond our walls. Are you bold enough?"

"Yes," Jennet said. "Which way do we go?"

"Yonder," the taller man said, pointing toward the stone wall. "Beyond Stronghold, to the west, lie the meadows of Tir. Go there, and fulfill your quest."

As he spoke, the wall shimmered and an arched wooden door appeared, just tall enough for Jennet and Tam to pass through.

"The princess's life depends upon your success," the woman said. "Good luck, and make haste."

Tam glanced at Puck, who nodded to the doorway. Whatever the sprite was up to, it lay outside the city walls.

Jennet strode to the door, which swung open at her approach. Puck darted in front of them, slipping through the archway like a blown leaf. When Jennet stepped through, she let out a strangled gasp, and Tam hurried after her, hand on his sword.

A second later, he understood why. As he passed through the arched doorway, the world tilted. Golden light swirled across his vision, and queasy dizziness settled in his stomach. He blinked and stumbled, trying to regain his bearings.

The city was gone. The simple meadows and forests surrounding it, gone. He and Jennet stood on a narrow path winding through a grove of white-barked trees. The sky above them was full of pearlescent light, like the edge of dawn. Or twilight. He shivered.

Now they were truly in the Realm of Faerie.

9

JENNET TOOK A BREATH, exhaling the vertigo out of her system. To her relief, Tam appeared beside her a heart-beat later. She expected to be standing in the middle of a faerie ring, but instead pale-barked trees surrounded them, glowing faintly in the half light.

"Puck," she said "Are you here?"

"Where else would I be?" The sprite appeared before them, floating cross-legged in the air.

"We're back in the Realm now, aren't we?" Tam said. "How did you do that?"

"Doorways exist to be passed through."

The sprite grinned and snapped his fingers. A ball of white light bloomed above his palm. It illuminated the trees, making odd shadows twist and dance at the corners of her vision.

"Yes, but *where* in the Realm?" Jennet peered

between the white-barked trunks, the back of her neck prickling.

"At the edges," Puck said. "A place where winning or losing carries a high cost indeed."

"What are we supposed to do now?" Worry gave her words a sharp edge. "Is the FullD interface unsafe? Are the Courts really giving up trying to break into the human world? What about—"

"Cease," Puck said. "I cannot answer your questions. I can only show you the way you must take in order to discover the answers."

Tam folded his arms. "So, we're not there yet?"

"Not yet," Puck said. "The Twilight Kingdom lies deeper than you know."

The sprite wasn't nearly as full of mischief and merriment as usual, and she tasted fear, metal on her tongue. It took a lot to subdue Puck, who had stood unflinching against the wrath of both the Dark Queen and the Bright King.

"Listen, and listen well," he said, his voice hushed. "I shall reveal to you one of the Great Secrets of the Realm. Few mortals know of it. Aye, even few of the fey folk themselves. But just as the Realm of Faerie lies across the veil from your world, so the Twilight Kingdom lies hidden beyond the Realm, a dark jewel at the heart of all our fey magics."

"If it's a kingdom," Jennet said, the words sticking in her throat, "who rules it?"

She couldn't imagine what could be worse than the Dark Queen and Bright King.

"The Elder Fey." Puck's words shivered ominously through the grove, making the leaves on the white-barked trees tremble. The ball of light in his hand dimmed.

Okay, maybe that was worse.

"I've never heard of them," Tam said.

"You hadn't heard of the Seelie and Unseelie Courts, either," Jennet said. "Not until you entered Feyland."

"The Elder Fey hold the oldest power," Puck said. "Little do they concern themselves with the Realm, and less yet with the mortal world. But they are keepers of the balance. Your task is to wake them from their deep dreamings so that they may set things to rights."

"Their deep dreamings?" Tam asked.

Puck shook his head. "I have told you enough—more than enough. Now is the time for action, not words. Are you ready?"

"Do we have a choice?" Jennet asked

The sprite folded his hand closed, extinguishing the hovering sphere of light, then opened it again to reveal a smooth white stone.

"Take this," he said, holding it out to her. "It may be of use to you in a time of despair."

She took it, the stone warm between her fingers, and slipped it into the pocket of her robes.

"Follow the pathway," Puck said. "A ring awaits to

take you beyond the Realm. Bard Thomas and I have done what we can to transport you close to the Elder Fey—but you will have to make your own way further into the Twilight Kingdom."

"Puck," Tam said, "how dangerous are these Elder Fey?"

The sprite regarded him a moment, bright eyes unblinking. "There are no mortal words to describe them. Take care, Bold Tamlin and Fair Jennet. Take every care you can, and even then it may not be enough. And now, I must bid you farewell, 'ere our presence here is felt."

"But…" Jennet stretched out her hand.

Too late. Puck was gone, and all his hints and knowledge gone with him.

"Is he going to just abandon us in there?" Tam said.

It was a bad sign, if Tam was complaining about the sprite leaving. Usually he objected to Puck's help.

"He won't." She tried to keep her voice confident. "asnHasn't Puck always shown up at the last minute to lend a hand?"

Tam just shook his head and started up the pathway. A few moments' walking brought them to a clearing, where a circle of thin-stalked mushrooms shed an eerie, purplish glow. A low humming emanated from the circle—a sound that made her nerves tremble.

"The portal to the Twilight Kingdom." She moved forward a hesitant step.

"Wait," Tam said.

He strode over to her and folded her into his arms. She lifted her face and their lips met in a kiss that felt as real as anything. Sparks flew through her, burying the fear. For a moment, nothing else mattered. Only Tam, only the sound of their breathing, the taste of his mouth. Only the small, still world captured in their kiss.

He gave her one last squeeze, then let go.

"Ready?" he asked, holding out his hand.

She took it, his fingers warm around hers. "Ready."

Together, they leaped over the boundary of glowing mushrooms. Landed in the center of the ring.

And fell into darkness.

10

Tam gripped Jennet's hand, though he couldn't feel it. An icy wind rushed around him, chilling him to the bone, and his heart pounded with the panicky sensation of falling.

He forced the frigid air in and out of his lungs. They'd be all right. Puck wouldn't let them die on the way to the Twilight Kingdom—that would defeat the purpose.

The sense of falling stopped, though it didn't seem he had landed anywhere. A pale glow seeped into the air, and he felt Jennet's fingers clasped in his once more. He looked over at her, shocked to find they were lying on the ground. Eerie purple mushrooms surrounded them, and the grass beneath them was black and silver, smooth as silk.

Definitely not in the Realm any more.

Jennet lay still, her eyes closed, her pale blonde hair almost white where it spread out over the black grass.

"Jennet?" he said. His voice was creaky.

Her eyelids fluttered open. She glanced around, then levered herself up.

"The Twilight Kingdom," she whispered. "I can't believe it."

"Me either."

He had thought Feyland was strange, but this—this was a whole new level of freaky. Tree-shaped foliage grew around them, like a wavery reflection of trees glimpsed in a pond covered with dark oil. The air held a harshness, a strange tang that human lungs weren't supposed to breathe. Overhead, the sky glowed an uncanny purple. They were not in the midnight forest of the Dark Court, nor the bejeweled brilliance of the Bright.

Bard Thomas's words echoed in his mind. *A between place.* He had once called Feyland that, a place where all kinds of magic existed.

What more was possible in a place like the Twilight Kingdom?

Tam took a deep breath and raised his arms. Slowly, his body rose into the air. Giddiness trembled through him. It was working! He paused, hovering six feet off the ground.

"Tam." Jennet's eyes were huge. "What are you doing?"

"Haven't you always wanted to fly? For real—not in a game, not in dreams, but really *fly?*"

Tucking his arms in, he swooped forward and skimmed above the glowing circle of mushrooms. Exhilaration bubbled in his head, like he was drinking pure fizz.

"Wow. I…" She shook her head and rose to join him in the air. "This is amazing."

"Definitely better than walking."

It felt as easy as walking, though—something he could do without conscious thought. All he had to do was decide where to go, and his body followed.

He smiled at Jennet. Despite the eeriness of the Twilight Kingdom, their impossible quest to wake the Elder Fey from their deep dreamings—whatever those were—and the danger awaiting them, he was filled with joy. He'd never thought he'd experience such real magic. Not Tam Linn, destitute kid from the Exe.

Then again, he never thought he'd have a girlfriend like Jennet, either. The world was full of possibilities.

She pivoted in the air. "Which way?"

"The light seems stronger over there." He pointed.

"Let's get above these trees."

They rose higher, until the wavery foliage lay beneath their feet. As he'd thought, there was more light to the left; an orange glow cast into the dimness, illuminating the rugged silhouette of low mountains. Between them and the mountains spread groves of the odd trees, and a river shining silvery-pale, the way water takes on light at dusk.

"Race you to the river," Jennet said, a teasing flash in her eyes.

Before he could reply, she was off, her hair and robes streaming behind her. Tam leaped into the air, making sure he was flying parallel to the ground. Those robes of hers had to be giving her some wind resistance. Sure enough, he was gaining on her.

"How fast do you think we can go?" she called to him.

"Let's find out."

Half-closing his eyes against the rip of the wind, Tam imagined he was a bullet, a train, something faster even than thought. He shot forward, and Jennet yelped in surprise as he flew past her.

Without warning, he crashed into something—hard. His head throbbed, his lungs clenched, and his whole body whimpered in pain.

"Tam," Jennet screamed, "catch yourself!"

Belatedly, he realized he was falling out of the air, the dark ground hurtling up at him.

Float, he thought, and at the last second levitated enough to land with a jolt beside the river instead of splattering all over. Jennet descended and grabbed his shoulders, her fingers digging into him.

"Are you all right? What happened?" She scanned his face, her own full of worry.

"I hit something. I'm ok."

"You better be."

She pulled him into a tight hug, and for a moment he let himself feel nothing but the shape of her body against him, her hair softly brushing his cheek. But the throbbing ache of impact wouldn't be pushed away for long. He let out a pained breath and stepped back, squinting into the sky.

"Whatever I hit was invisible, but plenty solid."

"At least we made it to the river." Jennet folded her arms. "Next time, no racing."

"I win." He smiled at her, though he felt a bruise forming on his forehead.

She rolled her eyes, his joking clearly easing her worry. No need to tell her how much he actually hurt.

"Let's cross and see what's on the other side." She floated up, then stayed there, unmoving. "Hey. I'm stuck."

"Can you come down?"

"Yeah." She descended onto the soft black grass. "Just not forward. It's like a wall of air built up beside the river."

He rose again and, careful of his bruised head, tried to fly across the river. No luck.

"That's what I ran into," he said.

Jennet studied the silvery glow of the river. "In some fairy tales, magic can't cross running water. Maybe that's what's going on."

"How do we get across? It's at least twenty feet wide."

"Swim?"

Tam glanced at the viscous water and shook his head. "That water doesn't look normal. There has to be a bridge. somewhere."

"We don't have much time before Mr. Chon calls the beta team back."

"He won't be able to reach us in here." Tam frowned. "Puck and Thomas wouldn't leave us without some kind of exit." He hoped.

"Come on." Jennet paced upriver, toward the orange glow cast against the shadowy sky.

"Don't walk," Tam said, flying up to her.

"Right. I forgot."

She rose to join him and they sped over the twilight landscape, the river shining on their right. Just when he thought they'd have to try swimming after all, Tam spotted a dark span arching over the water. Slowly, they descended to the velvety grasses beside the bridge.

"I hope there's not a troll underneath," Jennet said.

"Or something worse. At least we still have our weapons."

He and Jennet had arrived with their gear intact, though he wasn't sure how much good his sword would do in the Twilight Kingdom. It might work fine, or it might turn to a feather or a strand of silk. He wasn't taking anything for granted.

The bridge rose before them, made of some glossy,

semi-translucent substance—obsidian or darkest amethyst. Tam set one foot on it, his boot making a clinking sound. He took another step, and sent out a small chime.

"So much for sneaking across," Jennet said.

She joined him, her quieter footsteps making the structure hum. The sound of them walking over the bridge was like synth-trance music—all woo and thrum and random chiming.

"This will alert any creature for miles," he said. "Did you notice how quiet it was, before?"

The Twilight Kingdom was a hushed place. Well, it had been. The noise of their passage filled the air as they reached the center of the bridge. The back of Tam's neck prickled in warning, and he drew his sword.

"Halt!" a voice said.

A figure materialized on the span in front of them—a tall, glowing woman clad in shining robes made of spun metal. She had sharp cheekbones and eyes slit like a cat's. Long, serrated wings rose from her back, and her pale hair fell, tangled and wild, past her waist. In her right hand she held a sword pulsing with purple light.

Tam shifted into battle stance, his shield appearing on his left arm, but the faerie didn't rush to attack. Instead, she lifted her sword and regarded them, her eerie eyes unblinking.

"Who dares brave the paths of the Twilight Kingdom?" she asked, her voice sibilant and strange.

"Are you… an Elder Fey?" Jennet asked.

The faerie woman laughed, a shimmer of violet through the air. "Nay. The elders sleep deep within the heart of the mountain, in a place not made for such as I." Her amusement faded as she studied them. "Yet I ask again, who are you?"

"We are adventurers from the mortal world," Tam said. He knew better than to give the fey folk their names.

The faerie's pale eyebrows rose. "The mortal realm? That is a place much removed. What great need brings you here?"

"Does it have to be a great need?" he asked.

"Of course." Her words hissed though the still air. "There is no other way to reach our kingdom."

"We're here," Jennet said, "because the Realm of Faerie is trying to open a gateway into our world, the human world. They've nearly succeeded at least once."

The faerie nodded, her hair tumbling like silvery cobwebs about her face. "And why should I grant you passage over this bridge? The doings of the realms are of little concern to us."

Tam tightened his grip on his sword.

"We're supposed to wake the Elder Fey so they can restore the balance," Jennet said, her voice tight. "Isn't that important enough?"

The woman narrowed her catlike eyes. "It is best to

let the Elder Fey slumber. To wake them is to court death."

"It's not as if we have a choice," Tam said. "Are you going to let us across?"

The faerie woman tipped her sword and Tam tensed, moving his weight to the balls of his feet. He wasn't going to strike the first blow, but he was ready.

"Tam," Jennet said in a low voice. "I think she would let us by, if you don't push it."

"We don't have time to hang around chatting on bridges," he said.

The woman smiled, sharp and crystalline. "So eager for a fight, mortal? Very well, I will cross swords with you."

"Right." Raising his sword, Tam strode forward to face their opponent.

11

THE FAERIE'S strike came faster than Tam could blink. He barely got his shield up in time as the air hummed with the aftermath of her blow. He stepped forward and swung hard, but she fluidly blocked his blade with her own. The force of it shocked him to his toes. The sound of their blades colliding rang out like a huge silver bell, vibrating the air with a noise he could almost *see*.

The faerie smiled, showing pointed teeth, and attacked again. Her blade blurred with the speed of her blows, and Tam stumbled back. He couldn't attack in return—it was all he could do to defend himself.

"Tam!" Jennet cried as the faerie's sword descended.

He tried to bring his shield up to deflect the sword. Too slow. Ears ringing, he watched the edge of the blade sweep toward him.

Just when he was sure it was all over, the blade bit

into a length of wood mere inches from his face. Jennet's mage staff. She stood defiantly between him and the faerie, staff held crosswise with the blade still embedded in the wood.

"Stop." Jennet said.

The word seemed to expand, pressing outward like a sonic echo. Light flared around him and Jennet. The river below shivered.

The faerie wrenched her blade free and stepped back. Her cat eyes were wide, a look of faint surprise across her sharp, inhuman features. She stared at them a moment, motionless, then brought the flat of her sword to her left shoulder, the blade facing straight up, and bowed. Her shining hair floated about her, as though unaffected by gravity.

"I will battle you no more," she said. "The Twilight Kingdom has found you worthy. You are granted passage."

"What does that mean?" Jennet asked.

"It means you will not be hindered by those like myself, who guard the kingdom."

"But we'll be hindered in other ways?" Jennet asked.

The faerie shook her head. "I cannot answer that— but every journey has dangers. Your presence here is necessary. At least until your task is complete."

The faerie began moving her wings in slow arcs. She rose, her metallic robes swirling around her, her hair fanning out like moonbeams. Lifting her sword, she pointed across the bridge to the dark land on the other side.

"Your way lies ahead, mortal travelers. Make haste."

Tam slid his blade back into the scabbard then followed Jennet down the bride. Her footsteps set the bridge humming once more, his own strides chiming in cross-harmony. When they stepped onto the silky black grasses on the far side, he let out a long breath, grateful for the quiet.

The air shivered, filled with static, and letters shimmered in the air in front of them.

:xjk & Jenn333 rejkfjlk blta log outt:

"Did you see that?" Tam blinked, the glowing words etched across his eyes.

"Yes." Jennet squinted. "I think Mr. Chon's calling us back. Somehow, Puck is forwarding the message here."

"We can't leave yet—we've barely gotten anything done."

"I know. But…" She pulled in a breath. "Look!"

From behind them, a line of silver light etched across the dimness. Tam turned to see the cat-eyed faerie at the apex of the bridge, her blade lifted high. The strand of brightness led from the tip of her sword to a clump of wavery trees a short distance away.

"Come on," Tam said, hoping they could still fly after crossing the river.

At least his head felt better, eased somehow by the strange magic of the bridge. Relief flowed through him as he rose into the air at the mere thought of flying. Jennet joined him, and they sped toward the grove. There was a clearing in the trees, and in the center glowed a ring of pale-stalked mushrooms.

Their ride home.

He didn't know how they'd get back to the Twilight Kingdom, but the message was clear. Time for him and Jennet to go.

Part of him was glad, too, although they hadn't yet found the Elder Fey. The constant, dim light, the chiming bridge, the rasp of air in his lungs, all left him with an uneasy itch under his skin. Even the thrill of flying couldn't make up for the growing discomfort.

"Do you think we have to transition back into the Realm, before we can get to our world?" Jennet asked, floating down at the edge of the faerie ring.

"One way to find out," Tam said, taking her hand.

JENNET BRACED HERSELF, but she still lost her breath as frigid and icy blackness enfolded them. The sick sensation of falling ripped through her, and she squeezed Tam's hand, hard, although she couldn't feel it.

She and Tam landed in a circle of moon-pale mushrooms, and she stumbled forward a step. A sky stitched with stars curved above the limbs of white-barked trees. Tam steadied her, and the tightness in her throat eased.

They were back in the Realm—and Puck waited just outside the faerie ring.

"Hurry." The sprite beckoned. "The Dark Queen has sensed your passage, and has set the Hunt on you."

"Damn," Tam said, tugging her out of the ring. "How far to the next portal?"

"Not far." Puck turned and started down a dark, fern-edged pathway.

"I wish we could still fly," Jennet said as they hurried down the path.

The dark night was split by an eerie howl that raised goosebumps on her arms. The Wild Hunt had caught their trail. She picked up her skirts and ran.

"Come!" Puck called. "Once you return to your world, you will be safe."

He lifted his hand and summoned a ball of light to illuminate the way. A dim clearing lay ahead, pale dots of mushrooms circling the velvety moss.

High yips and the keening cry of pipes reached them, carried by a dark breeze. Fear clutched Jennet's stomach.

"Farewell, Puck," she gasped.

Without pausing, she leaped into the center of the faerie ring. Silver glinted at the corner of her eye as Tam followed.

Dizzying golden light enveloped her senses. The queasiness was welcome after the cold intensity of their passage to the Twilight Kingdom.

A moment later, she and Tam stood in the arched doorway set in Stronghold city's walls. The sky was a cheerful blue overhead, and the sound of simulated birdsong filled the air.

"You ok?" Tam asked, grasping her shoulder. "You look pale."

"I'm all right." She studied his face. Dark smudges lay under his eyes. "This multiple-realm-jumping takes a toll. But at least we escaped the hunt."

As Puck had promised, the fearsome hounds hadn't followed them. How long would that last, though? The faeries had been weakened, but they drew their strength from interaction with the human world. Would her and Tam's presence in the Realm make the fey folk strong enough to break through?

:Tam and Jennet, turn in your quests and log off immediately. You're late. The rest of the team is already out:

The words scrolled across her vision.

"Do you see that?" she asked.

"Crap—we didn't do the quests." Tam shook his head. "Do you think they know where we've been?"

"I have no idea—but Tam, this is the proof we've been looking for! If VirtuMax saw us enter the Realm, just think how things would change."

She gripped his arm, hope and excitement zinging through her.

"Jennet." Tam's voice was sober. "I've been thinking hard about this. What do you think will happen if we convince the company that other worlds really do exist? Worlds full of magic?"

"They'll pull the game." Even as she said the words, cold realization settled over her. "Won't they?"

He folded his arms, his eyes desolate. "VirtuMax doesn't care that their FullD put me in a coma, or that your hands got severely burned. They don't even care that Thomas died using the sim equipment, except that they lost their lead developer. It's all about money. And power."

Jennet shivered and stared across the virtual lake. Tam was right. VirtuMax was focused on one thing only —releasing the game and making millions of dollars. Would they really shut down the project if they knew the truth?

No. They'd do everything they could to ally with the leaders of Feyland, then turn the magic to their own ends. She felt sick that she hadn't realized it before.

Still, she couldn't let go of the idea. "We could try telling them, though. My dad would—"

"Your dad got kicked off the project. Even if he believed us, he couldn't stop the game's release. And I'm not willing to give Dr. Lassiter the keys to the Realm, are you?"

Jennet rubbed her left palm. The VirtuMax CEO had a reputation for ruthlessness, and from what they'd seen of Roy's shaky grasp of right and wrong, Tam's fear was well founded.

"Then what do we do?" she asked.

"Keep trying to reach the Elder Fey. Hope that Puck is able to hide our travels to the Realm."

Beside the shore, the quest givers waited expectantly.

"Let's go talk to them," Tam said. "Maybe we can finesse this somehow." He strode up to the woman NPC.

"Welcome back, travelers," she said. "I see you have returned successfully from your expedition to the meadows of Tir. Quickly, give us the herbs you have collected, so the princess may be saved."

Relief whooshed through Jennet. Puck had managed to cover their absence, at least in-game. What the VirtuMax people had seen on their monitors was another question. One they'd have to deal with soon.

She scanned her inventory, and there were the quest items—Rue, Sweetmeadow, and Briarblossom. She handed the herbs over, and a soft *ding* rang through the air, signaling their quest was complete.

"Now what?" Tam said.

"Thank you, adventurers." The taller man gave them a digitally perfect smile. "You have performed a great service to the crown. Make your way to Stronghold Castle to claim your reward and discover what new adventures await."

:Tam and Jennet, turn in your quests and log off immediately. You're late. The rest of the team is already out:

"Next time," Tam said, stepping away from the group of NPCs.

"What are we going to say about the game-play?" Jennet asked in a low voice.

He shook his head. "Depends on what the techs saw. Be vague—say the quest was challenging but not too hard, stuff like that."

:Tam and Jennet, turn in your quests and log off immediately. You're late. The rest of the team is already out:

"Ok, ok, we're coming," Tam said, raising his voice.

Jennet hit the X command. A second later she was in her sim-chair, the smoky material of the FullD visor between her and the real world. Too bad she couldn't stay there, hiding. She stripped off her gloves and removed the sim helmet.

Mr. Chon stood beside her chair, his face tight with impatience. This wasn't going to be pretty.

"Miss Carter," he demanded. "Where have you and Mr. Linn been?"

"Um."

In the next chair over, Tam pulled off his helmet, brown hair falling across his eyes. The rest of the beta team gathered behind Mr. Chon, looks of concern on their faces. Even Roy seemed anxious—but then, he knew what kind of trouble Feyland held.

"Jen," her dad said, "We've been worried. Chon lost the vid feed from your FullD systems, and you're ten minutes late coming out of game." There was an edge of panic in his voice she hoped the others couldn't hear.

"We're okay," she said. "Safe and sound."

Though her calf still ached where the spider had bitten it. She surreptitiously rubbed the spot through her jeans. Injury carryover could be serious, but it looked like she was the only one who had sustained damage into the real world. So far.

"You lost the vid feed on us?" Tam asked. "When?"

"As soon as you went outside the walls of Stronghold," Mr. Chon said. "There's obviously a glitch in the game we'll need to work out."

Tam glanced at Jennet, relief in his green eyes. Their journeys to the Realm, and then the Twilight Kingdom, weren't traceable.

"You did see us return and complete the quest, right?" Tam asked.

Mr. Chon nodded. "You'll have to put the details into your log, as precisely as you can. I especially want to know how the mechanics of the Manticore fight went."

"Right." Jennet let some of her weakness show, and swayed. "I'm not feeling that great. Mind if I take a break, get a glass of water?"

"Of course," her dad said, overriding Mr. Chon. "Are you sure you're all right?"

He helped her out of the sim chair and gave her a searching look. Obviously he suspected something had happened to her and Tam in-game. Maybe she could explain it, later.

"Very well," Mr. Chon said. "Everyone else, continue inputting your game-play descriptions. You have the day off tomorrow, but the next afternoon I expect you all promptly at three. We have a lot of content to get through."

Jennet caught her lower lip between her teeth. No kidding. More content than Mr. Chon could even imagine.

12

THE 6 A.M. alarm shredded Tam's sleep. Rubbing his eyes, he forced himself out of his sleeping bag to get ready for school. Mom's bedroom was ominously quiet and dark, and the Bug slept soundly, despite Tam's rattling around in the kitchen.

"Mom?" He tapped on her door. "Should I get Peter up?"

She preferred that Tam use his little brother's name, though the Bug didn't much seem to care. He probably liked thinking of himself as a bug—in all senses of the word.

Tam heard the rustle of covers, and then his mom cracked the door open. Her eyes were hollow and haunted, her hair tangled about her face.

"I'll make him breakfast," she said softly, tying the belt of her tattered bathrobe.

"Don't forget to eat something, too," he said.

He brushed a kiss over her forehead and swallowed the pleas that wanted to spill out. *Don't leave us. Get better. Please be here when I get home.*

She curved her lips at him in a smile that didn't touch her eyes, then went into the bathroom.

Tam glanced to his sleeping brother. Moving silently, he slipped into the bedroom. Mom kept their cash in a battered blue jewelry box on her dresser. Quickly, he peeled off a few bills, put them back in the bottom of the box, then pocketed the larger roll.

When his mom emerged from the bathroom, he was at the front door, shrugging on his pack.

"Have a good day, honey," she said.

He nodded, not trusting his voice, and went out into the bleak morning of the Exe.

Fear and urgency beat through him, giving rhythm to his steps, echoing every breath. Mom was on the verge of leaving—he'd seen it enough times now to know—and there was nothing he could do, except be there for the Bug.

Even seeing Jennet in their shared World History class wasn't enough to calm his churning fear. He hid it, though, ducking his head until his hair fell over his eyes, and keeping his mouth shut.

At lunch, he scooted next to Jennet at the cafeteria table. Although they weren't supposed to spend time together, their friend Marny had talked them into having lunch with her. And if Marny chose to eat with both of her friends, well, it wasn't their fault they had to sit at the same table.

"I need you to hold something for me," he said to Jennet in a low voice.

"What?"

He reached into his battered pack and pulled out the roll of cash, keeping it below the level of the table.

"Tam." Her blue eyes widened. "I can't take that. Don't you need it?"

"I need it to be out of my house right now. For a little while. Come on Jennet, I trust you."

"All right." Frowning, she held open her satchel.

Tam dropped the wad of money inside, and felt the tightness around his ribs ease a little. Jennet would keep the money safe, and in a place where his mom couldn't find it. When Mom left—the certainty of it was a stone lodged under his heart—at least she wouldn't take all their cash with her. He and the Bug would have enough to get them through, this time. Even if…

He shook his head. Mom would come back. She always came back.

"Hey, guys." Marny slid her lunch tray onto the table and took a seat across from them. "How's the beta testing going?"

"Interesting," Jennet said. "Are you sure you don't want to join the team? You're a prime player."

"You know how I feel about simming." Marny shuddered, her bobbed black hair swinging around her cheeks. "Nothing will convince me to stick my head in a helmet and sit in one of those chairs ever again."

Tam knew better than to ask. Not only was Marny claustrophobic, she'd been charmed against her will into playing Feyland with Lassiter. It would take a long time for that experience to wear off.

"So, the test is interesting... as in freaky?" Marny leaned across the table. "Are the faeries still running around in-game?"

She knew what had happened to Tam and Jennet, though she hadn't experienced the dangerous magic of Feyland inside the game. Still, she'd seen enough to believe.

"Kind of," Tam said. "They're not in the beta version we're testing. But Jennet and I ended up leaving the game and going into the Realm."

He was curiously reluctant to mention their further journey into Twilight Kingdom, even to Marny.

"And?"

"We're working on a solution," Jennet said, pushing her lunch aside. "Tam and I are supposed to wake up some powerful beings, and they'll fix things."

"Let me guess." Marny glanced between them, a frown on her round face. "*Dangerous* powerful beings."

"Probably." Tam set down his fork, tired of gumming the mushy cafeteria food.

"At least your uncle Zeg is in the beta," Jennet said. "I think he's enjoying it."

"Yeah." Marny smiled, her eyes sly. "He loves the chance to game. And the chance to bother VirtuMax. Did you know he spent last week fiddling with his gas car to make it smokier and noisier?"

Tam let out a snort of laughter. "Did he? Well, it worked. You should see the expression on the gate guards' faces every time we drive up."

He should have guessed. The Fanalua family liked to shake things up; challenge the perception of normal. Especially if it meant thumbing their noses at big business and fancy money.

The blare of the bell cut through the cafeteria. Jennet gathered up the remains of her lunch, then paused and touched his arm.

"See you tomorrow." Her eyes were full of unspoken wishes. Ones he shared.

He set his hand over hers, a fleeting warmth, then let go.

COLD WIND BIT through the Exe. Tam crouched in the crumbling alleyway near his house and pulled his battered brown coat closer. The yellow-eyed smoke drifters who lived down the block were all riled up.

Usually they stayed inside during the day, but this afternoon the men were scattered outside. One was banging on an abandoned dumpster with an old length of pipe. The hollow clanging echoing through the alleys had been Tam's first clue something was wrong. Two of the other drifters huddled beside the wall of the derelict building they called home.

But the one who worried him was the guy standing in the middle of the street.

The drifter's eyes darted back and forth. His right hand was stuck in his pocket, over a suspiciously gun-sized lump. Tam had to get past him to get home—and he had to make sure his mom stayed inside, away from the danger he could feel rolling down the street in thick waves.

"They were here!" the drifter yelled. "Right here! Come back!"

Typical smoke drifter yelling—disjointed and weird —but a shiver scraped Tam's spine.

"I din't like them, Skeever," one of the men curled up beside the building said. "Creepy dogs and shining girls. Get that noise out of my head."

Tam didn't think he meant the metal banging that ricocheted off the abandoned buildings. Fear scorched his mouth. Could the Unseelie Court have ridden here, in broad daylight? Or worse yet, the Wild Hunt?

He cast a desperate glance up the street at the blue-tarped roof of his house. There was only one reason the Dark Court faeries would be here. To find him.

Or his family.

Tam stepped clear of the oily puddle spreading halfway across the alley. Rubble from the eroding walls littered the cracked pavement. It didn't take him long to find a piece of concrete with a good heft to it.

He slid back to where the alley opened onto the street, the concrete cold in his hand. Throat tight with fear, he took aim and flung the hunk of rubble as hard as he could. It hit the side of the dumpster with a loud *clonk*.

The drifter in the street whirled and started toward the noise.

As quietly as possible, Tam slid along the shadows at the edge of the pavement. He might be a hero in-game, but it was suicide to take on a nest of drifters by himself.

Almost past. Scarcely breathing, he forced himself not to make a dash for the stairs. Sudden movement would alert the men—just keep going, slow and steady.

"Hey!" one of the drifters leaning up against the building called. He lifted an arm wrapped in tattered rags and pointed at Tam. "Is it one of them things?"

Tam froze. I'm not here, he thought. Only shadows.

"Where?" The drifter they had named Skeever looked up, his yellow eyes wide. "Gimme that."

He wrenched the length of pipe out of the other man's hands, hopefully forgetting the gun in his pocket. Drifters were like that; barely able to keep one thought in their brains at a time. He turned his head, scanning the street. Tam knew the exact instant the man spotted him, those creepy yellow eyes locking onto him.

Adrenaline spiked through Tam, sizzling his nerves like lightning.

"I see you," the man said. "Damn little beastie. Can't get away this time."

Tam glanced at his stairs. Run for it? No, it was too far, and even if he beat the drifter to his door, he still had to get his keys out and undo all the locks.

"Argh!" the man yelled, lifting the pipe above his head and rushing forward.

Tam threw himself to the side. Dammit, he needed a weapon, he needed...

He felt the heft of his sword in his hand, the protection of his shield strapped onto his right arm.

The shock of it stopped him cold. His in-game weapons, here? The drifter brought his makeshift weapon down, and Tam forced his disbelieving body into action. He blocked the blow with his shield, then swiped at the drifter with the flat of his sword. He didn't want to cut the guy—not in real life.

The drifter seemed oblivious to the fact his opponent was now armed. Tam shot a quick glance to the others, glad to see they didn't look inclined to jump into the fight.

Fending off Skeever's blows, Tam backed down the street, toward his house. Unless the guy got a lucky hit in, he'd be okay, but there was still the problem of getting up the stairs and opening his door.

He couldn't believe his weapons had materialized, but the same thing had happened to Jennet when she was threatened in the Exe. While it was a good thing—very good, at the moment—it also meant the walls between the worlds were thinning. Which was severe, especially if the faeries had just been visiting his neighborhood.

The pipe clanged against Tam's shield, and the drifter frowned. He stared at the length of metal, then dropped it onto the cracked pavement and started patting at his pockets.

Oh crap. He'd remembered the gun.

Keeping his shield up—maybe it would stop a bullet, if he was super-lucky—Tam backpedaled toward his stairs.

"Gotcha," the drifter said, opening his mouth in a smile that exposed his missing teeth.

He drew the gun out and pointed it at Tam. The barrel wavered unsteadily, but it was still death staring Tam in the face. He swallowed, his throat parched, his body humming with panic.

This couldn't be it. He had too much to do!

And he couldn't leave Jennet.

Shifting his weight to the balls of his feet, he prepared to rush the drifter.

"Hi there!" a bright voice called from the top of his stairs.

Oh, no.

His heart cased in lead, Tam turned to see the small figure of his little brother standing on the steps. The Bug's brown hair was tousled, and he was still in his jammies.

The drifter's eyes went wide.

"Another one," he growled, swinging the gun toward the Bug. His fingers twitched against the metal.

"No!" Tam cried, throwing himself forward.

13

THE AIR EXPLODED with the sound of the gunshot an instant before Tam bashed his shield against the drifter's chin. Behind him the Bug wailed, high and thin.

Skeever collapsed onto the dirty street, and Tam lifted his sword. He brought the pommel down on the drifter's temple. He still couldn't kill the man, even if the Bug was…

Swallowing panic, he whirled and sprinted for the stairs. A small figure lay crumpled at the top in a sticky puddle of liquid. Blood.

"Oh God."

Tam took the steps in three bounds, and gathered up his little brother. The Bug was lighter than he'd expected, and warm, too warm.

"We have to call an ambulance, get you inside, don't die, oh crap, where's Mom?" Tam knew he was babbling, but he couldn't help himself. *Not his little brother. No, please.*

He sprinted into the house and carefully laid the Bug on the couch. No time, no time, but he had to close the door before Skeever and the other drifters headed up the stairs. Tam slammed the door and threw the deadbolts, then raced to his brother's side. The air was thick and sludgy, like breathing tar. His vision blurred, and Tam swiped his hand across his eyes, feeling wetness on his cheeks.

"Can you hear me?" He choked the words out. "Where were you hit? Please, Peter, open your eyes."

His brother moaned. Relief hit Tam in the chest. The Bug was alive, though his body began to shake, racked by convulsions. Tam grabbed him by the shoulders—shoulders that were soft, then oddly bony under his hands.

"I'll call the medics," he said. "Hold on. Just hold on."

Then the Bug opened his eyes, and Tam froze, relief turning to ice and chilling him to the bone. Bulbous eyes with irises the color of pale milk stared at him.

Whatever had been shot, whatever was looking at him, it wasn't his brother.

Tam scrambled back, reaching for his sword, but he'd left it outside in his mad dash to take care of his brother. Or rather, the creature he'd *thought* was his brother.

"What are you?" he asked. "And where's my brother?"

The thing smiled, showing sharp teeth. Its body shuddered, growing simultaneously squatter and bonier until a hideous fey creature lay on the couch.

"Not an easy one to fool, are you?" he said. "Tricksy is as tricksy does. Time spent in the Realm makes humans too clever by far."

Tam glared at the creature, his panic pivoting over to hot anger. "You're a faerie. One of those replacement things."

He remembered reading about them in Jennet's old book of tales and ballads. Human children were taken, stolen away by the faeries, and something *else* left in their place.

"A changeling," the creature said.

"Where's my brother?" Tam glanced around the single room, as if the Bug had been overlooked.

But he knew Peter wasn't there. And the thing that had taken his place appeared less like a human child by the second—his face growing wizened and dark, his pale eyes bulging.

The changeling gave him a sharp-toothed grin. "Your brother is a guest in the Realm."

"Give him back!" Tam raised a clenched fist.

"Ah, ah." The changeling held up his hand, the nails long and clawed. "No harm done to me, none will be visited on your brother."

Damn it. The faeries always had a loophole.

"What do I have to do to get him returned? Safe and

whole," Tam added. You had to be ultra-specific when dealing with the fey folk.

The changeling clambered to the back of the couch, and perched there like a flightless gargoyle. "Feed me."

"Will that return my brother?"

"No." The creature leered at him. "But it will keep him from starving."

"Where's my mom?" Tam asked, though he had the sinking feeling he knew the answer.

"Your brother was left unattended. A perfect invitation to the faeries. An unwanted child is always welcome in the Realm."

"He's wanted! Why did you take him?"

Another wave of anger sizzled through Tam's veins. He wished he could take the creature and fling it into the street for the drifters, or poison it. But he had to keep it safe, for the Bug's sake. At least, until he could get into Feyland and rescue his little brother.

The changeling narrowed its ugly eyes. "Those who rule the Realm require you to cease meddling in their affairs. In a fortnight, your brother will be returned to you, unharmed—*if* you do not stand in their way."

Meaning, if he and Jennet did nothing to stop Feyland's release. Which was out of the question, since clearly the fey folk had every intention of entering the mortal world through the game.

But letting the Bug remain a prisoner in the Realm wasn't an option, either.

"Fine," Tam said. "I'll get you something to eat."

As he rummaged in the kitchen alcove, his mind worked furiously. His heart was screaming at him to save his little brother, but he couldn't go charging into the Realm by himself. Jennet would come with him, no question. And this was important enough he'd swallow his pride and ask Lassiter for help, too.

In a twisted sort of way, he was relieved that Mom was gone, despite his anger. It would kill her to see her beloved younger son replaced by a hideous creature with bulging eyes and pointed teeth.

"Here," he said, handing the creature a plate of left-over synthi-meat, some stale crackers fished out of the trash behind the big grocery, and a mug of water.

The changeling wrinkled his nose, but grabbed the plate and gulped the food down in three bites. It guzzled the water, then slid off the couch and began to make a nest out of the Bug's blankets.

"Where is my brother being held?" Tam asked, though he was pretty sure he knew.

"I serve the queen," the changeling said, scowling. "Now go away and leave me in peace. I will answer no more of your pestiferous questions."

He burrowed into the rumpled mess of blankets until only the top of his head was visible. If Tam didn't know better, he'd think it was his brother in there—similar size and shape, even a close approximation of the hair.

No way was he letting the changeling go to school in

the Bug's place. He shuddered at the thought. The faerie would have to stay here while Tam was gone—and who knew what kind of trouble it would get up to. Apprehension trickled down his back.

Even though Jenet's dad had forbidden him to contact Jennet, he had to let her know about this dire turn of events. He fished his messager out of his backpack, and locked himself in the tiny bathroom.

Bug taken by faeries, he wrote. Meet me early tomorrow.

He waited five minutes, but there was no reply. Reception in the Exe was spotty, even though the buried cable of the 'net, the backbone of the country's tech, ran right under Crestview—which explained why VirtuMax had parked company headquarters there.

Nothing like delivering evil fairies direct and high-speed to people's homes worldwide.

Tam powered off his messager and cracked open the bathroom door. The lump of blankets on the couch didn't move, but no way was he sleeping with that creature next to him. He'd grab his bag and crash out in his mom's room.

What if the faeries had nabbed her, too? He didn't trust the changeling. Faeries were slippery when it came to telling the truth.

Moving quietly, Tam slipped into the bedroom. The open closet held most of Mom's clothes—but her yellow winter coat was missing, and her favorite scarf. He went to the dresser and opened the battered blue jewelry box.

The cheap bracelets and plastic necklaces winked up at him. He ignored them and hooked his fingers into the catches of the secret compartment, then lifted the bottom of the box out. The few bills he'd left that morning had disappeared. Nothing but faded velvet stared up at him.

He let out a long breath.

His mom was truly gone. Not into the Realm of Faerie, like his missing brother, but into the dangerous world surrounding the Exe.

Tam wrapped his arms around his ribs, trying to hold in the fear and sorrow.

At least he still had Jennet.

JENNET STUFFED her gloved hands into her pockets and paced the sidewalk in front of Crestview High. Grey light seeped from the eastern sky, but the rising sun was too weak to penetrate the thick winter clouds crouching on the horizon.

Her path took her near the black grav-car where her chauffeur, George, waited patiently. He lowered the tinted window and gave her a concerned look.

She'd lied to the house manager and Dad, told them she had an early make-up class, but she couldn't lie to George. On the ride down from The View, she'd confided she was going to meet Tam. His only response had been a quiet grunt.

But Tam wasn't there.

"Miss Carter," George said, "wouldn't you rather wait in the car?"

"If Tam doesn't show up soon, I will."

She walked to the corner again, cold air stinging her cheeks, and peered up the street. There he was! Relief eased her breath at the sight of Tam's familiar figure trudging through the dawn. She gave George a quick wave, then ran down the sidewalk toward Tam. When she was a few steps away he opened his arms, and she fetched up against his chest with a solid thump. His lean, strong arms closed around her, and she held him tightly in return.

"My mom's gone again," he said, an edge of bleakness in his voice. "And the faeries took the Bug. Came into the Exe in broad daylight, and left a changeling in his place."

"I got your message." She stepped back and stared into his troubled green eyes. "We'll get the Bug back. I was up all night, thinking about this. I'm pretty sure they'll take your brother to the Dark Queen's court."

"They did." His tone was hollow, with the same fear that echoed inside her. "Sneak me into your house, after school. We can go in-game on your FullD equip and get him out."

Her heart ached at what she had to say next. "Tam—we can't."

He grabbed her shoulders. "You said you'd help me."

"If we rescue the Bug now, he'll still be in danger. They could swipe him again, behind our backs."

"One of us would be with him, twenty-four-seven. I'll skip school, and—"

"What about the beta testing? The questions if people find out your mom has disappeared again? I know it's hard, Tam, but we have to leave him in the Realm for now. They'll keep him safe." She hoped.

"Just abandon my brother to the Unseelie Court?" His voice cracked at the end of the question.

She took his hands in hers. "Thomas is there. Didn't he look out for you when you were a prisoner in the Dark Court? And there's always Puck."

"Like he would keep anyone out of trouble."

"The Elder Fey are supposed to restore the balance. That means getting your brother back, too." She squeezed his fingers. "Our priority is to wake the Elder Fey. Once we do, everything will work out."

"Dammit, I want my brother home *now*." Tam's shoulders slumped, and he stared at the ground. "The changeling told me if I kept him healthy, the Bug would be treated well—at least by the standards of the fey folk. Not that I trust the faeries."

"So, we have a little time."

"Less than two weeks," Tam said. "The faeries want to make sure Feyland launches. They're holding my brother hostage to make sure we don't do anything to stop the game."

It was a brilliant piece of evil. Tam couldn't make the choice to sacrifice his little brother, even for the good of all humanity. Or if he did, it would haunt him forever, make him a walking ghost. Either way, he'd suffer.

No question the Dark Queen was behind this. She had a far bigger score to settle with Tam and Jennet than the Bright King did—and she was ruthless.

"All right," Jennet said, trying to sound calm. "Next time we're in-game, we'll finish up in the Twilight Kingdom. I bet the queen doesn't even know we're trying to wake the Elder Fey."

Tam lifted his head, his expression shadowed. "Jennet, we can't do this by ourselves."

Fear, metallic and sharp, filled her mouth. "We'll figure it out, Tam. We always do."

Though this time, the odds were more impossible than ever.

At lunch, Marny set her tray down beside them, then took one look at Tam's face.

"Ok, spill it," she said.

Jennet shot her a half-smile, glad there was one other person they could talk to. Not that Marny could do anything to help, other than lend one of her broad, sympathetic shoulders.

Marny listened, her dark eyes narrowed. She nodded when Tam told her his mom had taken off again, and her eyes widened as he explained about his little brother being stolen by the Dark Court.

"So the faeries stole your brother, but left a substitute in his place?" she asked.

Tam nodded, misery clear in the set of his mouth.

"I want to meet him. It. Whatever."

"What?"

"Look." She spread her hands wide. "You two have to deal with things in-game. The last thing you need to worry about is some freaky fairy dude pretending to be Tam's little brother. Even though I don't sim, I can help with this."

"She's right," Jennet said. The knot of tension behind her ribs loosened a tiny bit. "We can't deal with the changeling, and beta testing, and the Twilight Kingdom —not all of it."

"At least your mom's not around," Marny said. "Crappy that she's gone, but the timing is decent. Considering. And this way, if she comes home and you guys are, um, unavailable, I can run interference."

"Ok." Tam swiped a hand through his hair, letting it fall back into his face. His eyes were smudged with exhaustion. "You can come over after school today and meet the changeling. Provided it's still there."

"It will be." Jennet rubbed at the scar on her palm. "From what I remember, changelings have to stay close to home. Their pretend home, I mean. I'll read up and let you know what else I find out."

"Good," Marny said. "This should be interesting."

14

Tam waited for Marny outside school. He'd already waved goodbye to Jennet as George drove her away. She wanted to come along, he could see it in her eyes, but it wasn't worth the chance of trouble. Bending the rules was one thing, but they couldn't risk Tam getting kicked off the beta team—not with so much at stake.

A bright red grav-car swerved around the corner and shot down the street, leaving grit swirling in its wake. Lassiter. It hadn't taken him long to talk his mom into restoring the privileges he'd lost as a result of tangling with fey magic. Tam rubbed his face and frowned.

So far, nobody suspected the "technical glitch" during the last beta session had been something more. But Lassiter had been in the Realm, all the way to the Bright Court. He'd be the first to notice something was going on.

Question was, would he keep quiet about it?

The last students exited the battered metal doors of Crestview High, Marny among them. She joined Tam on the sidewalk.

"Ready?" she asked.

"You sure about this?"

"Hell, yeah." She smiled at him. "I'm tired of you and Fancy-girl having all the adventures."

"Adventure isn't all it's cracked up to be. Especially where the Realm of Faerie is concerned."

Marny shrugged. "It's a change of pace. Come on."

She started down the sidewalk, and Tam lengthened his stride. Marny was tall, in addition to being solidly built. She could pin the changeling down with one hand if she had to—which was part of why he felt somewhat okay with this plan.

When they reached Stark Way, the pot-holed street marking the beginning of the Exe, Marny hung back. She knew enough to let Tam lead from there. Despite her bulk, she followed agilely through the stinking and trash-heaped alleys. Oily puddles reflected an equally filmy sky.

This time of year held less danger from the roaming gangs, but he and Marny were in Jackal territory. Tam stayed alert, listening for the crazed, cackling laugh that was the gangs' signal to attack. Things stayed quiet, though, all the way to his place. The smoke-drifters down the block were holed up in their dilapidated building, no doubt dreaming weird, disjointed dreams filled with otherworldly creatures.

"Watch the steps," Tam said, pulling out his keys.

"Right." Her voice subdued, Marny stayed behind him.

Their footsteps creaked on the stairs, and he glimpsed a shadow behind the wire-webbed windows. Breath catching in his throat, he unlocked the multiple deadbolts and pushed the door open. It was quiet inside. Too quiet. He held up his palm, signaling Marny to wait.

One step inside. Another. The back of his neck prickled and Tam wished he had his sword.

"Hiiiyyaaa!" a voice screeched.

A figure launched itself from the top of the bookshelf, right at Tam. He caught a glimpse of gleaming eyes in a wizened face, sharp teeth bared, before the changeling landed on him like some kind of rabid animal.

"Hey!" Tam cried. "Get off."

Heart thumping double-time, he tried to shake the creature loose, but it clung to his shoulders with sharp-clawed hands, pulling at his hair.

"Gotcha!" the changeling said, screeching with laughter.

That laughter ended in a squawk as Marny swiped the creature off Tam. It hit the floor and glared up at both of them.

"Nice," Marny said, her tone dry.

"What is this?" the changeling hissed. "Another human to see me? Sheer folly."

Tam turned and shut the door, snicking the locks home. "What was that about, jumping on me?"

He resisted the urge to kick the changeling. Someone, somewhere, was keeping track, and he didn't want to put the Bug in danger. Though he didn't mind the force Marny had used to dislodge the thing.

"Tee-hee. 'Twas all a bit of fun. Surprised you, did I?" The changeling grinned up at him and leaped to its feet. "Now feed me."

"Quite a houseguest you have there," Marny said. "As annoying as your little brother is, I prefer the Bug to *this*."

"What you think matters little to me," the changeling said.

Marny rolled her eyes at Tam and followed him into the kitchen. He flipped the electric kettle on to boil, then rummaged around in the cupboards. Not much to eat, beyond dried noodle packets and a couple of protein bars.

"Here," he said, flipping a bar through the air to the changeling.

The creature caught it and held it up to the light. "What is this item?"

"Food," Tam said, then shook his head as the changeling bit into the wrapped protein bar.

"Feh." The creature spit on the floor. "Mortal sustenance used to taste much better."

"You don't eat the wrapper," Marny said. "Peel it, like this."

She grabbed a bar from Tam and tore off the shiny plastic wrapping. The changeling watched her, then stripped off the wrapper and popped the whole bar into his mouth.

"Still tasteless," he said, wrinkling his already-wrinkled face into a sour expression.

"At least we agree on that," Marny said, handing her unwrapped bar to Tam.

"What?" he said. "You don't like synthesized nut-flavored protein bars?"

She curled her mouth. "I prefer my uncle Zeg's cookies."

"Me too, but I don't have any of those lying around. Tea?"

"Yeah—mint if you've got it."

Tam pulled out two mugs, then ate the protein bar, trying to ignore the dry non-flavor.

"So," Marny said to the changeling, "what's your name?"

"Are you trying to trick me, mortal?" His gleaming eyes narrowed.

Her eyebrows rose. "As in...?"

"Names have power in the Realm," Tam said. "Generally, they aren't freely given out."

He poured hot water over the teabag in Marny's mug and handed it to her.

"Right," she said. "Than what shall we call him?"

"I've been thinking of him as not-Bug," Tam said.

"Catchy." Marny shook her head. "But we can do better. Changeling, what name do you use when you're in the mortal world? Doing, you know, baby impersonations."

The creature folded his spindly arms. "I am called by the child's name."

"Yeah," Tam said, setting his mug of hot tea on the counter. "Except we know you're not my little brother. Either you choose something, or we will."

"Yoda," Marny said.

"Too obvious." Tam tilted his head, looking the changeling over. "How about... Bilbo."

"Nah. If anything, it's a Gollum."

"Stop," the changeling said, baring his pointed teeth. "If you insist, you may call me Korrigan."

He leaped onto the counter and took a guzzling sip of Tam's tea.

"Hey, that's mine!" Tam said. He made a grab for the mug, then reconsidered. "Fine. Drink up."

A malicious light in his eyes, Korrigan slurped the tea down. He finished, wiped his mouth with the back of his hand, and then squatted on the counter like an evil toad.

"Mortals," he said. "I cannot set foot over the

threshold unless Tamlin is with me. Since I am trapped in this wretched space, what is there to do here that will amuse me?"

"What do you normally do?" Marny asked. Tam noticed she kept a tight grip on her own mug.

"I squall and mewl like an infant. I flail my arms and legs, and lie in the cradle."

"Doesn't sound all that fun," Marny said.

"So you usually pretend to be much younger children," Tam said. "Why did they send you this time?" He let the comment about his "wretched" house pass.

The changeling frowned—a particularly unlovely expression on its ugly face. "It is how the thing is done. There cannot be a taking without a replacement. Most stolen children are but infants. You brother is a special case."

"Yeah, a hostage." Tam crossed his arms.

He was tired of Korrigan, tired of Feyland, tired of his entire life, with a bone-deep weariness that turned the edges of everything gray.

"Tam," Marny said in a low voice, "did you get any sleep last night?"

He shook his head.

"Go lie down," she said. "I'll show Korrigan a few basic Screenie games, ok? That should keep him busy and out of trouble."

"Just don't let him onto the 'net," Tam said.

"Bug's account is locked-out, right?" Marny glanced

to the corner of the living room, where their netscreen setup was.

"Yeah. Log him in to that, it should be fine." Tam couldn't help the yawn that pried his jaws open.

"Get some rest." Marny pushed his shoulder. "I'll introduce the changeling to the joys of Kart racing."

"Show no mercy," Tam said, already heading for the bedroom door.

She gave him an evil grin. "I won't."

15

THE CAFETERIA WAS noisy as usual, which meant Jennet could ask Marny how her meeting with the changeling went without anyone listening in.

It had been hard, watching out the grav-car window yesterday as Marny and Tam headed for the Exe. The ache of not being with Tam clogged Jennet's throat. Would her dad ever relent and let her see Tam openly? Would he ever understand about Feyland?

Tam and Marny were already at their usual table. Jennet put her tray down, wrinkling her nose at the limp spaghetti sprawled over the plate. The whole room smelled like tomatoes and overcooked pasta.

"How was meeting your first faerie?" she asked, scooting across from Marny.

"Quite the experience." Marny set aside her roll. "He's a freaky little creature."

Tam gave a wry nod. "Welcome to life among the fey folk. Did he ever manage to beat you in Kart racing?"

"Not yet... but Korrigan is pretty fierce. I bet he spends all morning practicing."

"Korrigan?" Jennet glanced at Tam. "He told you his name?"

"No. Just what we should call him."

"Right." Of course the changeling wasn't going to give Tam and Marny any kind of power over him.

"You guys go up to the compound today, don't you?" Marny said. "Do you think you'll get back into the Dim Land?"

A faint smile ghosted over Tam's lips. "You and the nicknames, Marny."

"It keeps things from getting boring."

"We have to return to the Twilight Kingdom, somehow," Jennet said. "The beta team plays today after school. Tam, I'm allowed to offer you a ride up."

"How very kind." There was an edge in his voice.

"Cut the drama," Marny said. "Say yes, Tam. Or would you rather drive up with Roy Lassiter?"

"What about Zeg?" Tam asked. "Doesn't he get the offer of a luxury ride to The View?"

Marny shook her head, the ends of her black hair swinging past her round cheeks. "He prefers to drive himself, you know that. Come on, Tam, don't be stubborn."

"He wouldn't be Tam if he weren't stubborn," Jennet said.

"Fine." The bell blared over the din of too many students talking, and he pushed his tray away. "I'll meet you after school."

BACK IN THE beta version of Feyland, the testing team split into their smaller groups and parted ways in Stronghold City. Roy offered Spark his arm, which she ignored, and Zeg and Jennet's dad went off together, talking. Obviously they were building some camaraderie from their adventures.

Jennet and Tam headed for Stronghold Castle. The wide cobbled streets of the city were clean and shining, and a crisp breeze fluttered the green banners at the tops of the turrets. Snatches of music and laughter drifted from the open doorways of shops and taverns as they passed. The setting was completely at odds with her mood, and Jennet let out a low sigh.

Tam's little brother was a captive of the Dark Court, they had a quest to complete in a place nearly impossible to get to, and the new FullD system featuring Feyland was on track to release in less than two weeks.

Impatience spiced her blood, every heartbeat urging *hurry, hurry*. But there wasn't anything she could do about it, except act as though she were playing a simple computer game.

She glanced at the perfectly aligned streets, the flowers that were all variations on a theme, the passersby who took no notice of two real players in their midst. Finding a faerie ring in the middle of Stronghold seemed improbable at best.

"How are we even going to get back to... you know where?" she asked.

"We have to start with the castle quests," Tam said quietly. "At least make it look like we're playing how Mr. Chon wants us to. Be patient."

The tall silver gates of the castle rose at the end of the street. Guards stood at either side, staring straight ahead. They didn't even glance at Jennet and Tam when they reached the gates—but an NPC stepped forward, blocking their way. It wasn't Puck in disguise this time. Jennet swallowed disappointment and curled her fingers around her mage staff.

"Welcome to Stronghold Castle." The green-liveried herald bowed. "State your business."

"We're supposed to speak to the princess," Tam said.

Mr. Chon had instructed them to pick up some simple quests in the city while the techs kept an eye on their FullD equip. The project manager wanted to figure out why Jennet and Tam's systems had malfunctioned last time they played—not that he'd be able to.

The herald moved back a pace. "Welcome to Stronghold Castle. You will find Princess Paloma in her garden. Proceed to the courtyard, then turn left."

The garden? That sounded promising. Jennet traded a look with Tam as they strode to the courtyard the NPC had indicated.

"Princess Paloma?" Tam said. "Chon sure went for the cutesy titles."

"At least she's not named after a fruit."

Their footsteps rang on the flagstones of the courtyard, which featured a burbling fountain in the center— statues of mermaids and fish spitting water. A columned opening to their left revealed glimpses of greenery. Princess Paloma's garden.

Jennet breathed shallowly as she and Tam strode between the columns, hoping they'd be transported back to the Realm. No luck. Instead, they stepped onto a lush green lawn dotted with uniform blue flowers. Before them, a half-dozen court ladies sat on an arrangement of benches. They wore long-sleeved dresses in soft hues of azure and rose and tall, pointed hats with gauzy veils draping off the top.

All except the girl in white, who had a circlet of gold holding back her dark hair.

Tam stepped forward and made her a bow, and the ladies surrounding the princess giggled.

"Your highness," he said. "We are pleased to find you in good health."

On their last quest, Jennet and Tam had supposedly found herbs to cure the princess of whatever dire illness she'd had. Good of Tam to remember—but then, he was a pro.

"Greetings, brave knight and fair lady," Princess Paloma said. "Have you come for your reward in healing me?"

Jennet moved to Tam's side. "We have."

The princess looked at them with eyes of deep purple. For a moment, Jennet thought she saw midnight stars hidden in their depths. Then the princess clapped her hands, and a small figure wearing a green tabard came running in from the courtyard.

"Follow my page to the royal treasury. There, you may each select one item in payment. Choose carefully, then return to show me your gifts."

"Thank you," Tam said, bowing again. "We will."

A soft ding filled the air—the signal their quest had begun.

"Come with me, adventurers," the page said, in a high, familiar voice.

Puck! Jennet tried not to grin too widely as she and Tam followed the sprite through the garden. He had managed to tame back his wild tangle of hair, but his knobby wrists and long fingers stuck out of the page's livery.

The sprite took them along a gravel path leading to tall double-doors. Jennet desperately wanted to pelt Puck with questions. Instead, she pressed her lips together and let the crunch of their footsteps fill up the silence. Thick hedges grew to either side, and she didn't see any way out, or anything that looked like a gateway to the Realm.

A few paces from the doors, Puck grabbed their hands and leaped into the hedge.

"What? Hey!" Jennet threw up her arm, fending the sharp branches away from her face.

"Shh," Puck said. "Be still a moment more."

He released them, and wove his fingers in strange patterns that left a shimmer in the air. The chime of fey magic echoed around them.

"There," the sprite said. "You are shielded from sight and sound. Now it will appear you and Tamlin have entered the castle to complete the quest."

The sprite grasped their wrists again and pulled them through the back of the hedge. Jennet stumbled, and Tam caught her elbow, steadying her.

"Wait, Puck," he said. "I'm not going anywhere until you tell me how my brother is."

The sprite cocked his head. "Your brother suffers no harm."

"Yet." Tam's voice was cold.

"Indeed, he is fascinated by the Dark Court, the magic and the creatures that dwell therein."

"He better not get *too* fascinated. I want him back safe."

Jennet rubbed her scarred palm. She'd read too many tales of humans gladly ensnared in the Realm, staying there while time outside sped past. When they finally returned, their families were long dead, their world utterly changed.

"Fear not, Tamlin. Bard Thomas guards your brother as one of his own. He will not let the youngling suffer ill treatment."

Maybe not—but she had the gnawing suspicion that the Bug would be permanently altered by his stay in the Realm. The sooner they got him back, the better. Which meant getting into the Twilight Kingdom, *now*.

"Come on," she said, pushing against the dense foliage. "Let's get this done."

They emerged from the hedge into an opening enclosed by the tall shrubbery. White-spotted red mushrooms encircled grass that gleamed silvery, as if touched by moonlight.

"Nice work" Jennet said.

Puck grinned. "Go, go. I will stay here and maintain the illusion of your quest."

Together, she and Tam stepped into the ring. Golden light rose up in a wave and she doubled over, stomach cramping. Dizziness hummed in her ears, and she blinked furiously. This was no time to be sick.

The vertigo passed, and they stood in a mossy circle bound by white-spotted mushrooms. Tall trees surrounded them, starlight filtering between their leaves. A path led, as one always did, between the pale-barked trunks.

"You all right?" Tam asked.

He laid his arm over her shoulders, his green eyes lit with concern. She pressed the back of her hand against her mouth, then straightened.

"Yeah. Let's find the circle to the Twilight Kingdom."

The moment Jennet and Tam stepped over the boundary of red mushrooms, a long howl shivered the night sky.

"Crap," Tam said. "The Hunt. They must have been waiting for us. That next ring had better be close."

Heartbeat jamming her throat, Jennet grabbed his outstretched hand and they pelted through the dark forest. Over the sound of her breath, she heard the yips of spectral hounds, the low, mournful cry of a horn.

The Wild Hunt had caught their scent.

16

THE CRIES of the Wild Hunt grew louder, drowning out the pounding of Jennet's footsteps. The back of her neck prickled, and she was certain if she looked behind them she would see the horned figure who led the hunt.

Legs burning with strain, she and Tam burst into a clearing lit by the glowing purplish mushrooms. Without stopping, he tugged her into the center.

Cold blankness wrapped around her. The air turned to ice, and for a panic-stricken second she couldn't breathe.

When sensation returned, Jennet found herself sprawled and gasping on the dark velvet grass of the Twilight Kingdom. Tam crouched beside her, his hands covering his face.

"Tam?" She carefully sat up, her bones aching with the memory of frost.

"Yeah. Just…cold."

He dropped his hands. The eerie glow of the mushrooms made him look sickly, and his eyes were leached of color.

She grabbed his shoulders and pressed her lips against his, willing him to be all right. It was like kissing a marble statue, and fear crashed through her.

Finally, his mouth warmed beneath hers. His arms came around her, and he started trembling, kissing her like she was the only true thing left in the universe. They clung together, until the cry of some twilight creature broke the moment.

Still, Tam didn't let go, and she was glad. He rested his lips against her forehead, the warmth anchoring her back into her skin.

"We can't keep doing this," she said.

"What, kissing?"

It was a feeble attempt at a joke, and she didn't laugh. He'd looked terrible just then, like he was about to die. Her fingers dug into his shoulders, as if by holding on hard she could keep them both safe.

"I don't think humans are supposed to travel between the worlds so frequently," she said. Or at all.

"We don't have a choice."

She wanted to yell and kick things. Wanted to turn her back on the stupid pixilated world of Feyland and the dire magic of the Realm. Wanted to tell Puck she quit. Game over.

But Tam was right. The only option was to go forward—into the Twilight Kingdom.

"We have to find the Elder Fey tonight," she said. "I'm not coming back here again." Not when it drained them so much.

His arms tightened around her. Then he let go and clambered to his feet, giving her a hand up.

"Time to see where we are." He floated straight up into the air.

The purplish sky shimmered behind him, the light hurting her eyes, as though they were being x-rayed. As they cleared the trees, she could see the silver slash of the river off to their right. On their left was the orangey glow they had seen last time, illuminating jagged peaks.

"Over there," she said.

Tam nodded, and they took off. The wind rasped at her skin, carrying a bite that wasn't quite cold. More like tiny bits of sharp sand grating invisibly against flesh. Her hair streamed behind her, and her mage robes whipped about her legs. Eyes pricking with tears from the flight, she kept pace with Tam. It was too hard to speak, to draw in lungfuls of the painful air.

They traveled over the dim landscape, passing hollows where violet light puddled and the sound of jangled chimes drifted up. Jennet scanned the ground ahead, watching for the telltale shimmer of dusk on water. No way did she want to slam into a wall of air—not at this speed.

When they next reached water, though, it was unmistakable. A huge silver mirror of a lake stretched before them, endless in either direction. The stark mountains jutted up across from them on the far shore, and the orange light pulsed in the air like heat waves.

Tam angled down, and Jennet landed beside him on the satiny grasses of the lakeshore.

She glanced around. "No bridge."

"Maybe we can fly across."

He flew to the water's edge and hovered there, sliding back and forth against the invisible barrier of air. Mouth set in a frustrated twist, he dropped back to the ground.

Jennet paced the shoreline, stabbing at the dark soil with the end of her staff. "Maybe there's a boat hidden in those bushes up there."

She didn't expect there to be, but they had to try *something*. Impatience flared in her veins. They didn't have time for this.

"Stupid rule, about not flying over water." Tam voiced her thoughts. "Alright, let's try the bushes."

It was a quick swoop over to the dark-leaved mass of foliage. As they got closer, Jennet saw dark berries shining amid the sharp-edged leaves. Long thorns studded the branches.

There was no boat drawn up on the shore.

"Berries," Tam said, eyeing the bushes. "Remember the banshee quest?"

"You think picking the berries will call some kind of creature?"

From the poisonous look of the fruit, whatever came couldn't be good.

Before she could stop him, Tam reached into the thicket and plucked a single berry. Nothing happened— no crash of thunder, no enraged faerie demanding they stop stealing her fruit.

"Where do I put this?" he asked, holding the shiny orb between his thumb and forefinger.

"Let me try something."

She closed her eyes. *Basket*, she thought, imagining the woven sides, the curved handle. In the Realm, they could summon objects with a thought. She opened her eyes. No basket.

"That would have been too easy," Tam said. "If we could summon a berry container, we could summon a boat."

"I'm not sure I'd trust an imagined boat to carry us safely over that." She gestured to the lake.

The surface moved strangely, as though made of liquid metal—mercury, instead of water. She didn't want that stuff touching her.

"Then we keep picking." Tam dropped the berry into his cupped hand.

Jennet reached into the bush. Her fingers closed over the smooth surface of a berry, oddly hard and slick to her touch. It wouldn't come loose. She tugged, and her hand slipped. A thorn needled into the pad of her thumb.

"Ow!" She pulled her hand free. A drop of blood welled on her thumb, dark and shining.

"Don't let it—"

Tam moved to her side, too late. The drop fell. The instant it hit the ground, a tremble went through the land. The lake shivered, and a high, distant drone cut the air, setting her teeth on edge.

"That was bad," she said, pressing her finger hard against her thumb to keep any more blood from dripping.

"I think so."

The trembling ceased, the lake stilled, and silence fell.

The skin between Jennet's shoulder blades prickled. "I think we're being watched."

"Me, too. But by what?" Tam set his hand to his sword and pivoted, scanning the shore.

She couldn't see anything but the long silver lake, the jagged, orange-lit mountains, the dim purple air. For a long minute, they stood still, breathing. Waiting. Nothing happened.

"My turn again," Tam said.

"Careful," she said in a low voice. "Those thorns are sharp."

He slid his fingers between the dangerous branches

and grabbed for another berry, then winced and let out a hiss of pain.

"Too sharp." He pulled his hand out of the bush

Jennet grasped his hand and frowned at the long scratch marring his skin. It looked black in the eerie light.

"I'm ok," he said, reaching for the bush again. "I didn't even get a berry that time."

The scratch sparkled and, quick as thought, a drop of his blood rolled off his hand and plunged to the grass.

"Dammit," he said.

This time, the ground shook. Waves lapped the lakeshore, and the air buzzed with a clashing chord, like two discordant voices shrieking into the dimness. Jennet gripped her mage-staff tightly, the wood solid under her grasp. Her ribs tightened and her lungs burned from the abrasive air.

Still holding the single berry in his cupped palm, Tam drew his sword.

"Give me the berry," Jennet said.

She plucked the fruit from his hand. As she picked it up, the berry suddenly softened. Her fingers crushed the soft flesh and a single drop of juice plummeted, shining like an obsidian tear.

The clamor in the air smoothed into a distant fanfare of brassy trumpets, tuneful and bright. The ground gave a last twitch beneath their feet, then subsided. The lake, however, frothed wildly, silver waves whirling in a vortex at the center.

"Look," Jennet said, her voice small in her throat.

Something was rising from the water—a pale prow, the long line of a mast. A single sail billowed, shimmering, as a boat rose from the middle of the lake. In the center, a shining figure wearing a hooded robe woven from mist and starlight steered the boat. Right toward them.

"I think our ride's here," Tam said.

She caught his hand, tangling their fingers together.

The boat drew up to shore, the side angled toward the dark velvet grass where they stood, and the figure raised its head. All was shadow within the confines of its hood.

"Blood and need calls me forth," it said in a hollow voice. "Board, and I shall bear you across the water."

Jennet shivered. Half-remembered myths of black rivers and death flitted through her mind. Still, what choice did they have? They were far removed from the mortal world.

"Do you promise to keep us safe?" Tam asked.

"Put away your sword, mortal. I make no promises, but you shall be granted safe passage to the far shore."

Tam slid his sword into the scabbard, metal hissing on metal. He squeezed Jennet's hand, and together they stepped onto the pale deck. The boat remained eerily still as they boarded—no dip and shift as the boat took their weight.

In unspoken accord, they moved to the center where the mast stood, slender and gleaming. The entire boat looked fragile. The figure gestured, and the boat glided smoothly away from shore.

Jennet leaned closer to Tam. "I hope it doesn't decide to dump us overboard halfway across the lake."

"I think we're ok. The blood and need and all that."

Unconvinced, she watched the shore recede. Behind them, their wake was a vee of silver spreading across the water. Wind ruffled her hair—they were going fast, although the craft remained steady as a grav-car.

When they passed the midpoint of the lake, the tension binding her ribs eased. Tam squeezed her hand again. There was something about the silent figure and eerie water-lit air that made her reluctant to speak. As if words would break whatever spell was keeping them safe.

Sooner than she would have imagined, the rough crags of the mountains blocked half the sky. Orange light echoed off the metallic surface of the lake. The boat entered the shadow of the peaks, and cold crept through Jennet's bones.

"Our journey is ended," the hooded figure said as the boat slid up against land. "This way will not be open to you again. Farewell."

Tam jumped to shore and reached for Jennet, steadying her as she stepped across. On this side of the lake the grasses were not black velvet, but singed silk, crackling under her feet. The air dried her tongue with an acrid tang.

Without another word, the hooded figure turned the boat. It sped, a pale blur, back toward the center of the lake. Partway there, the craft began to submerge, the water licking up over the deck, swirling about the figure's robes. A heartbeat later, only the tip of the mast was visible—and then it was gone. A single ripple spread out, viscous, from the middle of the lake.

Jennet shivered and eyed the crags rising before them. The grasses gave way almost immediately to dark, volcanic-looking rock. She could see no path, but in there, somewhere, were the Elder Fey. She took a step, the rock gritty beneath her feet.

"Wait," a thin, familiar voice said.

"Puck?" She squinted through the dim light, seeing nothing but flat black grasses and jagged shadows.

"There," Tam said, pointing.

Puck stood a few feet away. A dim, translucent version of him, anyway.

"You must return posthaste," the sprite said. "Come this way. A ring awaits."

"How do we know you're the real Puck?" Tam asked, his eyes narrowed.

Jennet was glad he asked. It was creepy seeing a

ghostly figure in place of the merry sprite she was accustomed to.

"Foolishness." Puck shook his head. "Your brother, the Bug, languishes in the Dark Court, and you want to play at riddles with me?"

"Good enough." Tam strode forward.

"But…" Jennet hung back. They were close to the Elder Fey, she could feel it, the knowledge burning along her skin. "We can't leave *now*. We're almost done."

"It is past time for your return to the mortal world," Puck said. "We cannot hide your absence any longer. Your mortal bodies are in danger of slipping into the sleep-state."

"No way are we going into a coma over this." Tam caught her hand. "If we did, who would wake the Elder Fey and save my brother?"

"But…" They were so *close*.

"Trust me. We'll get another chance. Right, Puck?"

The ghostly figure tipped his head. "One last chance, aye. But come now, ere the risk grows too great."

They followed the wispy figure down the shoreline to where a thin grove of trees stood. Within it was the usual circle of pale-stalked mushrooms shedding their purplish light. Puck leaped into the middle of the faerie ring, and winked out.

Tam squeezed her fingers. "We'll wake the Elder Fey. Third time's the charm, right?"

She sent a wary glance behind her, to the jagged

mountains rising against the orange-lit sky. Then why did she feel like they weren't going to have that chance?

17

THE TWILIGHT KINGDOM disappeared the moment Tam stepped within the circle of glowing mushrooms, and icy cold seized his bones. Coughing from the frigid air slicing his lungs, Tam landed in the center of another ring, Jennet beside him. At least this time they'd both managed to stay on their feet.

"Hurry," Puck said, dancing just outside the boundary of eerie mushrooms. "Ere the hounds catch your scent once again."

Tam was glad the Wild Hunt wasn't waiting this time as their welcoming committee.

Jennet swayed, and he caught her elbow.

"You all right?" he asked.

"Yeah." She blinked and straightened her shoulders. "Let's go."

White-barked trees rose above them as they hurried

down the path behind Puck. The stars were pinpricks of light in an impossibly dark sky.

"Here," Puck said, stepping into another clearing with the usual white-dotted mushrooms in the center. "I shall see you anon."

"What about the quest in the beta game?" Tam asked.

"All is in readiness for your return," the sprite said. "As before, the items you need will be provided to you."

"But we have no idea what we're supposed to have been doing," Jennet said.

Tam thought back to accepting the quest in-game. It felt like a hundred years ago.

"We're supposed to be choosing something from the castle's treasury," he said. "Just describe a generic treasure room, Jennet. You know, piles of gold, shiny weapons. Think like a game designer."

"Enough chatter," Puck said. "Go."

A long, wavering wail curled through the sky. It wasn't the howl of the Hunt, but the Unseelie Court boasted plenty of other nasties.

Tam stepped into the center of the faerie ring with Jennet. Giddy golden light swirled over his senses and they tumbled into the clearing in the hedge outside Stronghold Castle. On the grass surrounding them a faint echo of white-spotted mushrooms faded.

Jennet pushed her hair out of her face. "Back to the princess?"

"With the gifts we chose out of the royal treasury."

Tam checked his inventory. A small silver box had been added to his items. "I guess I got a box. A new sword would have been nice."

"Boys." Jennet shook her head. "Oh, sweet. I got a box, too. And there were probably piles of jewels lying around the treasure room."

Her hand went to her throat, as if feeling an imagined necklace there.

"Girls." Tam gave her a half-smile, then pushed his way out of the hedge. He knew she was rolling her eyes at him, behind his back.

Their footsteps crunched on the gravel of the empty pathway as he and Jennet headed to the green garden of Princess Paloma. As before, the pastel ladies-in-waiting sat on benches surrounding the white-garbed princess. Soft music played in the background, and the princess watched them approach with her unblinking violet gaze.

"Your highness." Tam swept her a bow. From the corner of his eye, he saw Jennet curtsey.

"Brave adventurers," Princess Paloma said. "Let me view the rewards you chose from my treasury. What have you claimed, Knight?"

She held out her hands, and a rectangular silver box about four inches long appeared. Tam flicked through his inventory. Yep, she'd taken it. He raised an eyebrow at Jennet.

"I have gold and arms aplenty, shining in splendor,"

the princess said, "yet you selected something so simple. Shall I open it?"

Tam shrugged. "Go ahead."

The princess lifted the lid, and her ladies gasped as brilliant light flooded the garden.

"Ah," Princess Paloma said. "One of the most powerful items in my treasury. The Talisman of Aroka."

She reached into the box and drew out the source of the brightness—a teardrop-shaped jewel suspended on a thick silver chain. Maybe the box wasn't such a dud after all.

"What does it do?" Tam asked.

"When invoked, it lends the wearer three times his normal strength and heals him of mortal wounds. Wear it well, brave Knight."

Princess Paloma set the box aside and stood on tiptoe to lift the chain over Tam's head. The talisman slipped down to nestle under his armor, its light fading. Tam blinked, glowing afterimages of teardrop-shaped gems burning against his lids.

"Lady Spellcaster," the princess said, turning to Jennet. "Let us see what reward you have brought from my treasury."

Again, she held out her hands, and again a plain silver box appeared. Princess Paloma nodded and lifted the lid. Once more, silver radiance streamed out of the box and the ladies-in-waiting stirred with excitement. The princess reached into the box and drew out a flat disc of milky stone that seemed lit from within. It, too, was strung on a silver chain. Princess Paloma held it up.

"Another wise choice," she said. "The Talisman of Shejin. When invoked, this talisman lends the wearer three times their magical power, and heals them of mortal wounds."

The princess placed the chain over Jennet's head. The glowing disc slipped beneath her robes and the light dimmed once more. A soft ding filled the air—the signal their quest was complete.

"You have chosen worthy items," Princess Paloma said. "Guard them well. The talismans can be invoked but once, so take care to use them only at your time of greatest need."

:Beta team, log out in five minutes:

The message scrolled across the lush green grass of the princess's garden.

"Thank you, your highness," Jennet said, curtseying to the princess.

Tam bowed. Princess Paloma waved her hand in dismissal and turned back to her gaggle of pastel-clad ladies. Clearly he and Jennet were done here. He jerked his head toward the tall columns marking the edge of the garden. Eyes full of questions, Jennet followed.

When the two of them reached the courtyard with its fountain, Tam halted beside the splashing water. Who knew if VirtuMax could listen in to their conversations?

"At least we're not late, this time," Jennet said in a low voice.

"Yeah." Tam fingered the silver chain around his neck. "And apparently we managed to do a good job with the quest."

"I still wish we'd been able to finish up in... you know where. Do you think we were really in danger—physically, I mean?"

"I do. Much as I distrust the faeries, I don't think Puck has a reason to lie. Not about this."

"At some point, we're going to be discovered." Worry shadowed her light-blue eyes.

"How? VirtuMax has no way of monitoring us once we step through the rings."

She shifted uncomfortably. "This 'vid-feed malfunction' trick of Puck's can't work forever. Maybe it's time to try something different."

Something hovered behind her eyes that he didn't like the look of. Jennet's plans usually meant putting herself in serious danger.

:Beta team, log out:

"We'll talk later." She took a deep breath. "See you out there."

Tam still couldn't get used to how easy it was to exit the new Feyland. No searching for a faerie ring, no queasiness. Just a quick selection of the X, and he was out. He pulled his gloves off, then glanced down the row at the rest of the team. Zeg and Jennet's dad were still geared up, and Mr. Chon stalked over to stand in front of their sim chairs.

"Mr. Carter, Mr. Fanalua, can you hear me?" He fiddled with his mic and headset. "Time to exit the game."

"One sec." Zeg's voice came from the speakers in Tam's helmet. "We're finishing up a fight, then we need to go turn in."

Lassiter rose from his chair at the end of the row. "Seriously? We finished our quest ages ago and were just exploring."

"Hey," Jennet said. "Monk and Priest are not the most deadly combo, you know."

"No doubt." Lassiter laughed. "Death by slow erosion. No wonder they're still in battle."

Spark pushed back a strand of her bright hair. "Maybe you should join them, Roy. It wouldn't hurt to switch the teams up a little."

Lassiter looked like he'd bitten into something sour.

"We will be reconfiguring the small groups," Mr. Chon said. "Tomorrow, when we assemble, I'll assign new questing partners."

Jennet shot Tam a wide-eyed look. "But—"

"Miss Carter." The team leader's voice was cool. "We lost signal from you and Tam again today. The techs think there's a short in your systems... possibly because they're situated next to one another. Tomorrow, we'll be switching everything up."

Damn. Tam crossed his arms. How was Puck going to get them out of this one? Jennet was right—the sprite couldn't keep messing with the FullD systems.

"Whew!" Down the line, Jennet's dad pulled off his helmet. "Good thing Zeg's a top-notch healer. We barely beat that last ogre."

Zeg stripped off his gear and gave Jennet's dad a grin from behind his frizzy beard. "You're starting to get the hang of things."

"Only because you're keeping me alive."

"Everyone, input your impressions of the gameplay today," Mr. Chon said, "then you're free to go. We have another session tomorrow afternoon. Be prompt."

Jennet glanced at Tam, her face pale and worried. How were they going to get back into the Twilight Kingdom if they weren't questing together?

18

JENNET WISHED she could talk to Tam, but her dad wasn't staying behind tonight to go over the data. She had to be content with a small wave to Tam as he and Zeg headed out through the shiny glass doors of VirtuMax headquarters.

"Jennet," her dad said, holding the door open for her, "all right with you if we walk home?"

She nodded, though her stomach clenched. Walking the few short blocks to their house would still give him too much time to ask questions—and she could tell he was suspicious about what she and Tam had been doing in-game.

Technically, they hadn't even been playing Feyland. Instead they'd been using magical faerie rings to travel to realms far removed from the mortal world, on a quest to stop the fey folk from taking over. Yeah, it all sounded so plausible.

Zeg's guzzler rumbled past, the exhaust fumes hanging in the still air. Jennet lifted her hand again in farewell.

"I like Zeg," her dad said. "Despite his tendency toward the theatrical."

"Me too. You should meet his niece—my friend Marny."

"Maybe we should invite them over for dinner some night."

"Maybe."

How awkward that would be, especially since Tam wasn't welcome anywhere near her house. She pressed her lips together as she and her dad turned down the wide, empty sidewalk.

"I've been thinking," he said—always a bad sign. "We should find a choir here, like the one you used to sing with."

"I'm not sure Crestview has anything like that, Dad. Besides, I don't really have time right now."

Part of her did miss the music, and her choir director had always said she had a great voice. But ever since entering Feyland and battling the Dark Queen, Jennet hadn't much felt like singing.

"There's more to life than school and gaming." Her dad gave her a concerned look. "Speaking of which, I find it strange that you and Tam are having system issues. Anything you'd like to tell me about that?"

"Meaning?" She tried to keep her voice innocent.

"Jennet. You and Tam have a history of... shall we say, poor physical reactions to the FullD systems."

"I would call going into a coma way beyond poor, personally."

"Maybe it's something in your body chemistry." He frowned. "Your neural interface is glitching with the equipment."

"Or maybe we're telling the truth!" She stopped and turned to face him, hands on her hips. "Dad, that's the answer that makes the most sense."

He studied her for a moment, his eyes tired, the lines around his mouth more pronounced.

"Faeries and magic? I know you believe—"

"What about Tam's leg getting hurt the night you kicked him out of my life?" she demanded. "How could a faulty neural interface cause a stab wound?"

Her dad ran his fingers through his hair. "I didn't get a good look at his leg that night. There were bigger things to deal with. You might remember Security bursting into the house and waving guns around? By the time I'd dealt with them, you'd bandaged Tam up. I have no way of verifying what you're saying."

"I'm not lying."

Anger warred with fear in her stomach. She wanted to yell at her dad, wanted to storm home to her bedroom and slam the door. But something held her back, a shaky anxiety she'd always had at the thought of making him angry with her. She folded her arms tightly across her body and blinked away hot tears.

"Why won't you believe me?" She hated the way her voice shook.

"I certainly believe there's something about you and Tam that reacts strangely when you play Feyland." Her dad cleared his throat. "Which is why I think it's best that you stop playing altogether. I'm recommending to Mr. Chon that he remove you both from the beta team."

"What?" She halted, cold air stabbing her lungs. Shivering, she pulled her thick wool coat tighter. "You can't do that."

"Of course I can. I'm your parent. It's my job to protect you." His voice was calm and reasonable, and Jennet wanted to scream.

"Please don't." The words clogged her throat. "Don't kick us out yet. Give us one more chance."

One last try to wake the Elder Fey. To save their world.

Her dad folded his arms, his mouth twisted in thought.

"I suppose you could stay for one more round," he said, and relief gusted through her. "If I upset Mr. Chon's plan for tomorrow, he won't be pleased."

"Switching up the teams, you mean?"

"Yes. But after that, the two of you are done. Understand?"

Her eyes were cold now, the wetness of tears quickly chilling in the winter air. "All right."

"It's for the best, Jennet. I'm just trying to look out for you. And Tam, too." He set a hand on her shoulder. "Let's get home. I'll have Marie fix you some hot chocolate."

As if she were still a little girl, and that would make everything better.

Ducking her head, Jennet trudged up the sidewalk. If she and Tam didn't wake the Elder Fey tomorrow, everything was lost.

TAM WAVED to Zeg from the top of his stairs, then carefully opened the door, not sure what kind of mess he'd be walking into. The changeling was even worse than his little brother. Maybe because Korrigan didn't have to pretend to be a human boy, at least not in front of Tam.

Or in front of Marny, who had agreed to hang out with the creature again while Tam was beta testing. Bad enough that Korrigan was left on his own during school hours. Tam couldn't imagine leaving the faerie unattended for the entire day—and then pretty much the whole night, while Tam slept.

When he'd gotten up that morning, after crashing

hard on his mom's bed, he'd found the living room draped in green cobwebs. Strange, fleshy-leaved plants sprouted in the corners, and a jungle-like smell permeated the air—thick and vegetal. He'd commanded the changeling to clear it all up, then dashed out the door, late for school.

No magical jungle greeted him as he pushed the door open. Instead, Marny and Korrigan sat on the couch, facing the netscreen. Brightly colored cars zipped around a track, and the scream of the virtual crowd was deafening as Marny's vehicle sped over the finish line. *Winner!* flashed in bright yellow letters across the screen.

"Noo!" Korrigan cried, flinging down his controller.

"I win. Again," Marny said, and glanced up. "Hey Tam. How'd the testing go today?"

"Good." He sent a significant look at the changeling. "I'll tell you about it tomorrow at school. Zeg's out there waiting for you."

No way would either of them let Marny walk home alone through the Exe.

"I know—the sound of his car is unmistakable." She got off the couch. "See you later, Korr. Better work on those driving skills."

The changeling made a face. "I shall master this ridiculous mortal game yet."

"He's totally hooked, poor guy." Marny shook her

head, then gathered up her knapsack. "See you tomorrow."

Tam held the door. "Watch that step," he called after her.

One of these days, he needed to do some scavenging and replace the weak tread. But first there was the little matter of fighting off evil faeries and saving the world.

19

IN THE BETA-TESTING hub the next afternoon, Mr. Chon stopped everyone before they took their usual sim chairs. Jennet curled her fingers into her palms, the nails digging in. When she'd told Tam at school that her dad was pulling them off the team, he'd frozen for a heartbeat. Then he'd folded his arms, green eyes hard with determination. They were going to wake the Elder Fey today, no matter what.

"We're mixing the groups up this afternoon," Mr. Chon said. "And the seating arrangements as well. Jennet and Spark, I want you two down at the end. Gear up and enter game right away. Talk to the Elvish ambassadors at the front gates of Stronghold—you'll be questing in Pelemor Forest today."

"But... shouldn't we wait for the others?" Jennet asked.

Mr. Chon shook his head. "I want a staggered entry. Groups will be starting gameplay fifteen minutes apart."

That was going to make meeting Tam in-game a lot trickier. Jennet moved to her new chair and picked up her gloves, turning them restlessly in her hands instead of slipping them on.

"Who's in after the girls?" Roy asked.

Mr. Chon glanced at his tablet. "Yourself and Mr. Carter will be running the Sands of Scouring questlines."

"Great." Roy rolled his eyes. "Babysitting duty again."

Ignoring him, Mr. Chon gestured to Tam, Zeg, and Coranne. "You're the last group, and I'm sending you into some difficult play. You three are the perfect party to tackle the mid-sized bosses we've created in the Dire Swamp. Tank, healer, and damage—very well balanced."

"Hey, I'm a tank, too." Roy's lips twisted in a scowl.

Mr. Chon sent a sharp glance toward Jennet and Spark. "Ladies, I need you two in game. Yesterday."

Of course Spark was ready to go—seated and geared up—while Jennet hovered beside the chair, mind whirling.

"Good luck," Tam said, his voice strained.

Jennet met his gaze, sure he could see the panic in her eyes. Tam wasn't going to be entering Feyland until half an hour after she and Spark. Plus, he had Coranne Smith with him, who was a spy for VirtuMax, no question.

She swallowed, fear tightening her throat. "See you later," she said.

Hopefully not too much later, but she couldn't see a way they could make this work. She pulled her helmet on, and the outside world receded.

"You in yet?" Spark asked over the headset.

"Almost." Jennet's Spellcaster materialized in the castle gardens. "I'm at the castle. You?"

"The tavern. Meet you at the front gates."

Maybe they would knock the quests off quickly, and she could go find Tam. And maybe the sky would start raining roses, too. Jennet shook her head and hurried through the cobbled streets of the city, heading for the tall gates. The heavy sensation in her stomach was the feeling of swallowing leaden truth. Everything was working against them. It was going to be impossible to reach the Twilight Kingdom today.

But she had to try.

Jennet passed through the gates, walking past a row of guards who didn't even glance her way. Outside the city walls an elegant blue pavilion stood, open on three sides. Silver streamers glittered in the breeze, and she could see the bright magenta flash of Spark's hair under the billowing cloth.

"I'm at the tent," Spark said. "Come on over."

Her fox-eared avatar stood before a pair of tall, pale figures. They, too, had ears pointing out of their silvery hair, but the elves' ears were long and delicate. Large, luminous eyes the color of the ocean watched Jennet approach—but there was no hint of consciousness on their angular, computer-generated faces.

Not truly fey folk, which was a good thing. So why was she disappointed no magic lingered about their stately figures?

Spark tilted her head as Jennet approached. "Did you change your avatar?"

"No. Why do you ask?" A sudden chill crept over Jennet's skin.

"Your hair seems a different color. Maybe it's a trick of the light." Spark shrugged one shoulder and turned to the elves.

Jennet glanced down. Sure enough, the black hair she'd chosen for her character had lightened to pale brown. Was fey magic seeping into the game already— or was it only her character that was affected, like with the spider bites?

She swallowed back fear, wishing that Tam was beside her.

"Greetings," Spark said to the elves. "Welcome to Stronghold city."

"Young Kitsune." The figure on the left inclined his head. "We have traveled far, and must send word home to our forest of our safe arrival. Will you and your Spell-caster companion be our messengers?"

"We'll deliver your messages," Jennet said.

"Good." The other elf's voice was higher pitched, and

her features had a more feminine cast. "We shall provide swift steeds to carry you to Pelemor Forest."

She made an elegant gesture, and two pale horses appeared outside the pavilion. Their manes and tails looked made of spun silver, and their saddles of beaten gold. Pretty, but not too comfortable.

The elves stood there, waiting expectantly. The horses pawed the ground. Clearly she and Spark were supposed to jump on and ride away—but how?

She scanned the bottom of her screen, and saw a silvery *M*. For *mount?* She selected it, and a moment later was perched on one of the horses.

Spark tilted her head up at Jennet. A second later, she, too, was mounted.

"Travel well and speedily," the male elf said.

He snapped his fingers and the horses burst into motion, heading away from the castle. They didn't take the road up into the forest Jennet's party had adventured through, nor did they veer off in the direction Spark and Tam had come to reach the city.

Instead, they galloped straight ahead, through golden fields stitched with bright orange flowers. The horses carried them swiftly and smoothly over the landscape. The sky was the color of a painting overhead, and the drowsy buzz of insects filled the air. After a few minutes, they reached a wide, dusty road, and continued along it. Jennet glanced behind them at the little puffs of dust rising from their passage. Good programming, that.

"Hey," Jennet said, "have you ever played a game where things weren't what they seemed?"

She hadn't planned on asking the question, but now that she had, she found herself hoping Spark knew what she meant.

The magenta-haired girl shot her a look. "You mean puzzle or illusion games?"

"No, ones like this—you know, questing, epic fantasy-type stuff. But one where the storyline isn't actually what's going on."

Jennet pressed her lips together. She wasn't explaining it well, but then, there really was no good way to explain fey magic seeping into a game.

"Not that I know of," Spark said. "Are you telling me you think Feyland is like that—there's some bigger meta-game going on underneath?"

"Maybe. Yeah."

Though it wasn't planned to be that way. At least, not by the human programmers.

The shadow of wings crossed the road ahead of them. Spark glanced up, then threw herself off her horse.

"Incoming!" she yelled.

Jennet was right behind her, her feet hitting the dusty road. She raised her mage staff, blue-white mage-fire crackling from the crystal set in the end.

Above them, the sun was blocked out by the descent of a huge red bird. It let out a hoarse cry, its talons extended in attack as it hurtled toward them. Shading her eyes with one hand, Jennet fired a magical blast that hit the creature in the chest.

It screeched and veered toward her. She ducked as the wind of its wings whipped her hair across her face, and skidded for cover behind her horse. The animal just stood there placidly, ignoring the fight exploding around it.

Spark had her bow out and was firing confidently, but despite the arrows sticking out of its chest, the bird seemed unaffected. When Jennet's next bolt of blue fire hit it, though, the creature cried out again.

"I think it can only be harmed by magic," Jennet called.

Spark nodded and set aside her bow as their enemy wheeled away, huge scarlet wings beating. The bird gained altitude, climbing higher into the blue.

Jennet squinted up into the brightness. "Think it's leaving?"

"No way." Spark held up her hands, palms out. "Get ready."

Sudden red blurred the air as the bird tucked its wings and plummeted toward them, a deadly missile of beak and bone and talon. Jennet shot—and missed, her magefire blasting empty air. The sky shuddered, vibrating with the bird's descent.

A wall of orange fire rose in front of them, heat rippling the air. Jennet glanced at Spark, then raised her staff. Her blue-flickering Sheet of Flame joined Spark's fire—a double dose of magical energy shimmering between them and the bird.

Their enemy hit the flames. It let out a horrific screech as its feathers caught fire, but it kept coming. Jennet and Spark dove to the ground as bladed talons whistled through the air over their heads.

Jennet's horse whinnied high and scared as the bird, deprived of its human prey, fastened its talons into the horse instead. Wings still smoking, it rose, bearing the animal with it, and began to flap away.

"Wait," Jennet cried. "Come back here with my mount!"

She tilted her staff and sent a bolt at the retreating bird, but it didn't turn around. Soon it was just a dark blot on the horizon.

"Great."

She turned back to the road, now blackened with fire. A single scarlet feather lay where her mount had stood.

Spark picked the feather up and shook her head.

"Too bad it took your horse."

Especially when speed was essential. "Maybe we could both ride yours."

"Worth a try." Spark mounted. "Come on up."

Jennet hit her *M* button, and a second later was sitting atop the horse… but Spark now stood on the road. Jennet blinked, and they had changed places again.

"A single-occupant horse," Jennet said, scuffing the dirt with her foot. "How un-useful."

"Put it in the recap notes." Spark's voice was dry. "Guess you're on foot."

Jennet started down the road. Spark charged past her in a streak of silver, then pulled her mount to a stop several yards away.

"There's no speed setting on this thing," she said.

"Go ahead without me." Jennet bit her lip. "At least one of us should get the quest done. Either I'll catch up, or we'll run out of time."

Or die on the road, but she didn't feel like mentioning that part.

"You sure?"

"Yeah. See you in the forest." She waved, to show she meant it.

Spark lifted her hand, then turned and sped away. Far too soon, the road was empty.

Jennet had to admit, she liked Spark—and the gamer girl didn't seem as if she was trying to snag Tam away. Not that Jennet was worried he'd go. The two of them were solid, despite the world trying to keep them apart.

If anything, Jennet suspected Spark might be interested in Roy. Underneath all that ego was a decent guy—but still. Maybe Spark liked to take on projects.

Jennet shook her head and trudged down the road, the drone of insects loud in the stillness.

Had half an hour passed yet? Was Tam in-game

somewhere, inaccessible? She let out a sigh, defeat weighting her steps.

The dry grasses beside the road rustled, and Jennet whirled, staff at the ready. An instant later, she relaxed her guard as Puck tumbled out in a mad somersault.

"Greetings, Fair Jennet." The sprite swept her a low bow. "How fares it on this fine day?"

"Better, now that you're here. Transport me to the Realm, then go get Tam."

"Alas, I cannot. He has just entered this between-place, and is too well watched to separate from his companions."

She blinked at Puck, fear scratching her skin.

"But we have to get to the Twilight Kingdom today—this is our last chance! At least take *me* there."

The sprite floated up, cross-legged in the air, until he was face to face with her. His expression was serious, the merry twinkle in his eyes extinguished.

"You cannot succeed without Tamlin," Puck said. "Sending you alone into that place would spell your certain death. And the doom of the mortal world."

"But..." She tried to breathe, panic tightening her ribcage. "I have to go, today. Tam and I are off the beta team after this. We won't be able to get into Feyland again."

Puck held her gaze. "Fair Jennet, this is not the only game-portal to the Realm. You have entered through many others. Find a way."

"There isn't a way."

Her FullD prototype systems were totally off limits. Though she was willing to risk her dad's wrath, HANA, their House-Activated-Network-Assistant, had been programmed to set off alarms if Tam ever set foot inside. She still hadn't figured out the override codes, and even if she did, the entire staff knew he wasn't allowed in.

But she didn't have any other choice.

The sprite nodded, as if he could read her thoughts. "You and Tamlin are clever and brave. You will find a path back to us."

He slowly drifted back down to the earth. A breeze riffled the grasses and, for a moment, Jennet felt the dry, dusty warmth against her skin. She wrapped her arms around herself, pushing down the fear-flavored despair. They had to find a way through this.

"How's the Bug doing?" she asked. Tam would want to know, and she was worried about the kid, too.

Puck grinned. "He and I are merry playmates."

"Don't let him eat or drink anything."

"Fear not, Fair Jennet. Thomas guards him well. He will not be unduly snared into the Realm."

"He already has! And we're going to get him out as soon as possible."

"Muster your allies," Puck said. "The battle will not be easy. The Courts have joined forces—an unheard of thing—and their combined might is fearsome."

"What?" She stared at the sprite, ice edging her bones. Each court was bad enough alone, but together? "Why didn't you tell us before?"

She and Tam were in deep trouble. No way the two of them could face off against the combined rulers of the Realm, and win. Not when it had taken all their skill to defeat the king and queen individually.

"It was not necessary for you to know, until now," Puck said.

"I can't believe you and Thomas didn't—"

:Jennet and Spark, finish your quest. Logoff in five minutes:

The sprite lifted his head. "I must away. Find your portal to the Realm again. Soon."

He leaped into a handstand. A moment later there was nothing but glittering air where he had been, and the echo of chiming laughter that almost sounded like sobbing.

20

Tᴀᴍ sʜᴏᴠᴇᴅ his hands into the pockets of his battered brown coat and tried to keep the cold brick wall of Crestview High between him and the winter wind. White mist curled from his lips to blend with the dawn shadows. Although Jennet hadn't messaged him to meet her before school today, he was there, waiting.

Yesterday, at the end of beta testing, she'd given him a serious look—one that said they needed to talk. Which of course they did, although they'd gotten a temporary reprieve. Since neither of their systems had malfunctioned during the testing period, Jennet's dad hadn't made a big announcement about pulling them off the team.

Maybe he'd said something on the quiet to Mr. Chon, but nobody had told Tam not to show up for the next session in two days. Not that he and Jennet had two days, if the near-panic he'd seen in her eyes was any indication.

The lights of a grav-car swept the early-morning dimness from the air, and Tam unclenched his cold fingers. The black car slid up to the curb, and Jennet got out.

"Tam?" she called softly.

"Here." He stepped away from the building.

Her face lightened when she saw him. She ducked back into the car, then re-emerged with her satchel and a sleek silver thermos. Tam couldn't see George through the tinted windows, but he waved, knowing the driver was looking out. The grav-car's lights flashed in acknowledgement.

"I hoped you'd be here," Jennet said. "I brought hot chocolate."

Tam took the thermos she held out to him and unscrewed the lid. Steam rose, curling around his face with delicious, chocolate-scented warmth.

"I saw Puck in-game yesterday," she said. "He told me a couple important things."

"What did Spark think of that?"

"She wasn't there. We got separated during our quest. I'm not sure if that was Puck's doing or a game flaw."

"Did you ask about my brother? Is he ok?"

"Puck said they were 'merry playmates' and that Thomas is keeping an eye on him."

From what Tam knew, there wasn't much merriment in the Dark Court, but he trusted the bard to keep his brother safe until they could get him out. Which had to be soon. He tipped the thermos and took a mouthful of hot chocolate, trying to erase some of the chill chasing through him.

"Puck neglected to mention one small detail." Jennet's voice trembled on the words. "The Dark Queen and the Bright King have joined forces."

"What?" The chocolate curdled on his tongue. "Can they even do that? I thought they were polar opposites. Fire and water, you know."

"I guess when the fate of their Realm is at stake, they'll do whatever it takes."

He screwed the top on the thermos, twisting it down tight. "We won't let them win."

"How can we stop them?"

"You're shivering. Come here."

Tam set the thermos down and took Jennet into his arms. Her hair smelled like flowers and light, and every good thing in the world. Every good thing that could so easily be lost to the treacherous powers of the fey.

He was scared too, though he wasn't about to show it. Although he and Jennet had won against the Bright King—barely—the Dark Queen had defeated them. Her magic was too strong. Together, the king and queen would be unbeatable.

Jennet held tightly to him, and the places where their

bodies touched warmed enough to push back the cold. Enough to push back the dark fear. The clouds on the eastern horizon brightened from grey to white as the sun tipped over the edge of the earth.

"Jennet, things are too chancy with the beta testing," he said. "Even if we stay on the team, they'll keep us split up. You know that."

She drew back and stared into his eyes. "We're going to have to sneak onto my systems. I've thought about it, and if we—"

"No."

"Tam. We have to get into the Realm."

"We will, but you're not the only one with FullD prototypes sitting around."

She tilted her head, and he saw the moment realization hit, her blue eyes widening.

"Roy's systems," she breathed. "Tam, you'd do that?"

"It's safer for everyone. And if I have to make good with Lassiter, well…" He shrugged, though the words were bitter.

It was the only way forward he could see. Even if it meant patching things up with the walking ego that was Roy Lassiter.

"All right. He owes us, anyway." Jennet leaned into him again, and he held her close.

For a minute he could forget the aching emptiness where his mom should have been, his fear for the Bug trapped in the Dark Court, the impossible quest hanging over them. There was only the feel of Jennet in his arms, fitting perfectly against him as the sky brightened.

AFTER SCHOOL, Tam and Jennet waited outside the building for Roy Lassiter.

"He didn't leave already?" Jennet said.

"His car's still in the lot." Tam folded his arms. Lassiter's fancy red grav-car was impossible to miss.

Students poured out the battered double-doors of Crestview High. Used to be, Lassiter was easy to find in a crowd—surrounded by admiring fans, the golden boy of the school. Now he was just another student in a sea of them, and he'd made it clear he blamed Tam and Jennet for that change.

"There he is." Jennet touched his arm. "Want me to come along?"

"Not yet."

If Jennet was there, Lassiter would use it, and Tam wasn't sure he could hold his temper if the guy started making digs at her.

Tam strode forward. "Hey, Lassiter."

"What?" The other boy narrowed his eyes. "I'm not giving you a ride to The View, if that's what you're after. Besides, there's no beta testing today."

"I know. Let's talk." Tam jerked his head, indicating they should move out of the stream of students.

"I have nothing to say to you."

"It's about Feyland."

Lassiter frowned. "Make it fast."

The guy might dislike him, but they'd shared an experience no one else had. They'd both come face to face with the Bright King of the Seelie Faeries and stared into the heart of that dazzling power.

But where Lassiter had craved it for his own, Tam had just wanted to keep Jennet safe. Only one of them had been the winner.

"All right, Exie," Lassiter said, crossing his arms when they got to the rusty parking-lot fence. "You have one minute. Make it count."

"I need your help."

Lassiter's eyebrows shot up. "Do you? And why should I help you?"

"Because you're one of the only people who understands what's going on. That Feyland is way beyond ordinary."

"Ordinary. Like I am now."

"No." Tam dropped his voice. "Anyone who's been touched by fey magic is special. You know that. You've felt it. But if the faeries break through into our world, everything will change—and not for the better."

Lassiter was quiet a minute. The calls of students echoed against Crestview's brick walls, underscored by the roar of the buses pulling away. Jennet waited, expression tense, near the front doors, and Tam gave her an imperceptible shake of his head.

"You still think that's their plan?" Lassiter finally asked. Some of the arrogance had drained from his voice.

"I know it is."

"How?"

"In beta testing, when Jennet and I 'shorted out' the FullD systems, it wasn't an equipment glitch. We went into the Realm."

And beyond, but he didn't want to tell Lassiter too much. Yet.

"You say."

Tam shifted his backpack higher on his shoulder. He had to convince Lassiter to help them.

"Also—my little brother has been replaced by a changeling."

"A what? The faeries stole your brother?" The other boy tipped his head and laughed, though it sounded forced. "Right. Tell me another one."

From the corner of his eye, Tam saw Jennet marching over. She must have caught the last part of their conversation.

"It's true, Roy," she said.

All humor was gone from Lassiter's face. "Prove it."

"After everything with Feyland, you don't believe us?" Tam wanted to take Lassiter by the shoulders and shake him. Hard.

"It's not my problem," Lassiter said. "And your minute is up."

Jennet turned to Tam, her blue eyes worried. "You'll have to take Roy to your house and show him the changeling."

"No." Tam took a step back.

No way did he want to expose his admittedly rundown house to Lassiter's arrogant gaze. The Viewer boy judged him plenty, without Tam adding more fuel to that fire.

"Admit it," Lassiter said. "It's all lies. Some story you two cooked up. Otherwise, why not let me see the so-called evidence, Exie?"

Tam unclenched his fists. Jennet was right—the only way to convince Lassiter was to let him see the changeling. And since the creature couldn't leave the house without Tam, this was the easiest solution.

Much as he hated the idea.

"Fine," Tam said. "But then you have to help us get into Feyland—on your sim equip."

"Yeah, if your fake faerie magically changes my mind. Which I doubt." Lassiter narrowed his eyes, his thumb rubbing his wrist-chip implant. "Wait a sec. Is this some kind of trap? Lure me into the Exe and then you and your ghetto posse jump me, steal my car? Cut out my chip?"

Jennet let out an exasperated breath. "Roy, make up

your mind. I'll come too, to keep you safe and hold your hand in the scary Exe."

"Jennet, you're not supposed to visit me," Tam said.

Planning to meet at Lassiter's was already stretching the rules way thin. It was too soon to risk everything. Once they'd woken the Elder Fey, he'd give everything he had to get his brother back from the Dark Court—but not until then, although his skin itched with impatience every time he thought about it.

"I can take care of myself," Lassiter said.

"Great." Jennet said. "Let me run inside and get Marny. She's going with you."

"What?"

"Why?"

"Guys, somebody's got to changeling-sit while we're at Roy's." Without waiting for a response, Jennet headed back into Crestview High.

"You think you can pull something on me?" Lassiter curled his mouth.

"Either you'll believe the truth staring you in the face, or you won't." Tam was done arguing about it.

When Marny and Jennet came through the doors, the big girl made a face. She wasn't fond of Lassiter, and he returned the dislike. Back when he'd had a touch of fey magic he'd bewitched her—and pretty much the entire school— into falling in love with him. When Marny got free of his enchantment, she'd told him the hard truth about himself. A truth he wasn't going to accept any time soon. Being average was hard.

"Message me when you get up to the View, and I'll meet you at Roy's," Jennet said. "Good luck."

She smiled at Tam, then headed for the curb where George waited in the Carter's black grav-car.

"Come on." Lassiter led the way to where his shiny red car waited in the parking lot.

"I'm sitting in back," Marny said. "Tam can enjoy the pleasure of your company."

"Don't mess anything up," Lassiter said.

Marny rolled her eyes, but waited for him to wave the doors open.

"I don't suppose you have a real address I can put into the navbot," Lassiter said as he slid behind the wheel.

"Not so much," Tam said. "I'll tell you how to get there."

Once, Tam's street had been on the map—literally—but for the last ten years the Exe had been a grayed-out area, a bruise on one side of Crestview. Now The View perched on the other side, squashing the city uncomfortably in between.

Lassiter drove too fast, but Tam didn't say anything. All was quiet in the back seat, though as the car heeled around a corner he glanced over to see Marny bracing herself.

At the outskirts of the Exe, Lassiter slowed.

"You sure it's safe?" he asked.

"Of course it's not," Marny said. "Just do what Tam says, and we should be all right."

Tam guided Lassiter down the pitted streets, worry gnawing at him. Marny was right—it totally wasn't safe. Bad enough that George had brought the Carter's grav-car into the Exe. Now here was Lassiter's tricked-out red car, screaming *money* at the top of its lungs. And it was going to be parked right outside his house.

On the other hand, coming in on foot would have been equally dangerous. In his car or out, Lassiter made an obvious target. Tam directed him to drive around the back way, so at least they wouldn't have to pass the drifter's squat.

"We have to make it fast," Tam said as the old auto shop came into view. "Pull up over there. And put the alarm on."

"Of course," Lassiter said. "It's triple-alarmed."

Like that would make any difference if someone wanted to damage or steal the thing.

"You seriously live here?" Lassiter's tone held disbelief laced with amusement.

"Shut it," Marny said. "Welcome to the real world, rich boy."

Tam ignored the argument and pulled out his keys. As soon as the car stopped he slipped out and hurried up the stairs. Nothing he could do about Lassiter's opinion, though his stomach clenched at the thought of the ammunition he was giving the Viewer. But there was no going back now.

By the time Lassiter and Marny got up the stairs, he had the door open.

Inside, thorny vines covered the walls and hung from the ceiling, bearing bright orange flowers shaped like mouths. The changeling had been busy again.

"Korrigan?" Tam called as they stepped into the living room.

It felt more like an exotic jungle than a room. Slippery yellow-green moss muffled his footsteps, and was that a waterfall in the kitchen? At least it completely camouflaged the messy reality of his house.

"You have a way with decorating, Exie," Lassiter said. He reached a finger out to touch one of the flowers, then jerked it back when the mouth opened and hissed at him, showing needle-sharp fangs. "Jeez."

"Come out, Korr." Marny said. She reached into her pack and drew out a foil-wrapped bar. "I've got a treat for you."

"Protein bar?" The changeling appeared, dangling from a vine attached to the ceiling. He reached a clawed hand out. "Give it."

Marny waved it at him. "A little less jungle, please. And ditch the carnivorous flowers."

Korrigan screwed up his ugly face. "You mortals have no appreciation for the spice of danger."

"We have more than enough danger going on right

now," Tam said. He glanced at Lassiter, who was watching the changeling with wide eyes. "Seen enough?"

The other boy swallowed, all his bravado gone. "Yeah."

"So, you believe us?" Tam asked. He wanted to hear Lassiter admit that he'd been wrong.

"Fine, fine. You were right." The other boy kept glancing at Korrigan. "I guess if we can be transported to Feyland, its creatures can come out."

"You have no idea," Tam said. "Alright, let's go."

"One sec, let me vid this."

Lassiter pulled out the slimmest messager Tam had ever seen and held it up. He scanned the room, lingering on the figure of Korrigan who hung by one arm and foot, noisily munching the bar Marny had given him.

"Smile," Marny said to the changeling.

Korrigan opened his mouth in a hideous expression, his lips a gaping slash too wide to be human, his teeth pointed, his eyes slitted nearly shut.

"Nice." Lassiter flicked off the vid and pocketed his messager.

"Have fun, guys," Marny said.

Tam frowned at the changeling. "No more water features in the kitchen, ok?"

Korrigan grimaced at him, which was at least better than the changeling's horrific smile.

"I'll make him clean up," Marny said. "I have the rewards, you know."

"Protein bars." Tam shook his head. He'd never have thought the changeling liked them, not after that first experience.

"Go," Marny said. "And be careful."

"You too. Keep the door fully locked."

Tam stepped onto the landing, the feeling of being watched prickling between his shoulders. It was past time to get that excruciatingly obvious car of Lassiter's out of the Exe.

21

JENNET TAPPED out the answer to another math equation on her tablet, then glanced at her messager for the hundredth time. It lay silent and dark on the corner of her desk. Were the boys and Marny all right? It was too easy to get into trouble in the Exe. She bit her lip, worry shredding her concentration.

She couldn't do another math problem or she'd scream. Pushing away her homework, she grabbed the messager and stared at it. Could it be broken?

It dinged in her hand, and she jumped. Relief skidded through her when she saw the message from Roy.

:We're at the palace. Come on over:

On top of the danger of the Exe had been the danger Roy wouldn't believe them, even when confronted with the changeling. Thank goodness he'd shown a little sense. With Roy, you couldn't always be sure.

"HANA," she said, addressing the house.

"Yes, Miss Carter?"

"Let the staff know I'm going out to ride my g-board. And I'll be visiting Roy Lassiter's for a bit."

"Noted. Please return home before dark."

Five minutes later she was standing in front of the imposing façade of the Lassiters' mansion, her board tucked under her arm. Her cheeks stung from the cold, and her ears felt numb. The cameras mounted at the entryway swiveled onto her, then the massive doors slowly swung open. Always ones for a grand gesture, the Lassiters.

"Hey, blondie," Roy said, meeting her at the entry, all his cocky assurance restored.

She stepped into the cool stone-floored foyer and propped her board against the wall. "I take it you were convinced."

He nodded, the light sliding over his brown hair. It was a muddier color than Tam's and not as straight. Once, under the influence of fey magic, he'd sported a head of bronzed hair with the most perfect hint of curl. But that was back when he'd been impersonating his better self. At least physically.

And though he still looked as average as ever, she had to admit his personality was marginally improved.

"Where's Tam?" she asked.

"Getting the systems ready. Come on."

Roy led the way down the tall, canyon-like hallway.

Shadows shrouded the ceiling, and the few sconces shed weak puddles of light on the walls. At the far end towered another set of double doors. They silently opened and Jennet shivered, though she knew it was just the Lassiter's house network sensing their approach.

Beyond the doors lay the theater. True to its name, it came complete with rows of seats and a floor-to-ceiling screen. But what always stole Jennet's breath was the number and variety of game systems showcased along the walls—netscreens, moto-sense setups, and dozens of sim systems. Even though she'd seen it before, she still found it stunning.

"What did Tam think of all this?" She waved her hand at the display.

"Oh, he was impressed." Roy grinned at her. "But he tried not to show it."

Jennet raised an eyebrow. She was impressed, too. Not by the crazy display of tech wealth, but that Roy had actually left Tam alone with all that valuable equipment.

Roy led her to the FullD systems, partitioned off behind frosted glass panels. His mom, being the CEO of VirtuMax, collected a model of every prototype the company made—which meant the Lassiters had three complete FullD setups. Spot lighting from above illuminated the systems, gleaming off the helmets and supple synth-leather chairs. The LEDs on the gloves twinkled like precious gems.

"There you are," Tam said, glancing at her through the scrim of hair he'd let fall across his face—always a sign he was worried.

She was too, now that they were about to enter the Twilight Kingdom again.

"I'll take the middle system," she said, "since I've played on that one."

Roy nodded, then moved to the FullD on the left. "I'll be here."

"I don't think you can come with us," Jennet said.

"I've been in the Realm before." Roy narrowed his eyes. "Or are you saying you don't want me along?"

"Whether we do or not, Jennet and I are going even deeper than Feyland." Tam slid into his chair and pulled on the gloves. "You can try to follow, but don't be surprised if you get blocked out."

Roy's eyebrows lifted. "There's something beyond the Realm?"

"Yeah," Jennet said, picking up her helmet. "It's called the Twilight Kingdom. And it's freaky."

Roy took his seat and started gearing up. "Whatever. I'm still coming into the Realm."

Jennet didn't mind. Even if Roy couldn't make the passage to the Twilight Kingdom, it would be good to have another sword guarding their backs in the Realm. She pulled the helmet on and selected the familiar *F* key to launch the game.

Dizzying golden light filled her senses, and her stomach lurched. Oh yeah. Back in Feyland for real.

She blinked and took a deep breath as the disorientation faded. Roy's Mercenary stood to her left, wearing his gleaming gold mail. Bands of gold circled his upper arms, and he wore a huge two-handed sword strapped on his back. On her right was Tam's Knight, his silver armor shining in the sun. They stood in the middle of a faerie ring of white-spotted red mushrooms. A warm breeze swirled the leaves of the trees rising at the edge of the clearing, where a mossy green path led between the silvery trunks.

"Back to being a fox-girl?" Roy asked.

She glanced down at the vest and leggings she wore, the dagger at her waist. "Right. I made a Kitsune on your system."

It felt strange to be playing this character again. She scanned through her list of abilities, hoping they wouldn't have any big fights ahead.

"Will the Twilight Kingdom let you in as a different character?" Roy asked.

"They better." Tam set his hand on the pommel of his sword. "She's still Jennet, after all. Ready?"

She nodded, and they stepped out of the ring.

"Puck?" Jennet called, glancing into the forest.

"Aha!" The sprite's voice rang through the clearing, and a moment later he appeared, springing from the lower branches of a nearby tree. He landed nimbly before them and cocked his head. "You bring the Royal One into the Realm as well? A curious choice."

"Got a problem with that, little guy?" Roy folded his arms.

"Stop it," Jennet said. "We have more important things to do than argue."

"Jennet is right," said a tall figure striding out from between the pale-barked trees.

"Thomas!" she cried, flinging herself into his arms. "I wasn't sure we'd see you again."

He was solid and familiar. She blotted her eyes on the fine linen fabric of his shoulder, then let go of her fierce hug and stepped back

"Why can you come here?" Tam asked. "Judging by the mushrooms, we're in Bright Court territory."

"The fey monarchs have made a truce." Thomas regarded them with wise and weary eyes. "As the queen's Bard, I serve as ambassador, and am granted passage over the Seelie Court's lands."

"Who is this guy?" Roy asked.

"This," Jennet said, "is Thomas Rimer. Lead developer and programmer for Feyland."

"But…" Roy's voice went high. He cleared his throat. "But he's dead."

"Am I?" Thomas held out his hands and studied them. "I am not, perhaps, real in the sense that you know, but I exist nonetheless."

"Inside a computer game?" Roy backed up a step.

Tam turned to the other boy, the edge of impatience in his green eyes. "You know magic is real—you've used it yourself. Why is this any stranger?"

"Are we going to get trapped in here too?" Roy asked.

His knuckles were white, fisted tight, and Jennet suspected he wanted to bolt back into the ring and log out.

"I am not trapped," Thomas said. "Not in the sense you mean. No, I chose this."

Jennet squeezed the bard's arm. It was comfortingly sturdy under her fingers.

"Dad told me you had terminal cancer," she said. "I didn't know."

"The doctors didn't catch it until far too late."

"So you, what?" Roy made a wild gesture with one hand. "You programmed yourself into Feyland so you wouldn't die?"

"Nobody could do that," Tam said. "It was magic, obviously."

"Tamlin is correct," Thomas said. "Twas the magic of the Realm. My body was failing. I traded my life to serve the Dark Queen."

Suspicion blazed through Jennet like a falling star. Thomas had died last summer—when she'd lost her in-game battle with the queen and fallen ill. She'd been hospitalized in critical care, the doctors unable to tell exactly what was wrong with her. It had been grim, until the day she'd woken up feeling a hundred percent better.

Which was right around the time Thomas was found, his lifeless body in his sim chair, still hooked up to the FullD system.

She whirled on him. "Thomas! You sacrificed yourself for me. How could you do that?" Tears burned, hot and bright, in the corners of her eyes.

"Ah, Jennet." His voice was soft. "You were not destined to waste away, a victim of the queen's dark magic. I was dying in any case. It was an easy choice."

Tam put his hand on her shoulder. She drew in a deep, shuddering breath. Two good men had given themselves to the Dark Queen, for her. She had saved Tam, but…

"You can't ever come back to our world, can you?" she asked.

Thomas shook his head, sorrow lingering on his lips. "I cannot, as you know."

"I wish you could." She swallowed salt.

"Complete the task you have been set," he said. "Restore the balance. That will be payment enough."

"Restore the balance… what does that even mean?" Tam asked.

Puck, who had been uncharacteristically silent during this exchange, sprang into the air. "It means you must go, *now*, into the Twilight Kingdom and wake the Elder Fey."

At his words, a breeze rose, shimmering the leaves on the trees.

"But, my brother—" Tam began.

"He is well enough," Thomas said. "There is still time to free him—but your first task must be completed."

Roy stepped forward, his brown eyes full of questions. "Can I help?"

Jennet glanced at him. She'd never expected to hear those words come out of his mouth, especially spoken with such sincerity.

"Only Fair Jennet and Bold Tamlin can pass the borders of the Realm into the Twilight Kingdom," Puck said.

"Why?" Roy frowned.

"It is not your quest to complete, Royal One," Thomas said. "Be assured, your strengths will be called upon—sooner than you might think. Now, bide here with me while the others journey on."

"Quickly, quickly." Puck caught Jennet's sleeve and tugged her toward the mossy path.

"Thomas." Jennet's voice caught. "Will I see you again?"

"Most assuredly." He touched her shoulder. "Be of good heart."

Vision blurring, she let Puck haul her away. Tam was next to her, his calm strength steadying her until she could blink the tears from her eyes.

"Here." Puck stopped midway down the path and pointed into the woods. "Through the bracken fern, you will find your portal. The queen calls me now, and I must not tarry. Nor should you. Good luck, mortals!"

He whisked away into the underbrush and was gone.

Tam caught her hand as they left the path, heading for the faint, purplish glow a few yards ahead. Another faerie ring formed of pale-stalked mushrooms—their gateway to the Twilight Kingdom.

Tam pulled her to him and pressed a kiss on her lips, warm and firm.

"Here we go," he said. "Into the Twilight Kingdom."

Heart beating fast in her throat, she nodded. She desperately hoped it was for the last time.

22

ICY COLD GRABBED TAM; stealing his breath, freezing his blood. He was sure he was dying. Then the darkness lifted and he could see again. He knelt in the center of a faerie ring, Jennet beside him, while the tall, strange trees of the Twilight Kingdom waved over their heads.

In the purple light her skin was too pale, her eyes dark hollows in her face. Tam pulled her close, their bodies trembling as they tried to get warm. He coughed and tasted blood, metallic on his tongue.

"That journey's—not getting any easier," she said.

If anything, it was getting worse. The air rasped his lungs, and he blinked hard, trying to focus his vision in the eerie dimness. The Twilight Kingdom was not a place for mortals. Staying here too long, or returning once more, would kill them. He felt the truth of it down to his bones.

"Whatever it takes to wake the Elder Fey, we're doing it," he said. "Because we're not coming back here."

He stood, though his legs still felt weak, and gave Jennet a hand up. They rose into the air, past the wavery trees, until the landscape spread below them. The foothills of the mountains loomed, jagged and dark, just ahead.

"Do you feel it?" Jennet asked.

"Yeah."

The moment they cleared the trees, he'd been aware of a tugging sensation in his chest, pulling him toward the dark mass of the peaks. Something wanted them to go there. He only hoped it wasn't something looking for a human snack.

As he and Jennet approached, he scanned the barren slopes. He flew higher, the wind whipping his hair. Higher still. Until…

"There." Jennet pointed to an opening in the rock limned with orange light.

"I hope we're not flying into a live volcano. That could get messy."

"At least it would be warm."

Tam angled for the opening. It looked like a cave mouth, but as he got closer he saw it was too regular to be a normal cave. The opening was ten feet high and perfectly rounded at the top. A whiff of sulfur stung his nose. Slowly he descended to a floor paved with huge, smooth blocks of obsidian.

Jennet landed next to him. She looked better—or maybe it was the orange light softening the shadows on her face.

"A tunnel," she said, peering deeper into the opening.

He wasn't giving up the volcano theory. In addition to the smell, the air was warmer here. Soft gusts chased the last of the chill from his body.

"Let's go," he said.

"Tam…" Jennet gave him an anxious look. "I can't fly."

He imagined rising up into the air—but nothing happened. His feet remained firmly on the dark stone. Looked like the rules had changed again, once they were inside the mountain.

"Then we walk," he said.

One hand on his sword, he led the way. His armored feet rang over the smooth floor, though Jennet was silent behind him. The tunnel began sloping down, and the orange light grew brighter, the last sliver of dim purple sky disappearing behind them. As he'd feared, the temperature was rising.

He glanced at Jennet. Determination shone from her blue eyes, and she gripped her staff tightly in one hand. Crazy love surged in his blood, so sweet and strong he could barely breathe, could barely move. He would do anything to keep her safe. Anything.

"All right?" she asked.

"Yeah." No.

He wanted them out of there, back in the real world, the faeries defeated, his brother returned. But the only way out was to keep going forward.

Tam touched her cheek, then made himself turn and head down the tunnel. His footsteps clanged against the stone, the light and heat growing stronger with every step. The air itself felt thicker, viscous and sticky, as if he was wading through honey. A drop of sweat trickled down his back.

Jennet let out a gasping breath. Tam caught her hand and together they pressed through the hot, thick air. The orange light took on a searing edge, and he blinked at the brightness. If they didn't get to the end of the tunnel soon, he and Jennet would end up collapsing into little wet puddles of humanity on the floor. His throat burned, acrid and dry.

Suddenly, the tunnel opened out into an enormous cavern. The terrible pressure surrounding them eased, although the heat remained, scorching his skin. Tam halted, pulling Jennet to a stop as the path turned into a ledge. A drop-off of hundreds of yards plummeted at their feet, molten rock seething below in a lake of orange fire.

"Look," she said, her voice a bare thread of sound.

A dark island rose in the middle of the lake, steep-sided and made of shining midnight stone. The peak ascended to their eye level, and something lay there.

Something sinuous and winged. Something black-scaled and clawed. Its head was turned toward them, its eyes lidded closed. It lay perfectly still on its bed of stone, only the twin trails of smoke rising from its nostrils to show the creature was alive.

"Now what?" Jennet whispered.

Tam swallowed.

"Now," he said, "we wake the Elder Fey."

"The Elder Fey are *dragons?*"

"Apparently." It didn't surprise him, as though the knowledge had been there, waiting all along for him to recognize it.

Jennet glanced down at the fiery lake. Tam judged the distance to the sheer sides of the island across from them. Though the Elder Fey slumbered frighteningly close, there was roughly twenty-five feet separating them. Way too far for them to jump.

The ledge they stood on didn't lead anywhere, except back into the tunnel. There was no stairway or bridge, no way he could see to reach the island.

"We can't fly," Jennet said, "so how do we get over there?"

"Maybe we don't." Tam peered at the black dragon sleeping out of their reach. "Can you think of any way to wake it up?"

"Shoot magefire at it?"

He didn't like the idea. What if the dragon woke and attacked them? But they didn't have a lot of other options. He slid his sword out of its scabbard.

"Alright," he said. "Give it a try, but be ready to run back up the tunnel."

He didn't think the Elder Fey could pursue them into that small space, though he didn't want to put it to the test.

Jennet lifted her staff and fired a bolt of blue mage-fire at the dragon. The bolt hit, sizzling against the dark scales beside one wing. Tam braced himself for an attack, but the dragon continued to slumber.

"Try again." His fear began churning into frustration.

She struck again, aiming for the wing. The creature didn't stir. Another bolt of blue lightning glanced off its head, to no effect.

"I guess it's immune to magic." Jennet lowered her staff.

"Worth a try, though."

Tam squinted across to the peak, judging the distance. He hefted his sword, finding the balance point, then lifted it like a huge metal dart.

"Careful," Jennet breathed.

Taking a deep breath of overheated air, he drew his arm back. This had to count—it was the only sword he had. He took three long steps into the tunnel, then lunged forward to the very edge of the precipice, propelling his blade point-first toward the slumbering dragon.

"Tam!"

Jennet caught him around the waist and pulled him

back to safety. His sword flew, the gleaming silver blade flickering with orange light. Yes... yes....

No.

The sword clattered to the stone, a hand's breadth from the creature's head.

"Damn," he said.

Sweat dampened his neck, and the thickness of the air choked his lungs. Jennet slumped against the wall, a strand of hair sticking to her face.

Tam cupped his hands around his mouth, drew in a lungful of red air, and yelled, "Wake up!"

The words echoed in the cavernous space—but the sleeping dragon didn't stir.

"We can't have gotten this far, just to fail," Tam said. "There has to be a way."

"I keep waiting for Puck to show up. But I don't think he's going to." Weariness smudged Jennet's eyes.

"Now would be a good time." He pushed through the thick air to join her against the rock wall. "It's getting hotter."

Jennet nodded. Then a curious expression crossed her face. She drew her hand out of the pocket of her robes.

"Look," she said. "I'd forgotten." A white stone sat in her palm, glowing faintly. "From Puck, remember? To use in a time of despair."

"I think this qualifies." Tam picked the stone up and turned it between his fingers. "But *how* do we use it?"

"Throw it?"

"No. We can't risk losing it if we miss. Or wasting our chance, if we hit the dragon and it doesn't wake up." He handed the stone back to her. "Puck gave it to you. Which means you can use it."

"I don't know!" Frustration sent her words spiraling into the air.

Oh, oh, the syllables echoed back at them, magnified.

"Do that again," he said.

"What?"

Ut, ut.

Jennet looked at the bright stone in her hand, then closed her eyes. She hummed, low in her throat, and the sound amplified, filling the cavern. On the peak before them, one black wing twitched, and Tam caught his breath.

She opened her mouth and began to sing.

"*SLEEP, O babe, for the red-bee hums*
  The silent twilight's fall.
  Aoibheall from the Grey Rock comes,
  To wrap the world in thrall."

The song curled through the cavern, the rocks vibrating with overtones. Jennet's voice was clear and thin. As she sang, the melody gathered strength, growing more piercing and lovely.

"A LEANBHAN O, *my child, my joy,*
My love and heart's desire,
The crickets sing you lullaby
Beside the dying fire."

The heat that had been pressing heavily against his lungs, his thoughts, lifted. The lake of molten rock dimmed, the waves cooling to a sullen red while Jennet sang on.

"DUSK IS DRAWN, *and the Green Man's Thorn*
Is wreathed in rings of fog.
Siabhra sails his boat til morn
Upon the Starry Bog."

The midnight dragon stirred, one huge dark wing rising, flexing. Tam wished he had his sword. He took a step in front of Jennet and raised his shield.

"A LEANBHAN O, *the pale half moon*

Hath brimmed her cusp in dew,
And weeps to hear the sad sleep-tune
I sing, O love, to you."

One eye slitted open, brilliant gold. Tam's heart pounded, his head filled with the haunting, twining melody.

The dragon raised its head, a quick, sinuous motion, and fixed its impossibly ancient gaze on Tam and Jennet. Fear, icy and primal, sliced through Tam as though he were a mouse, transfixed in the shadow of some huge raptor.

The Elder Fey had woken.

23

JENNET TOOK another breath of fiery air and kept singing. She stumbled over a couple of the words, but the song poured from her mouth, haunting and lyrical. Her mother used to sing to her at night, a forgotten lullaby she'd buried deep, along with the pain of her mom leaving. Somehow the song had resurfaced when she most needed it.

"Jennet," Tam whispered.

Her name was a thread of sound, barely audible over the echoes of the song. She opened her eyes, then shrank back, pressing her shoulders against the hot stone behind her.

The dragon stood, obsidian claws scraping the peak it had slumbered on, and unfurled wings so dark they seemed to suck all the light into their shadowy folds.

Who wakes me?

The Elder Fey did not speak, not in human fashion, but the meaning sounded in her head, sibilant and displeased.

Tam cleared his throat and stepped to the front of the ledge. His right hand was fisted, knuckles white.

"Greetings," he said, bowing to the huge creature. "We are mortals, sent here by those in the Realm of Faerie." He paused, clearly searching for words.

The dragon blinked, slowly, rainbow lids coruscating.

I am not concerned with your tiny, transient lives. Leave, so I may return to dreaming the worlds into being.

Jennet pushed herself away from the rock and went to stand beside Tam.

"You are needed to restore the balance," she said, her pulse pounding in her veins, hot and panicked.

The balance is not at risk.

"It is." Tam's voice rose. "My little brother is captive in the Dark Court."

Mortals are taken by the fey. It is the way of things. The dragon opened its mouth in a huge, dangerous yawn, its teeth serrated and sharp as diamonds.

"Listen," Jennet said. "The faerie courts are trying to find a way to open a permanent gateway into our world —and they almost have! Doesn't that count?"

The dragon regarded them a moment with its unreadable eyes, then lifted its massive black head and

ANTHEA SHARP

let out a deep, crooning cry. The sound vibrated to the soles of her feet, and she clutched at her mage staff, fighting for balance. Tam stumbled back against her, then straightened, his hand going to his empty scabbard.

A bolt of blue hurtled into the cavern—a smaller dragon, gleaming like polished sapphire. It hovered in front of the black dragon, wings moving in graceful arcs, and dipped its head. If the two creatures were conversing, it was in a way not meant for mortal understanding. A moment later, the blue dragon was gone, disappeared through some invisible passageway.

The black dragon lowered itself onto the rock, as smoothly as oil gliding over water. It gazed at Jennet with its golden eyes.

Sing once more, while I await the messenger's return.

She glanced at the white stone, still glowing in her hand. Melodies swirled through her, half-forgotten, unbidden.

"Jennet?" Tam touched her arm.

The look in his eyes made her heart spill over. She took his hand and began to sing.

"*The water is wide, I cannot cross over,*
And neither have I wings to fly,
Give me a boat that can carry two,
And both shall row, my love and I."

234

. . .

The dragon let out a low sigh that blended with the ringing echoes. It was a sigh edged with old sorrows, brightened with hope. It was a sigh thousands of years old.

Enough.

"Do you think the dragon didn't like my song?" Jennet asked Tam in a low voice.

"I don't care." He squeezed her fingers. "It was perfect."

The blue dragon streaked into the cavern again and hovered in front of its leader.

"That was fast," Jennet said.

"I'm guessing time and space don't mean a lot to the Elder Fey."

"Is it getting warmer in here again?" She pushed a strand of hair behind one ear.

"Yeah. Look at the lake."

Jennet peeked over the side of the ledge, to see the molten surface shimmering bright orange once more.

The black dragon hissed, a sound like death. She shuddered, and Tam pulled her into his arms. The air grew harsh and thick, and gouts of lava fountained from the lake, spattering dangerously close to the ledge.

Was this it? They woke the Elder Fey, then died inside the Twilight Kingdom? She held tightly to Tam, fright battering her breath.

The fey have overstepped. Mortals, attend.

"We're listening," Tam said.

The blue dragon turned and came straight at them. Jennet flinched, but before crashing into them, it halted. It was small, compared to the black dragon, but still big —at least fifteen feet long. It fixed them with the same eerie golden eyes, and Jennet had the feeling it found them amusing.

Collect your blade, earthly knight.

The blue dragon held out one clawed foot. Nestled in the cage of sharp talons was Tam's sword. He reached for it, his face pale.

"Ow." Tam winced as the edge of one talon touched his skin. A single line of blood welled on the back of his hand, bright crimson, as he took his sword.

Collect your blade, fair maiden.

"I don't have a blade," Jennet said.

The Blade of the Elder Fey is in your keeping until the balance is restored. Once drawn, the blade will not rest until it tastes blood. Unsheathe it only when true battle is upon you.

The blue dragon held out a slim silver casing, presumably housing the deadly blade. Jennet glanced at Tam, fear pushing up through her throat. She really didn't want the thing.

"Everything here has a reason," he said, setting his hand on her shoulder. "Take it."

Slowly, she reached out. Her fingers looked tiny and

fragile in contrast to the deadly elegance of the blue dragon's claws. Just before she touched them, the dragon released the scabbard, dropping the Blade of the Elder Fey into her hands.

Heat rushed over her, and the molten lake seethed. The black dragon rose, wings beating like thunder. She choked on the air, too hot, too hot.

Fate is set in motion. Return now to your place.

The solid rock tilted under her feet, then disappeared. A hundred pairs of golden eyes, ageless and unpitying, regarded her. She heard Tam shout, as if from a distance. The blade seared her left palm—the one that still bore the scars of Feyland—until she screamed from the pain burning into her flesh.

The Twilight Kingdom whirled around her, and was gone.

24

"JENNET!"

Panic clawed through Tam. Her scream still echoed in his ears as he was plunged into a heavy mist. A moment later, he stood alone on a flat plain, silken wisps of grey surrounding him in all directions.

"Jennet!" he called again.

He turned in a circle, straining to see something. Anything. The light lay tranquil and heavy about him. His pulse beat loudly, like a broken clock in a place time didn't exist.

"Jennet?" This time it came out a whisper.

There was nothing but empty solitude in reply.

After a minute, or an eternity, he saw a figure coming toward him through the mist. A woman! His breath turned leaden when he realized it wasn't Jennet.

Just as quickly his disappointment pivoted to fear, heart clenching when he recognized who it was.

The Dark Queen of the fey.

Her midnight hair flowed like silk around the beautiful, dangerous planes of her face. Her dress swirled behind her as though it were part of the landscape, all shadows and fog. She met his gaze, her eyes fathomless and deep, with an expression that cut him to the heart.

"Bold Tamlin," she said in a voice like smoke. "What have you done?"

He didn't want to answer—couldn't answer, his mouth dry, his senses stunned.

In the real world, his memories of her were pale recollections of the dangerous radiance of her eyes, the yearning she conjured up in his blood. The true Dark Queen, standing before him, had the power to ensnare his mind. If he let her.

Swallowing hard, he conjured up Jennet's image and tore his gaze away.

"My knight," she said. "You have meddled where no mortal should go."

"I'm not your knight."

Cold washed over him, the ice of her displeasure. "There is still time to turn aside."

"I don't think so." He made the mistake of looking into her eyes again, and was caught, snared in promises and mystery.

She reached one delicate hand to trace his jaw, leaving searing frost in the wake of her touch. Tam shivered, senses clamoring with panic and need.

"Would you consign me," she said, "indeed, my entire Realm—to death? Would you deprive your own world of all traces of magic? Without you, we shall wither and die until there is nothing left but black emptiness. Is that what you truly desire, Tamlin?"

"Give me back my brother." He forced the words out through lips gone numb.

"Ah, bargains." She smiled, starlight and the darkness between.

"No bargains. Just return him to me."

"There is a cost to everything." Her voice dipped, resonant with promise. "What would you give me to restore your brother to the mortal realm, unharmed? Once, you offered yourself."

His lips shaped the word *no*.

Chill crackled through the air, and she narrowed her eyes. The mist blew in tatters about them.

"Everything beloved will be lost to you." Her words were a blade slipped beneath his ribs.

Could he do it, trade himself to the faeries again, to keep his brother safe?

He clenched his fists, fingers burning with cold. The only reason the Dark Queen wanted him was as a sacrifice to open the gateway between her world and his own. Once that happened, no one would be safe—not his brother, not anyone. It was a hollow hope she offered.

"No," he said, putting force behind it.

"Thrice you have denied me." The fury in her voice was like black ice, treacherous and deadly. The rising wind whipped her hair into a dark tangle. "I abandon you here, once-knight, to the fate you have earned."

A frigid gust made Tam close his eyes. When he opened them, she was gone, but the wind remained, cold and fierce. He wrapped his arms around himself, surprised to find he wore his jeans and long-sleeved shirt. No armor. No protection from the bitter air.

He couldn't just stand there, or he'd freeze to death. Hunching his shoulders, he headed in the direction from which the queen had come. Misery edged his thoughts, clear and brittle as frost on a fallen leaf. He'd had a chance to save his brother... but it was an impossible choice. The cost was too high, for everyone.

The knowledge didn't keep his heart from breaking.

A faint sound caught his ears, and he stopped, jerking his head up to listen. The whistling wind drowned everything out, even his own ragged breathing. Nothing. He waited until shivers racked his body, then bowed his head and trudged on, into the blankness.

The sound came again, and his heart bumped with sudden hope. The clear notes of a guitar, plucked in melody. Rising, falling. Barely breathing, he turned to the right and followed the trail of music.

The notes grew louder, and the fear wrapping him began to unravel. Ahead, the monotony of fog was broken by something on the ground. Tam stumbled forward, teeth chattering. Transparent mushrooms grew in a circle, an insubstantial faerie ring made of mist. His passage home.

A freezing blast shredded the ring into nothing but cloudy wisps, and Tam fell to his knees.

"No," he whispered.

Still, the music did not fail. Tam kept his eyes fixed on the place the ring had been. He felt lightheaded. It had to reappear. Please.

The faintest suggestion of mushrooms wavered in the air. The melody grew insistent, and he rose to his feet, his pulse crashing desperately in his veins. Holding his breath, he flung himself into the ghostly faerie ring.

Cold gripped him, the midnight ice of the Dark Queen's smile. He ached, as if his whole body was a bruise.

"Tam?" Jennet's voice, tight with worry. Her hand on his forehead, stroking back his hair. "Can you hear me?"

Music still dripped into the air, stronger now. He was so tired, and everything was black. Or maybe his eyes were closed. He pried his eyelids open, each one weighing a hundred pounds. Jennet stared at him, her face pale. Above her shone the white-barked trees of the Realm. He lay on his back in the middle of a faerie ring, moss as soft as velvet under his head.

"Thank god," she said, leaning over to press her lips against his.

At first he could barely feel the kiss, then heat began to spread through him, little sparks flaring painfully to life. He lifted his arms and encircled her, holding her close.

"Ahem." Roy Lassiter tapped Tam on the shoulder. "Enough with the happy reunion. Don't we have some fighting to do?"

Tam sat up, his hands and feet burning as circulation returned. Bard Thomas stood playing his guitar at the outskirts of the circle, and Puck hovered cross-legged in the air beside him. Thomas nodded at Tam, his fingers stilling on the strings.

"Thanks," Tam said. "I wouldn't have made it without your music."

"I am glad you heard it well enough to follow it back to us." The look in the bard's eyes suggested he knew where Tam had been. And who he had seen.

Jennet grabbed his hand. "When I returned without you, we were so worried. Thomas thought you'd gotten sucked *elsewhere*."

Midnight shadows whispered through Tam's mind.

"Yeah, I did."

He wasn't going to talk about the Dark Queen—not when they were still within her Realm. Maybe not ever.

"So, what went wrong?" Lassiter asked. "Are you going back in now?"

"No," Tam said. "We're done."

"What?" The other boy tipped his head. "You were only gone like ten minutes. How can you be done?"

"Time moves differently between the worlds," Thomas said. "What seems a minute to us is much longer in the Twilight Kingdom. Tam and Jennet have succeeded in waking the Elder Fey."

"So, now what?" Lassiter asked. "Puck here seems to think we've got an epic battle ahead."

"Indeed," the sprite said, his expression sober.

Tam gave Lassiter a questioning look and the other boy folded his arms. "Thomas brought me up to speed. The Twilight Kingdom, the courts joining forces. Lots going on. You could have told me."

"We did," Jennet said.

"Yeah, after the fun was over."

"Trust me, it hasn't been fun." Tam scrubbed his hands through his hair. "And it's not over. We have to get my little brother out of the Dark Court."

"The three of us?" Lassiter frowned and glanced over at Puck and Thomas. "Five of us?"

Thomas shook his head, his eyes weary. "I cannot oppose the queen—I serve her. And Puck is not able be part of your battles, either."

"It might work." Jennet looked from Tam to Lassiter. She lifted her hand, clenched around a silver scabbard. "I have this."

"No," Thomas said. "The three of you cannot prevail against the combined powers of the Bright Court and the Dark, even if you carry the Blade of the Elder Fey."

"Then what do we do?" Frustration burned Tam's tongue.

"Gather your allies," Puck said. He made a slow cartwheel and regarded Tam, a touch of his usual mischief showing in his eyes.

"But—"

A low, eerie howl echoed through the night, and Thomas looked up into the star-strewn darkness above them.

"The Wild Hunt," he said. "You must depart, quickly."

Lassiter offered Tam a hand up, to his surprise. His bones ached as he stood. It took a moment to find his balance before he followed Thomas down the fern-lined path weaving between the trees. It ended at a clearing where the usual white-spotted red mushrooms formed a circle.

"See you out there," Lassiter said, leaping into the center.

Jennet kissed Thomas on the cheek. "Thank you."

"Guard each other well," the bard said. "This is not ended yet."

Another howl shivered the night.

Much as Tam's heart begged him to stay in the Realm and storm the Dark Court to rescue his brother, he couldn't. Yet.

Swallowing bitter impatience, he caught Jennet's hand, and together they stepped into the faerie ring.

25

JENNET BRACED herself as golden light whirled about her senses. When her vision cleared, she was sitting in the sim-chair at Roy's, the guys on either side of her. She sat forward and slowly removed her gloves. Heart thumping with hope, she lifted her left hand.

The red burn scars she had borne since All Hallow's Eve were gone. Her palm was still pink, but the shiny, seared flesh running the length of her fingers had disappeared. She drew in a deep breath and rubbed her thumb over her hand. The new skin tingled, the whorls of her fingerprints restored.

Still, they hadn't won yet. She and Tam had succeeded in waking the Elder Fey, but the Bug was still trapped in the Realm. Other than fixing her hand and giving her a deadly blade, it was impossible to tell if the Elder Fey had actually *done* anything.

"Whew." Roy pulled off his helmet. "You two have some freaky experiences in-game, I have to say."

Tam stripped off his gear. "You should have seen the Twilight Kingdom."

"No thanks—I'll leave the crazy stuff to you."

"Now what?" Jennet said, looking at Tam.

His expression grim, he held her gaze. "Now... we have some explaining to do."

Roy nodded. "Thought so. I'll tell Spark."

"Tell her what?" Jennet asked.

"You have the hardest part," Tam said to her. "You have to convince your dad to sneak the beta team into VirtuMax late tonight."

"What?" Shock made her blink.

"Puck said we had to gather our allies. That means the beta-test team."

"With the exception of Coranne Smith," Roy said. "She'd never go for it."

"No kidding," Tam said. "Last thing we need is the company whistle blower."

"Wait." Jennet couldn't wrap her mind around it. "So, you're saying the plan is to get the rest of the team to come in-game with us?"

"In-Realm," Tam said. "We can't defeat the fey monarchs without the team. Zeg will come. Even if he doesn't believe me, he'll love the chance to break into VirtuMax headquarters after hours, just to say he did."

"I can convince Spark," Roy said. "I've got the vid of

Korrigan, after all. She might not buy the whole story until we get in-game, but she's always up for a challenge."

"Which leaves your dad," Tam said. "Jennet—you can do it. It's ok to stand up to him. He'll still love you tomorrow, I promise."

"Can't we do it without him?" Jennet shot Roy a pleading look. "You can get us into the building, right?"

He folded his arms. "Give me a few days to hack my mom's access codes, sure."

"We don't have a few days." Tam flung his gloves down on the sim-chair, his face tight. "We have to go in tonight. The Dark Queen knows what we did, that the Elder Fey are awake. My brother isn't safe."

"My car is approved for The View's gate access until midnight," Roy said. "I'll take you into Crestview to get Zeg, Tam. Then we'll swing back by Spark's VIP digs and fill her in. Jennet, you and your dad can meet us there. One hour."

"But…" She swallowed.

She'd never been able to convince her dad the danger of the Realm was real. Why would he believe her now?

Tam's messager beeped as he and Lassiter swooped out of The View in the red grav-car. He dug in his pack and pulled it out, hoping it wasn't Jennet with bad news. To his surprise, the message came from Zeg.

Tam scanned it, stomach tightening, and let out a quiet curse.

"What?" Lassiter said, taking a corner too fast. Good thing he liked to speed.

"Change of plans—we're heading to my place. Zeg's there. Marny called him when she and the changeling were attacked."

"Attacked?" Lassiter asked. "The hell. They okay?"

He ran a red light, and Tam braced his feet on the carpeted floor.

"I hope so. Zeg didn't say much. I'm telling him we're on the way." Tam's fingers flew over the messenger.

"Why didn't Marny message you?"

"She knows how crucial our game-play was this afternoon."

Tam didn't mention how faulty reception was in the Exe. She might have tried to message him, with no luck. He leaned forward, willing the car to go faster.

"Did evil faeries track them down?"

"No. The changeling *is* an evil faerie, remember?" His messenger beeped again, with Zeg's reply. "Damn. It was the smoke drifters down the street."

All the activity had drawn too much attention to his place. Leaving Marny with the changeling had endangered her, and it was his fault. He shouldn't have ignored that prickle between his shoulders. In the Exe, disregarding the danger signals left you dead.

He wouldn't discount faerie involvement, either. It

would be easy enough to stir the drifters up, then point them in the direction of his house—and it seemed like exactly the kind of thing the Unseelie would do. Especially if the queen commanded it.

"But the drifters are gone, right?" Lassiter said. "Defeated?"

"They might have backed off for now, but..." Tam shivered.

Smoke drifters were unpredictably violent once provoked. He had to get everyone out of his place and lock it down tight before the drifters returned. Tomorrow, he'd go back and keep a low profile until the drifters calmed again.

"You ever think of moving?" Lassiter asked.

"No." As if his family had anyplace else to go.

"Well, you should."

Lassiter seemed blissfully unaware that people didn't *choose* to live in the Exe.

"Turn left here," Tam said when they got to Stark Way. They'd made it to the Exe in record time.

"The city ought to replace these streetlights," Lassiter said as the grav-car slipped into a wide pool of shadow.

"They ignore this neighborhood," Tam said. "Go right at the next street."

His block was quiet—but it was an aftermath kind of silence, thick with tension.

"Stay with the car," Tam said as they slid to a stop behind Zeg's battered guzzler. "I'll go get them."

"Here." Lassiter rummaged beside his seat, then handed Tam a small black object. "It's a taser. Just in case."

Trust Lassiter to have a weapon—not that it would do much good against crazed smoke-drifters. Tam pocketed it and nodded his thanks.

"Be right back." He hoped.

The cold night air carried the smell of rot that permeated the Exe. Tam carefully mounted the stairs. They creaked under his feet. When he got to the seventh tread, he stopped, heart twisting. The stair was gone— just a hole where something, or someone, had crashed through. Fresh gouges splintered the railing, testimony to violence.

The landing showed more evidence of the fight. The door was dented, and the glass in the living room's wire-webbed windows was broken, crushed bits hanging together around the rusted wire. Somebody could get through that shattered opening, if they wanted to. He hoped there was a big enough sheet of metal to cover it downstairs in the abandoned auto shop.

"Guys?" He tapped the door. "It's me, Tam."

The peephole slid open, and he caught a glimpse of frizzy beard. Then the locks snicked, and Zeg opened the door.

"Tam," Marny said. She jumped off the couch and gave him a rib-cracking hug.

"Good to see you, too." Alive and unhurt, thank god. "What happened?"

He pulled back and spotted Korrigan crouching in the corner, his ugly face fierce, his claws bared.

"A couple hours after you and Roy left, we heard someone coming up the stairs. The smoke drifters. They said if we gave them all the money we had, they'd go away. Then they tried to batter down the door."

"We fought them," the changeling said. "Mistress Marny laid about with her club, while I sent poisonous crawlies to bite and torment."

"Club?"

"Yeah," Marny said. "One guy started coming through the window, so I bashed him with the lamp. Between that and Korr's bugs, we drove them off. Then I called Uncle Zeg."

"They haven't come back?"

"Yet," Zeg said from his place by the door. "But they will. Grab anything important, Tam, anything you want to keep for good, and bring it down to my car. We're clearing you out of here."

The pit of his stomach felt empty and cold. "This is my home. I can't just leave."

"Now that you can accompany me, we may leave." Korrigan scrambled into the kitchen and began piling up protein bars. "We must take these, and the screenie system."

"Tam." Marny set a hand on his shoulder. "It's not secure here any more."

"But what if my mom…" He swallowed, hard, forcing his voice not to tremble. "What will Mom think, when she comes home?"

"You can't stay here." Zeg moved to the net system and began winding the cords. "I'll take this down. You get your stuff."

Numbly, Tam gathered a few items of clothing for both him and the Bug. His brother's favorite book. The tattered bald teddy bear that had been Mom's when she was a girl.

Marny put the belongings in the middle of one of the Bug's blankets. It made a pitifully small heap. "Anything from the bedroom?"

"Yeah," he said. "Picture album, jewelry box."

"Go get them."

In the bedroom, Tam also grabbed Mom's favorite dress, the one with the green flowers, and her last bottle of meds. Nothing else seemed worth saving.

Zeg came inside, bringing the chilly air with him. "Hurry," he said, his voice tight. "There's something going on at the end of the street."

Korrigan went to the door, dragging a plastic bag full of protein bars behind him.

"Let us away," he said.

Marny shouldered the blanket bundled with Tam's possessions. "Anything else?"

"No." Tam thought a moment. "There's a brand new Zing system downstairs."

Zeg shook his head. "Hopefully the drifters won't think of the shop—or be able to break in. We'll come get it tomorrow."

"Once we repair the window, we can bring everything back," Tam said.

Marny gave him a doubtful look, and Zeg stayed quiet.

"Come, come," Korrigan said, his voice high and impatient.

"Marny, ride with me." Zeg held open the door. "Tam, you and the changeling go with Roy."

"But—"

"Git 'im!" a rough voice cried from the street. "They're taking the loot!"

"GO!" Zeg shouted, pulling Marny with him down the stairs.

ZEG AND MARNY leaped over the broken step, with Tam and Korrigan right behind them. Half a block away, torches smeared the air with oily light as the nest of smoke drifters advanced. Skeever was in the lead, and Tam prayed he'd forgotten his gun.

"Hey!" Lassiter stuck his head out of the grav-car. "What's going on?"

He shot a glance at the torch-bearing drifters and went pale.

"Start the car!" Tam called, clearing the last step.

Marny reached Zeg's guzzler and wrenched the door open. It emitted a loud screech, and Skeever's head went up, his crazed eyes wide.

"Over there, idjits!" he yelled, shaking his torch toward the cars.

The drifters surged forward.

"Get in." Zeg gave Marny a push. "All of you, go!"

"Tam, hurry!" Lassiter yelled, sliding the passenger-side door open.

Tam dove for the grav-car, then stopped. Movement on the street behind the drifters caught his eyes. A frail, familiar form, in a yellow coat he knew too well.

"Mom," he whispered.

They had to get her out of there. The drifters hadn't noticed her yet, but they were primed for violence. When they did… Tam shuddered. He couldn't think of the consequences.

"My mom's out there," he said to Zeg. "I have to get her."

Zeg paused, one hand on his car door. "I'll help."

"No. Get Marny out of here."

Tam couldn't risk *everyone*—though he had no idea what he was going to do.

Zeg gave him a look, then glanced at Marny, waiting in his car. With a low curse, he threw himself into the driver's seat and slammed the door. The guzzler started with a coughing roar and then pulled away, leaving an acrid cloud of exhaust. The drifters started yelling. One of them flung a rock that left a dent in the shiny finish of Lassiter's car.

Pulse pounding, Tam scooped up Korrigan and tossed him into the back seat, ignoring the creature's angry squall as protein bars littered the ground.

"Gotcha!" a harsh voice cried.

Hard fingers closed over Tam's arm, and he pivoted to see the wild yellow eyes of Skeever glaring at him. Without thinking, he pulled Lassiter's taser out of his pocket and jabbed it at the drifter's arm.

Electricity arced from the end of the device, and Skeever convulsed. He doubled over with a strangled cry, letting go of Tam.

Heart racing, Tam leaped into the car. Lassiter peeled down the shadowy street, not waiting for the door to shut.

"Wait," Tam gasped, the after-image of white lines printed on his eyelids. "We have to go back."

"Hell, no. Close the door."

"Roy, my mom's back there. We can't leave her for the drifters."

"The timing sucks." He let out an angry breath. "Hold on."

Tam gripped the edge of the door as Lassiter wrenched the wheel. The grav-car spun into a U-turn, the dilapidated buildings spinning around them. Korrigan growled from the back seat.

"There." Tam gripped the open edge of the door. "In the yellow coat, behind the drifters."

Lassiter thumbed a switch on the dash, and the air was split by sirens and flashing lights. The smoke drifters milled, confused by the sudden noise. As they peeled past the mob, the reek of torches and unwashed bodies stung Tam's nose. He glimpsed wild eyes and makeshift weapons. Two of the men were carrying bottles with rags stuffed in the top. Homemade bombs. His blood chilled.

"Mom!" he yelled, leaning precariously out of the car.

"Tam?" She squinted at the lights, her voice thin and scared. "What's going on?"

He grabbed her arm and yanked her into the car. She landed awkwardly on his lap, and Tam waved the door closed. The air cracked with a gunshot, and he saw Skeever, his face lit garishly by Lassiter's lights, waving his gun.

Lassiter accelerated, the force of it pressing Tam into his seat.

A chest-vibrating *whump* exploded behind them. The sky lit with flames, the buildings around them reflecting the hungry orange light. Knowing what he'd see, Tam swiveled around in the seat, trying to shield his mom from the knowledge.

The top of the old auto shop was covered in fire, accelerant-fueled flames consuming his house. The blue tarp on the roof curled and melted, the metal scorched, and anything that could burn, did, blackening before his eyes.

Korrigan watched out the back window, his claws dug into the seat where he perched.

"Fire," he said, gleefully.

Tam turned back around, grief clogging his throat.

"What's going on?" His mom blinked at him. "Where are we?"

Her hair was tangled and greasy, and she felt way too light on his lap. Had she eaten a single meal since she'd left? At least she recognized him. She'd been coming home—and now they had no home to return to.

"We're…" He cleared his throat. "We're going to visit a friend. Don't worry, Mom."

Lassiter turned the corner, a little more gently than usual, and they headed out of the Exe. Away from the rising column of dense black smoke that marked the only home Tam had ever known.

Korrigan chomped on protein bars in the back seat, Lassiter shot glances at Tam, and his mom sat quietly, still sunk in some half-dreaming stupor.

"Lucky we got her out of there," Lassiter said.

He didn't know how unbelievably lucky it was that Tam's mom had shown up right then. What if she'd come home a day later, to an empty, burned-out shell of a house? Tam might have lost her forever.

"Mom?" he asked softly, "What made you come back tonight?"

"The little girl," his mom said. "She was so pretty. Shiny wings. Said it was time to come home. She touched me, here, and brought me back."

His mom held out her wrist. On the inside her skin bore the mark of four delicate fingers, a glowing spatter of silver light. Tam's spine tingled with the recognition of fey magic. One of the faeries had led his mother home —out of her dreams and confusion, to a street filled with violence. It was impossible to tell if the creature had wished to do harm, or had simply interfered with no ill intent.

"Korr, you know anything about this?"

The changeling peered between the front seats, his bulbous eyes lit eerily by passing streetlights.

"I know naught—but the barrier separating the Realm and your world is much weakened. Many things have slipped free to wander, this night."

"Great," Lassiter said.

"We have to get in-game and shut the fey down, for good," Tam said. "Hey!"

Korrigan's dark claws had closed on his skin, pinching hard.

"Mortal boy," the changeling hissed. "Do not rob us of sustenance. We shall waste and wither, until the Realm is no more."

Tam pulled his arm away and rubbed at the red marks left by the changeling's claws. "I'm doing what I have to."

Letting the dark faeries, or the bright ones for that matter, invade the human world was not an option.

Halfway up the wide, landscaped street winding to The View, Tam spotted Zeg's guzzler squatted at the curb.

"Pull over," he said.

Lassiter did, his lights sweeping over the battered car. Zeg and Marny got out, Marny carrying the blanket with the last of Tam's possessions bundled inside.

Lassiter slid the doors of the grav-car open. "Special View taxi at your service."

"Thanks." Zeg settled his bulk in the back seat. "I figured the gate guards wouldn't let me through this time of night."

Marny sat beside him, tucking the bundle at her feet.

"Crowded in here," she said. "And no, Korr, you can't sit on my lap."

The changeling made a face and crouched on the floor, out of sight of the gate guards.

"We'll be at Spark's in a minute," Lassiter said. "Sit tight."

"Like we have any other choice," Marny said.

Tam held his breath as the car slipped under the gleaming silver arch of The View, but nobody stopped them.

When they reached Spark's mansion, he quit looking behind them for Security, and helped his mom out of the car. His mind skittered away from the thought of his house consumed in flames. Later. He'd deal with it later.

The bodyguard who opened Spark's front door didn't even blink to see them, though Tam knew his mom looked terrible. Not to mention the squat, other-worldly figure of the changeling.

Were such odd visitors commonplace? What kind of

life did Spark lead in the outside world? Sometimes he forgot they had an international celebrity in their midst.

"Hi," Lassiter said. "We'd like to see Spark."

"I'll inform Miss Jaxley you're here," the man said, then slid a sideways glance at the changeling. "Wait in the great room."

He gestured down the hall, and Lassiter led the way, obviously comfortable with the layout of The View's enormous houses. The spacious hallway smelled of flowers, real ones, in a big white cluster on a table by the door. Tam trailed after Lassiter, supporting his mom, who was still in a daze. Did she even understand all this was real?

The great room featured a huge window looking out over the lights of Crestview below. Tam settled his mom in a nearby chair, then studied the night panorama, his eyes drawn to the dark blot of the Exe. It was too far to make out the smoldering remnants of his house.

There was no going back, as long as the drifters were nesting down the street. Not as long as Skeever led them. And who knew if there was anything left worth salvaging.

Marny and Zeg stepped into the room and stood nervously by the doorway, Korrigan between them.

"Take a seat," Lassiter said to the changeling, pointing to the big couch in the center of the room.

Clearly he wanted Korrigan positioned for maximum effect when Spark walked in. The changeling bared his sharp teeth and hopped onto the plush beige upholstery, looking as unappetizing as a spider crouched on a piece of bread.

Confident footsteps sounded in the hall, and Spark Jaxley appeared at the door. She halted and surveyed her uninvited guests, one eyebrow going up. When her gaze found Korrigan, her other eyebrow rose, twin slashes of magenta surprise.

"Well," she said. "This is interesting."

JENNET'S DAD was late getting home, and then HANA hustled them in to dinner before Jennet could broach the topic of sneaking into VirtuMax.

And how would she even begin?

The chandelier over the table shed a perfect light—no shadows for questions to hide in. No easy way to convince Dad he needed to smuggle the beta team into headquarters.

She ate her food, barely tasting the lobster bisque, the perfectly done steak and vegetables. Dad was quiet, too. After the usual questions about how school was going, followed by her usual answers, he stared into space, chewing. His face held an abstracted expression she was used to—the sign he was deeply immersed in thoughts of work.

Finally, when their chef brought out the berry crisp for dessert, she grabbed hold of her courage.

"Dad," she said. "The team is meeting tonight at Spark's. We need to go over there."

He gave her a curious look. "A party? It's a little early for celebration, don't you think? The testing isn't over yet."

"Um." She twisted her napkin between her fingers. "Actually, we were hoping you'd let us into VirtuMax. There's something important we need to do in Feyland."

"You'll be beta testing tomorrow. Whatever it is can wait."

"It can't!" She took a deep breath. "We *have* to go in-game tonight."

He pinched the bridge of his nose. "You're asking me to break into my employer's headquarters so the beta team can play illegally?"

"It's not breaking in, if you have the keys and codes. And we're supposed to play."

"Not unsupervised, after hours."

"You used to be the program manager."

"That still doesn't make it right," he said. "In fact, you could argue it's even worse. Think of how that would reflect on me, as if I'm trying to take over, or even sabotage the project."

She wished—but Dad was too honorable for that. No, the only way to deal with this was from inside the game.

Marie, the house manager, came in to collect their plates. She gave Jennet a sharp look. The woman could sense when trouble was in the air, especially if that trouble had to do with Tam.

"Will there be anything else, Mr. Carter?" she asked in her clipped accent. "Coffee?"

"No, thank you." He waved her away.

Jennet set her wrinkled napkin on the table and waited for Marie's footsteps to fade. What else could she say to convince him? She swallowed, her throat dry.

"Dad. Thomas is in there—in the Realm. You could see him, talk to him."

He shook his head at her, blue eyes faded and weary. "I don't know what you think telling me stories like that will accomplish."

"Come on." She hated the hint of whine in her voice, but couldn't erase it. "Find out if I'm telling the truth about Feyland. After everything that's happened, don't you wonder, at least a little?"

He didn't say no right away, and tentative hope flickered, an ember in her chest. She bit her lip on further pleas and promises. There was no guarantee Thomas would be in-game—except that he was bound to the Dark Court as the queen's bard.

Finally he sighed. "It's just a game, honey. I've played it too. Remember?"

She shouldn't have brought up Thomas. Dad still

hadn't fully dealt with his death. Frustration flashed through her. If only she could make him understand.

"At least go over to Spark's with me."

Somebody had to talk him into taking the next step. Roy had seen the changeling, after all, and Zeg would be there, too. Maybe faced with a united front, her dad would agree to let them into headquarters. Even if he still didn't believe her.

"Is the team there now?" he asked.

"Yes." Surely they would be. "If you just talk to Roy about Feyland—"

"Jennet." He said her name heavily, like a stone dropped into a pool, ripples spreading from the word.

She leaned forward, hands clamped tightly together below the edge of the table.

"What?"

"I'll go with you to Spark's," he said, "but this is the end. No more wild stories about the game. No more..." He swallowed. "No more talk about Thomas. Please. After this, you don't raise the subject of faeries in Feyland ever again. Agreed?"

He met her gaze, held it. Heart thumping, she stared back at him. They had to get in-game, rescue Tam's brother, and stop the fey monarchs. Or the faeries would break through into the mortal world, and Dad would find out the hard way she'd been right all along.

"Agreed," she said.

Win or lose, everything changed. Tonight.

GEORGE PULLED the grav-car up outside Spark's mansion. The second he slid the door open, Jennet jumped out. She wasn't taking the chance that Dad would change his mind and turn the car back around.

The chill night breeze at the edge of the bluff ruffled her hair. Below, the lights of Crestview twinkled as if everything was right with the world—except in the dark smudge of the Exe, where only a few sullen streetlamps glowed. The clouds over the city were lit with orange city-shine. No hint of stars, not even a moon.

Roy's sporty red car was pulled up in the driveway. Jennet stuck her hands in her pockets, clenching them as though she could squeeze away the nervousness racing through her. At least the rest of the team had arrived.

"I can't believe you kids are pulling Zeg into this mess," her dad said, getting out of the car.

"We need a healer. And he believes us."

Her dad shook his head and strode up to the mansion's front doors. They opened immediately, and one of Spark's bodyguards gestured them into the warmly lit foyer.

"The others are down the hall," the guard said, "waiting for you in the great room."

Jennet bit her lip and followed the sound of voices spilling from the room ahead.

Tam's voice cut through the babble of conversation. "Look, as soon as they get here—"

"We're here," Jennet said, stepping over the threshold.

The spacious room was fuller than she expected. Tam stood near the door. He touched her arm, his expression tense. Zeg was a couple paces away, and for some reason he had Marny with him. Roy stood by the window, arms crossed, and Spark leaned against the back of a small sofa. Jennet blinked in surprise to see Tam's mom perched on one of the chairs, looking fragile and confused.

But the biggest surprise of all sat on the plush couch in the center of the room.

"What the hell is that?" Jennet's dad asked, freezing in the doorway.

The squat creature regarded them from bulbous, milky eyes, then smiled with needle-sharp teeth. It was hideous, and unmistakably not from their world.

"That," Tam said, "is a changeling from the Unseelie Court in the Realm of Faerie."

"I..." Jennet's dad stared at the creature.

"Hard to take in, I know," Zeg said. "I've seen a lot of things in my life, but this is one of the strangest."

"Is it real?" Her dad's voice shook, the tiniest bit, but Jennet heard it.

The changeling got to his feet, clawed toes gripping the upholstery.

"Shall I conjure up my crawlies, the better to convince you?" he asked in a high, creaky voice.

"No need," Marny said. "You're proof enough, Korr. Plus, your bugs are hideous."

"Can I... touch it?" Jennet's dad asked.

He held his hand out toward the changeling. Korrigan hissed and swiped his black claws at Jennet's dad, snagging the sleeve of his jacket. The changeling pulled with uncanny strength and Jennet's dad stumbled over to face the faerie.

"Close enough, mortal?" Korrigan asked, baring his sharp teeth.

"Let him go," Marny said.

The changeling narrowed his eyes and disentangled his claws from the cloth. Jennet's dad hastily stepped back, his face pale.

"All right," he said, straightening his jacket. "I believe you."

"Finally," Tam said.

Jennet's dad frowned. He stared a moment longer at the changeling, then scrubbed one hand over his face.

"I owe you an apology," he said to Tam, then turned to Jennet. "To both of you. Honey, I... you have to understand how impossible your stories sounded. I thought you were making up wild excuses."

Jennet crossed her arms. It wasn't easy to forgive his blindness.

"This would have been a lot simpler if you'd believed me in the first place," she said.

"I know." Regret laced his voice.

"Hey," Zeg said. "We all make mistakes. The thing is to keep moving forward. Speaking of which, it's getting late and we have plans to make."

Despite the delayed anger simmering hotly in Jennet's stomach, her dad looked so lost and weary that she touched him on the shoulder. He covered her hand with his and gave her a sad smile. She couldn't quite smile back. They had a lot to talk about—later.

"Zeg's right," Spark said. "Everybody, sit down. We need to sort things out."

Roy snagged a chair and made himself comfortable. "I'm thinking we wait until after midnight to sneak into headquarters, in case anyone's working late."

"I've asked the cook to throw together some pizzas," Spark said. "No commando raids on an empty stomach."

Jennet wasn't hungry, but she knew Tam was always up for something to eat. She glanced at him, and he caught her hand and pulled her over to sit with him on the sofa. Her dad didn't say anything. How could he? The reasons he'd banned her from seeing Tam were all untrue. Judging by the shadows in his eyes, he was sorry for it.

"Ok." Tam leaned forward and rested his elbows on his knees. "You've all met Korrigan. He's the changeling that..." He threw a look at his mother, swallowed, then continued. "That was left in place of my brother."

"I don't understand," Jennet's dad said.

"Dad, the Dark Court faeries stole Tam's little brother and are keeping him hostage. Our job tonight is to rescue him."

"Let me see if I get this," Zeg said. "The game of Feyland actually leads to fairyland? Which is a real, magical place?"

"Yes," Tam said.

Zeg pursed his lips, a glint of excitement in his brown eyes. "That'll be something to see. So, we go in-game, find this Dark Court place, and rescue Tam's little brother."

"Except it won't be that easy," Roy said.

Spark nodded. "I assume we're in for an epic battle."

"Yeah," Tam said. "Thing is, there are two courts, and apparently they've joined forces."

"I take it this is a bad thing?" Zeg asked.

"Extremely." Tam sat up straighter. "Which is why we need everyone's help. Jennet and I can't defeat the king and queen, not by ourselves." Roy made a noise, and Tam shot him a look. "Not the three of us either, Roy. You don't know what the Dark Queen is like."

"Miss Jaxley," the metallic voice of the house computer announced, *"The cook would like you to know that pizza will be served in the dining room in five minutes."*

"Thanks," Spark said. She pushed away from the

couch. "Come on, everybody. Tam and Jennet can explain about these different courts, and we can plan strategy while we eat."

TAM MADE himself stop after eating six slices of pizza. The team was ready to go, everything planned. At least, as planned as they could be when dealing with the treacherous magic of the Dark Court.

Tam hugged his mom's thin shoulders. She smiled up at him, her expression still half-dreaming.

"Stay here with Marny," he said. "I'll be back in a while."

He hoped.

He didn't mention Korrigan. Small kindness that his mom didn't seem to think the changeling was her son. It was hard to tell how much she understood. She seemed to be taking everything in stride, from his missing little brother, to their house blowing up, to the appearance of weird faerie creatures.

He looked over at Marny. "Take care of her."

"No worries. But Tam, about your house... you know, the apartment behind Uncle Zeg's has been empty since Grandma Tina passed on."

"Later." He chopped his hand through the air. "When we get out of the Realm I'll deal with it."

And if they didn't get out, it definitely wouldn't matter.

"Ready?" Zeg asked in his calm, rumbling voice.

Spark opened the front door of her mansion and the beta team slipped into the chilly night. Thankfully, it wasn't spitting sleet, though frost glinted on the pavement and edged the dead grasses of the lawn.

They were walking the few blocks to VirtuMax headquarters. Jennet's dad and Zeg went first—just two friends out strolling in the winter night. The rest of them would take the long way, and meet up at the back door of VirtuMax in ten minutes.

Tam jammed his hands into the pockets of his battered brown coat, mind racing with contingency plans.

"So we'll be our avatars when we reach the Dark Court?" Spark asked.

"Yeah," Lassiter said. "If you enter the Realm using the game, that's how it works."

"And if you don't?" She gave him a curious look.

"Then you're just yourself," Jennet said.

Tam could see the memory shadowing her eyes of how the Bright King had taken her in her sleep and transported her to his court. He shivered. He'd been able to use the game interface to go rescue her. Good thing, too—it would have been nearly impossible to defeat the king wearing just the sweats and t-shirt he slept in.

"Headlights," Lassiter warned. "Looks like Security doing a sweep."

They'd discussed the possibility, and how to deal with it. Tam drew Jennet close and she snuggled in against his side, while Lassiter laid his arm over Spark's shoulders. She frowned a little, but it was all part of the plan. Nothing to worry about, just a few Viewer kids heading to Lovebird Lane, away from the all-seeing eyes of the house networks.

The blue and white grav-car slowed, a high-powered beam playing over them. Tam turned his face away. Chances were Security wouldn't recognize him, but still. Lassiter lifted his hand in a wave, and the light shut off. For once, Tam was grateful the guy was the CEO's son.

As soon as the car slid away, Spark shrugged out from under Lassiter's arm.

"Aren't we almost there?" she asked.

"Yeah," he said. "Just around the corner."

They rounded the block. Ahead, the pale, square buildings of VirtuMax headquarters rose from the flat plain of empty parking lots. Lone splotches of light illuminated the lines painted on the pavement. Lassiter led them around back, keeping to the shadows.

When they got to the overhang sheltering the back door, Tam unclenched his cold fingers. Zeg and Mr. Carter were there, waiting. Mr. Carter quickly keyed the door open.

"All in," he said. "Stay quiet and follow me."

Zeg had a small handheld light, a blue LED that washed the walls in a ghostly glow. The six of them moved through the dim corridors of VirtuMax, their shoes making hushing sounds and random squeaks on the polished floor. Tam had a sense of where they were headed, but it would have been impossible without Jennet's dad.

Of course, they weren't in the clear yet. The long, dangerous night still stretched ahead.

The corridor terminated in a thick steel door with a strip of red lights over it. A keypad blinked on the right. Mr. Carter held up his hand, and the team stopped.

"I'm not sure I have the newest codes," he whispered. "I get three tries, in three minutes, to open the door. If I fail, alarms will trigger, both here and at Security."

"Now you tell us," Lassiter said. "You know, given a day or two, I could have hacked my mom's account."

Tam jabbed him in the ribs. "We don't have two days. My brother's in serious danger."

And he didn't want Jennet's dad thinking about how easily Lassiter could get into the system.

Mr. Carter flipped open the clear cover on the keypad and entered a complicated series of numbers. Tam held his breath. The lights over the doors stayed red.

Again, Mr. Carter's fingers flew over the pad. Again, nothing happened.

"One more try," Zeg said. "Take your time."

Jennet's dad shook his head, his face grim. "I don't have the right codes. Listen, I'll stay here, say I was coming in late to get some work done. I'll stall Security as long as I can. The rest of you get back to Spark's."

"No, Dad." Jennet stepped up and laid her hand on his arm. "I know you can do it."

"We're wasting time," Lassiter said. "Try again."

"I told you, it's not going to work. They've changed the access codes."

Zeg flashed his light at the old-style watch strapped to wrist. "Better come up with something. The alarm's going off in less than two minutes."

THE BETA TEAM stared at one another, faces illuminated by the red lights over the door. Jennet curled her nails into her palms until her skin stung. They couldn't fail, not now.

"Dad…"

"I'm sorry," he said. "You all need to get out before the alarms go off."

"Wait," a high clear voice said. "Do not depart."

"Puck?" Jennet whirled, searching the shadows.

The sprite stepped forward, his clothing like frayed oak leaves, his hair tangled about his face. She heard her dad suck in his breath.

"Lift me toward the mechanism," Puck said, gesturing at the keypad.

"Can't you fly up there?" Lassiter asked.

"Too much iron bounds me on all sides. I must save my magic for what is essential."

Jennet grasped the sprite and held him up before the lock. He weighed little more than twigs and tatters. The magic of the fey folk tingled against her hands.

"Hurry," Tam breathed.

Zeg checked his watch again. "Thirty seconds."

Puck shuddered, a leaf trembling before the wind, then reached one long-fingered hand and gently touched the middle of the keypad. Blue fire ran from his fingers and curled about the keys, shimmering. Jennet held her breath. Please work.

"Fifteen seconds."

Roy jiggled from foot to foot. The fire sizzling over the lock sparked, then winked out. The lights above the door blinked from red to green, and the click of the latch releasing was loud in the tense silence.

"You did it!" Jennet wanted to hug Puck, but he felt way too fragile.

The sprite grinned at her. "Say not that you doubted me, Fair Jennet."

Jennet's dad inspected the keypad. A faint sizzle of smoke wafted from between the keys. "Did you break it?"

"It doesn't matter," Tam said. "We're in. Let's go." He pushed the door open.

"Take care, mortals. Stay brave and true," Puck said.

"Wait—don't abandon us." Jennet's fingers tightened, but it was like trying to grasp the breeze.

"I shall meet you anon, in the Realm." A heartbeat later the sprite was gone, leaving nothing but silent air between her hands.

"Puck?" she called. His name echoed in the empty corridor.

Tam grabbed her hand. "He said we'll see him in there. Come on."

The team hurried through the testing center, the darkness making the space seem cavernous. Scattered standby lights shone on the equipment—amber, blue, and red pricking the dimness like watching eyes. Jennet squeezed Tam's hand, glad she had him to hold on to.

When they got to the row of FullD systems, Jennet's dad went to the wall and slid his hand across a switch. Power hummed, and the sim chairs lit with strips of light, glowing along the sides.

"See you in there," Tam said, sliding into the closest chair and pulling on his helmet.

Jennet took the next chair, and in moments was ready to go. She hit the command to enter game, then gasped as giddy golden light swirled around her.

The beta version of Feyland was done behaving.

Stomach twisting, she landed in a grassy circle bounded by a faerie ring. Half the mushrooms surrounding her were moon-pale, the other half red, dotted with white. The two sides of the Realm, united.

Tam stood beside her. His silver armor shone strangely, one side lit as if by bright day, the other dusted with midnight shadows. She glanced up to see that the sky above them shared that same disturbing split.

Spark and Roy tumbled into the ring, followed by her dad and Zeg. Roy got to his feet and gave Spark a hand up, while Jennet went over to steady her dad.

"What was that?" he asked, one hand on his stomach.

"The transition into Feyland," she said.

"The Realm of Faerie, that is," Tam said. "Congratulations—you've just journeyed between the worlds."

Spark glanced at the white-barked trees enclosing the clearing, their sides lit in turn with fire, with frost. "Is it always like this?"

"No," Roy said, and Jennet's dad gave him a curious look.

"This is because the two courts have joined forces," Tam said.

Magic hung in the air, almost as tangibly as in the Twilight Kingdom. The curling wind bore the distant baying of spectral hounds, mixed with the faint chiming of pixies.

Jennet lifted her mage staff, the blue crystal at the end shedding a faint light oddly similar to Zeg's LED. She shook her head at the thought.

"Which way?" Zeg asked, pushing back the hood of his grey priest's robe.

"Here." Tam leapt from the circle and strode to the moss-lined path leading from the clearing. "Careful of the mushrooms, we might need this circle in order to come back."

If they came back.

Jennet hurried down the path after Tam. She knew he was burning with impatience to get to his brother, but the team needed to stay together.

At the edge of the grove she caught up with him, and fear fastened in her throat.

They stood at the top of a hill, the Realm spread out before them. Stars shot, flaming, through a midnight sky. Shadows pushed at the noontime sun. Flowers bloomed at their feet, then withered to dust. The land trembled as though it were dying. Or being reborn.

At the bottom of the hill—leagues away and only a few paces—two pale roads met in an uneven X. A lamp hung from a post at the center, flaring, waning, flaring again. On the far side of the crossroads rose a circle of seven standing stones. The tall menhirs glowed faintly, rough granite suffused with starshine.

Horrible familiarity weakened her knees. Jennet clutched her mage staff for balance.

"Miles Cross," she whispered.

It was here the Dark Court had brought Tam as a sacrifice to open a gateway to the human world. Here that she had battled for his life against the Dark Queen, and emerged scarred. Her hands ached with the memory of searing fire.

Tam turned to her, his green eyes widening. "This is Miles Cross?"

She nodded. Of course he didn't recognize the place —it had been night when he was here before, plus he'd been under a fey enchantment.

The rest of the team came up behind them.

"Whoa," Roy said. "I've never seen the Realm look so freaky."

"Hold hands," Jennet said. "The way things are fluctuating out there, I think we need to be in physical contact to stay together."

She vanished her mage staff with a thought, then grabbed Tam's hand and reached back for her dad's. She could just imagine half the team disappearing between one step and the next.

"I'll be on the end," Tam said.

Of course—he wanted one hand free for his sword.

"I'll take the other side," Zeg said.

The beta team stood in a ragged line above the coruscating landscape of the Realm of Faerie.

"On three, we run to the crossroads," Tam said. "Don't let go, no matter what."

Don't let go. Jennet's palms burned with memory.

Tam counted, and the team took off. The first few steps weren't bad, then the grass under their feet bucked like a startled horse. Thick vines snaked out of the ground, tangling their ankles. Zeg and Roy stumbled, and Jennet went down. Tam and her dad hauled her up.

"Keep going," Tam said.

"Ow!" Spark cried. "Get them away from me."

Jennet looked over to see a half-dozen golden bees buzzing about Spark's head.

"Don't panic," Zeg said, and looped the line, waving his free hand around Spark's bright pink head. It didn't seem to help.

"Sizzle them," Jennet said.

Spark narrowed her eyes. "Get back, Zeg."

Flame scorched the air in front of Spark, and dead bees fell, cinder-crisp, to the ground. Jennet looked back to the white-barked grove crowning the hill. The team had come halfway down. Ahead of them, the crossroads shimmered.

"Move," Tam said.

Jennet's next step plunged her ankle-deep into a bog. Black muck clung to her foot as she pulled it loose with a sucking sound.

"Nice," Roy said.

Beside Jennet, her dad foundered to his knees. She tugged at his hand, but he was stuck fast.

"Go on without me," he said. "I'm not the best fighter, I know that."

Tam circled around Jennet, still holding her hand, and grasped her dad's arm. "We need you. And nobody is getting left behind."

On Jennet's other side, Spark raised her arm high. Jennet did the same. With Tam's extra boost, Jennet's dad pulled free of the dark bog with a hungry squelch. The smell of rotting vegetables filled the air, and she wrinkled her nose against the stench.

"Almost there," she gasped.

The beta team started forward again. The ground solidified under their feet, the bog and slick grasses disappearing until they ran over a surface smooth as glass. Miles Cross lay a few yards ahead, the lantern at the crossroads shining gold, then black, then gold again.

A fracture formed in the ground between them and the road, hairline at first, but quickly widening.

"Faster!" Tam yelled.

His end of the line reached the crack, now a good three feet across. He and Jennet jumped, her dad and Spark at their heels. Roy landed on his knees at the edge of the now-deep fissure. Zeg leaped, but his foot just missed solid ground. Jennet watched, horrified, as his body tumbled back into the crevasse.

"Zeg!" Jennet tried to yank her hand from Tam's, straining to get back to where Zeg dangled, his grasp on Roy's hand slowly slipping.

"*Pull.*" Tam's voice was sharp with fear.

"Quick," Roy said, his face white. "I can't hold him much longer."

Tam strained forward, Jennet right behind him. Her dad was a little slower, but Spark pushed against him with her shoulder. Roy cried out as the line stretched, with him as the breaking point.

"Again," Tam said, and lunged.

Jennet's arms burned, like they were going to come out of their sockets. How much worse did Roy feel?

With a sudden whoosh the pressure eased and the line staggered forward. Fear clenched her throat. Had they lost Zeg? She couldn't bear to look.

Roy let out a shout of relief, and she glanced over her shoulder. Zeg stood at the end of the line, massaging his wrist with his free hand.

"Don't stop now," Spark said.

She dragged the middle of the line forward, the rest of the team straggling behind her. Three more steps and they stood on the pale roadway of Miles Cross. Above, the sky continued strobing. The circle of standing stones shone white, then black, their shadows reaching hungrily across the road.

The team had made it—just in time.

The road vibrated with the sounds of distant passage, faint now, but moving closer. The cold, bright wind brought the drift of chiming bells, the guttural cries of goblins overlaid with a banshee's screech, a scattering of harp notes like golden coins spilled into the air.

The faeries were coming.

29

Tᴀᴍ ʟᴇᴛ ɢᴏ of Jennet's hand and flexed his fingers. His muscles coiled with tension. That had been too close—losing Zeg was unthinkable.

He shot a glance at his friend, who projected his usual calm solidity despite nearly falling to his death. Good thing Lassiter had held on, though it must have hurt like hell. Tam caught the other boy's eye and nodded his thanks.

"Do you hear that?" Spark asked. Her pointed fox ears twitched.

"What?" Jennet asked.

"Sounds like a kid singing."

Tam strained his ears, trying to pick out what Spark was hearing from the mixed sounds carried on the wind.

"So?" Lassiter rubbed at his left shoulder. "The faeries sound like all kinds of things."

"A kid singing *Crush It*? I don't think so. Unless the faeries listen to top 10 radio in here."

"My little brother," Tam said, hope and worry tearing into him. "He loves that song."

That had to mean the Bug was all right. Didn't it?

On their left, the ring of standing stones began to glow. Tam dimly remembered those eerie granite monoliths rising above him. In the center lay a rectangular slab and he shivered at the dark stains marring the sides.

"Here they come," Zeg said, his gaze focused down the road.

Tam and Lassiter moved to the front of the party. Jennet's dad stepped forward, but she pulled on his arm and drew him back to marginal safety.

"Let the heavy-armor fighters protect us," she said quietly.

Tam hoped like hell they'd be able to.

The dark shadow of the massed faeries resolved into individual shapes. In the front, a dozen figures in bright armor marched, lances prickling up, helms covering their faces. Behind them, redcap goblins cavorted, their teeth glinting and sharp.

Other creatures, half-animal in form, trailed them, shambling and mincing, growling and squealing. A delicate bevy of maidens followed, their hair like spun moonlight, silver bells edging their gossamer robes.

And behind them, the two fey monarchs rode side by side. The Bright King was mounted on a golden charger, his armor shining brilliant gold. The Dark Queen rode a chestnut horse, her dark skirts spread out like the midnight sky, her face beautiful as an eclipse. At her shoulder rode the Black Knight, on a horse as pitch black as his armor.

Tam drew his sword and settled his shield on his left arm. At his side, Lassiter gripped the pommel of his two-handed sword and raised it at the ready.

"Halt." The Dark Queen's voice was hard as ice. "What is this we see before us?"

The ranks of the fey folk parted to let the queen and king ride through. They halted behind the rank of spear-bearers and regarded the six humans blocking the road before them.

The queen tipped back her head and laughed, a sound that could crack bone. The Bright King leaned forward, his gaze going to Jennet, and Tam tightened his grip on his sword.

"Fair Jennet," the king said. "Do you truly think to oppose us? There is a better way."

Jennet shook her head, a strand of pale hair brushing her cheek. "I don't think so."

"It is not too late," the king said. "You may still join us. All of you."

"I claim Bold Tamlin for my court," the queen said.

"No," Tam said. "We're here for my brother."

"You must find him, first," the queen said.

"Fine." Tam took a step toward the faeries, scanning the throng for a glimpse of the Bug.

The queen threw her hand up, and his limbs locked, one foot lifted in mid-step.

"Hey!" Lassiter hefted his sword. "Let him go."

"You may seek," the king said, "but we do not give you leave to move from this place."

Crap. How were they going to find his brother? Panic bubbled high in Tam's throat, and he forced it back down.

"Bug?" he called. "Can you hear me?"

The queen smiled darkly. "He is forbidden to speak."

Damn the faeries and their impossible quests. But there was always a solution, if only he could puzzle it out.

"Tam," Jennet said softly behind him. "He can't speak... but maybe he can sing."

Hope pricked him, sharp and bright. Hadn't Spark thought she heard the Bug earlier?

Tam wasn't much in the singing department, but he had to try. He drew in a ragged breath and started, his voice unsteady.

"Down, down, tonight it's all the way."

Jennet joined him partway through, her clear voice bolstering his. Then Spark took up the song in a husky alto.

"We gonna rock it til the break of day.

No need to rush, rush it."

That must be Lassiter. He couldn't carry a tune, but at least he was trying.

"Oh baby, then we crush it," sang a high, fearless voice from within the bunch of gossamer-clad maidens.

They melted away like frost in sunlight, revealing Tam's little brother.

Tam's heart clenched, hard. His foot fell to the ground, and he staggered as his body unfroze.

"Bug?" he said. "You ok?"

"Hi, Tam." His brother smiled at him. "I'm ready to go home now."

"That's the plan."

The Dark Queen shook her head. "Alas. We have other plans for you, mortals."

She brought her hand down in a sharp gesture. Quick as thought, the Black Knight slid from his horse and strode through the ranks of bright-armored lance carriers. They followed him, a dozen spears tipped in deadly formation.

"Attack!" the king cried.

The fey folk let out a cacophony of cheers. The Black Knight raised his sword and veered toward Lassiter.

"Take cover," Tam yelled to his brother, then lifted his shield as the lancers charged.

Wickedly barbed points clanged against the metal. One slipped past the edge of his shield, and Tam batted it away with his sword. A bolt of blue magefire streaked by and hit the nearest lancer square in the chest. The figure stumbled back, but they were still way outnumbered.

Lassiter's sword rang against the Black Knight's armor. Without a shield he was at a disadvantage, but so far he seemed to be holding his own.

The lancers charged at Tam again, and this time one of the spears pierced his forearm. Damn, that hurt. He glanced down to see a thin trickle of blood marring his silver armor.

"Heal!" he called.

A green glow settled over his arm, dulling the pain. Just in time, as the lancers surged forward. Jennet sent more mage bolts, but the magic didn't harm the fey folk, only pushed them back. Spark's arrows did better. One of the bright-armored figures lay motionless on the ground, a feathered shaft sticking from his helm.

Two of the lancers charged past. He couldn't let them reach Jennet and Spark. Tam backed up, keeping the rest of the attackers at bay with long, sweeping arcs of his sword.

From the corner of his eye, he saw Lassiter spin around from the force of the Black Knight's blows, and he winced in sympathy.

"Heal!" Lassiter called out.

Zeg's spells kept them in the fight, but they were

struggling already. Not a good sign, when the king and queen hadn't even joined the battle yet.

A flutter of orange robes signaled Jennet's dad springing into motion. He leaped at the closer of the approaching lancers and managed a solid strike to the head. One of Spark's arrows finished the enemy off, but the second lancer reached them. The lancer jabbed his spear into Spark's shoulder and she cried out, her hand going to the wound. When she pulled her fingers away, they were red with blood.

Jennet blasted the enemy, a second too late.

"Hang on," Zeg said, hands weaving in the air.

He sent a healing spell toward Spark, but Tam didn't have time to watch it take effect. The remaining lancers were attacking him hard, jabbing at his legs, his helm, any place they could reach. One thrust his spear between Tam's feet, and he stumbled.

"Hi-yah!" Jennet's dad yelled. This time his attack was parried, the sharp point of a spear gouging his arm.

The clash of sword on armor grew insistent. Tam glanced at Lassiter, to see the Black Knight land a fearsome blow to his side. Lassiter's eyes grew wide, and his sword point wavered, dipped.

"Roy!" Tam cried, struggling to fight to his friend's side.

Pain pierced through him as the lancers stabbed his arms and legs. Zeg's heals couldn't keep up with the amount of damage he was sustaining.

"Advance!" the Dark Queen cried, her voice cracking through the air like lightning.

A tide of redcap goblins swept toward them brandishing knives, their wicked teeth bared. The first wave ran into a sheet of flame, which only enraged the creatures. Shrieking, they clambered over the bodies of fallen lancers.

Tam had nearly reached Roy. In slow motion he saw the Black Knight lift his blade high overhead. Roy brought his two-handed sword up to block the blow. Faster than the eye could follow, the knight reversed his movement. His blade slid between Roy's ribs, and Roy fell to his knees. His sword tumbled to the ground, streaked with black blood.

"Tam," Roy gasped, his brown eyes meeting Tam's horrified gaze. "Sorry."

Slowly, he crumpled, eyes closing.

"No!" Tam leveled his blade at the Black Knight and threw the force of his anguish behind the blow. Silver pierced black armor, and the knight let out a bellow that shook the sky.

"Dad!" Jennet screamed, high and panicked.

Tam pulled his sword free and whirled to see Mr. Carter go down under a half-dozen goblins. There was no sign of Spark. Zeg cast heals desperately, but the goblins had reached him and were pulling viciously at his robes. He staggered, then fell.

Rage and despair rose through Tam like a bleak tide.

He turned and locked eyes with the Dark Queen. She smiled, a merciless blade honed to the cutting edge.

"Take them," she said.

A lancer brought his weapon down hard on Tam's head, and the world went dark.

30

Bitter cold and blackness. Then a whisper in her ear.

"Fair Jennet."

It hurt to breathe. She had to remember… had to…

"Lady, awake." A flutter of sound, moth-quiet. "Stir not."

Her eyes fluttered open, and she wished they hadn't. She lay in the circle of standing stones, propped up against one of them. Her hands were tied behind her. A golden cord wrapped around her aching chest secured her to the menhir.

In the center of the circle, Tam's little brother lay bound on the slab of stone. The Dark Queen stood at his head, the Bright King at his feet. Red and blue flames flickered along the edges of the stone.

"Brother," the queen said. "Our victory is complete."

The king nodded. "Once we open the gateway to the mortal world, the bargain between us is ended."

Jennet swallowed, her throat dry and tight. She had to get loose! Where was the rest of the team? Slowly, she slid her gaze to the right. Tam was tied to the stone next to her, and he was awake. Relief shivered down her spine. He met her gaze, and his lips formed a *sh*. She blinked once—to show she understood the need for silence. They couldn't act, not yet—though she didn't know how he could bear it when his little brother lay on the verge of being sacrificed by the faeries.

She looked carefully to her left. Fear clenched her stomach when she made out a huddle of orange robes and pale skin tied to the stone. Her dad. He'd gone down under an attack of redcap goblins.

"Puck?" she whispered, for it had been the sprite who had woken her.

"Aye, lady." His voice was a bare thread of sound in the shadows behind her.

"Is my dad okay?"

"He still breathes."

That didn't sound good. She swallowed back hot tears. They had to *do* something.

"Can you untie me?"

"I cannot work directly against the courts," the sprite said.

"Then why bother to wake me at all?" Desperation clawed through her.

"I cannot free you," Puck said, "but the fox spirit can. Be still."

Fox spirit? A moment later, Jennet felt a cold nose snuffle her palm. A quick snick of sharp teeth, and the bonds at her wrists fell away. Another snap, and the golden cord holding her to the stone parted, draping across her lap.

Jennet sent a wary look to the center of the ring, where the two monarchs were absorbed in elaborate preparation.

"Can you free Tam?" she whispered.

"Aye." Motion rustled behind her, then was gone.

Was the whole team here, tied to the tall stones? Moving her head slowly, she scanned the circle. Beyond her dad's slumped figure—oh, how she wanted to dash to his side—Zeg was bound to the next stone. His eyes met hers, and she swallowed a prayer of thanks. The next two menhirs were empty. Then her gaze snagged on Roy's body, and fear rose up to choke her.

She had thought her dad looked bad, but Roy... he seemed barely alive. His armor was rent open, a trickle of blood seeping over the once-shining bronze breastplate. His face was the color of ashes. Of death.

In the middle of the circle, the king and queen held their hands up. Light shimmered between their outstretched palms: red fire, purple flames, black radiance.

Jennet looked away, and a flash of russet fur caught

her eye. The fox, with Puck astride, darted from Tam's stone over to Roy's still form.

But where was Spark? Had she died, her broken body left at the crossroads? No, it couldn't be. Jennet forced herself to breathe. Her lungs burned, heat searing across her breast.

Wait. Not her lungs. She glanced down to see a milky disc of stone suspended from a silver chain, glowing fiercely on her chest. The Talisman of Shejin!

She looked over at Tam, where the teardrop of his own talisman shone brightly against his silver armor. The rewards from Princess Paloma's quest. She hadn't thought much of them at the time, but now... she squeezed her eyes shut, trying to recall the princess's words in the Stronghold Castle gardens.

Lends the wearer three times their magical strength, and heals them of mortal wounds.

Her eyes flew open and she locked gazes with Tam. Neither of them bore mortal wounds—but Roy did, and Dad too. To hell with the faeries. She couldn't wait another moment.

Jennet scrambled to her feet and lunged to where her dad lay slumped against the stone. She tore the talisman from her neck and slipped the silver chain over his head.

"Stop her!" the Dark Queen cried.

"Come on, Dad," Jennet breathed.

She tucked the glowing disc of white stone under his robes. A moment later, clawed hands dug into her arms as two redcap goblins grabbed her. She glanced over at Tam, who'd taken advantage of the distraction to slip over to Roy. The light of his teardrop talisman dimmed as he dropped it beneath Roy's sundered breastplate.

This had to work.

"Look to the knight as well," the Bright King called, his voice deep and resonant.

Two twiggy guards leaped from the shadows. Tam tried to draw his sword, but they caught his arms, pinioning them to his sides.

"Bring them." The queen gestured to the flat stone. "Three sacrifices will hold thrice the power. Our gate will never be closed."

Jennet struggled, but the goblins hauled her forward and forced her to her knees beside the stone. Across from her, Tam was pushed to the ground as well. His face was lit by red and blue fire, his mouth set in a determined line she knew too well.

"Tam?" His little brother's voice was scared, his eyes huge in his dirt-streaked face.

"I'm here, Bug. Hang in there."

"We must end this," the king said.

He strode to where Jennet knelt and placed a hand on her hair. His touch burned like liquid fire, and she heard the high, sweet chiming of pixies.

"Aye." The queen moved to Tam's side and tangled her pale hand in his brown hair.

He shivered and closed his eyes at her touch.

"Cheehooo!" The cry rang through the dark bright air.

Jennet looked up to see Zeg standing at the head of the flat stone, his teeth bared in a ferocious grimace, his hair standing wild around his head. He slapped his own chest three times, then bent, tore through the cords binding the Bug, and lifted Tam's brother from the stone.

"Stop!" The queen flung out her hand, a midnight sphere flying from her palm.

Zeg ducked and backed away, but a menacing growl made him halt. Behind him the horned master of the Wild Hunt stood, silhouetted against the stones. Red-eyed hounds milled just outside the circle, sharp teeth gleaming.

"Crap," Tam muttered.

"Return the boy," the king said.

In the heartbeat of hesitation before Zeg moved, a blur of red leaped from the darkness. The fox! It fastened its teeth on the goblin holding Jennet's right arm. Tam leaped to his feet and kicked the other goblin, and she was free.

She stood and held her hands up to the fierce sky. They had one more weapon at their command. She didn't know why she hadn't come into Feyland with the blade, but she had to summon it now.

Going on sheer instinct, she concentrated with every cell in her body, opened her mouth, and sang a high, clear note. The breath spun from her, moonlit and full, holding the note, expanding it. The stones around them began to hum, strands of light waking within the dark rock. Something settled in her outstretched palms—something long and silver and ancient.

The Blade of the Elder Fey.

"No," the queen whispered. For the first time, Jennet saw fear cross her perfect, deadly features. "Do not—"

"Too late." Jennet pulled the blade free.

It was thin, elegant, and utterly lethal. The moment it cleared the scabbard it began to vibrate, quivering like a wild thing yearning to be unleashed. Jennet wrapped both hands around the pommel, feeling the blade shivering against her bones.

"Fair Jennet, foolish mortal." The king's voice was laden with sorrow. "You have spelled our doom."

"Not yet," the queen snapped. "Are you a lapdog, that you lie down at the merest hint of *their* power?" She whirled to the huntsman. "Bring the boy. Now!"

Her voice burned the air with bitter frost. The horned figure strode forward, a head taller than Zeg. He set black-clawed hands on Zeg's shoulders and pushed him, still holding Tam's brother, to the center stone.

"Brother, is your weapon at the ready?" the queen hissed.

The king nodded.

Jennet glanced wildly between them, the blade in her

hands throbbing with power. She must strike, and now —but which one?

"Jennet," Tam said, his voice tight. "Take *her*."

"Oh no, earthly knight."

The queen had returned to Tam's side. She grabbed his hair and pulled his head back, exposing his throat. In her other hand she held a wickedly sharp black dagger, curved like a thorn. Or maybe it *was* a thorn, from the darkest tree that ever grew.

"Fair Jennet," the queen said, "harm me, and your champion dies."

The king moved toward Jennet and she took a step back, raising the blade. It hummed eagerly in her hands.

"I don't think so," she said.

"Then I shall take the boy."

Quick as light, he snatched Tam's little brother from Zeg's arms. In his hand he held a long golden dagger, sharp as a needle.

"Bug!" Tam cried, anguished.

Jennet's breath caught, jagged in her throat. Blood must be spilled to call the Elder Fey, she knew it with a certainty. But she could not attack either monarch without dire consequences.

She had only a heartbeat to act. Biting down hard on her lip, she took the sword and poised it over one arm. The blade trembled impatiently.

"Jennet, no!" Tam lunged for her, ripping free of the

queen's grasp. Her thorn grazed his neck, leaving a thin red line.

The razor-sharp edge of the Blade of the Elder Fey touched Jennet's skin, cutting softly, tenderly, to the bone.

A second later pain shocked her senses, so fierce she fell to her knees. Her arm bled like a fountain. Tam snatched the blade from her hand, and she turned her face up to the sky—now twilight, now blazing through her tears—and screamed.

31

Tᴀᴍ ᴡʜɪʀʟᴇᴅ, the Blade of the Elder Fey shaking in his grip.

"Save her!" he cried.

He didn't care who, only that someone had to.

Zeg had his hands up, weaving a glowing healing spell. The queen folded her arms, her gaze glittering like ice. The king held tightly to the Bug's shoulder, and his brother whimpered in pain.

"Let him go," Tam said.

"Our plans are in ruin," the queen said. "Take revenge, brother, ere *they* arrive."

The king raised his golden dagger. Tam leveled his blade at the king's throat.

"Don't," he said.

Golden eyes, deep with centuries, regarded him.

Unwavering, Tam held his gaze. *Harm my brother, and I'll kill you.*

As if reading the thought, the king lifted his hand, and Tam's brother ran to his side.

"Tam, Tam," he said, scrubbing tears from his cheeks with a grubby hand. "I knew you'd come."

"I'm here."

Still pointing the blade at the king, Tam gathered his brother into a tight hug. He didn't ever want to let go.

"Jennet?" he said.

He couldn't bear to look, to see her lying on the grass, her heart's blood spilled, her blue eyes staring sightless at the sky.

Zeg, face lit with green light, cast another spell. The stones surrounding them crackled and hummed, as if filled with electricity. A cold hot wind blew across the trampled grass.

The standing stones erupted in purple fire.

"They come," the king said. His voice was weary. "Sister, we shall pay a heavy price for our bargain."

"And what of our Realm?" She advanced upon him, dark hair whipping about her face. "Would you let us die, deprived of that which sustains us? I would live, brother!"

The air around them dimmed, growing harsh in Tam's lungs. A deep drum throbbed through the air. No, not a drum. Wingbeats. He tipped his face up to see an enormous black shape descending from the sky.

"A dragon," the Bug whispered.

It was a fearsome, incredible sight. Behind the black dragon came brighter motes of color—sapphire, ruby, amethyst, so bright Tam had to squint.

The king and queen stood their ground as the Elder Fey approached, but the other fey folk averted their gaze and huddled into whatever small shelter they could find. Still holding tight to his brother, Tam stepped back to where Jennet lay. Her blue dress was crumpled like a torn piece of sky. The deep slash in her arm still bled sluggishly, leaving an ugly smear on the green grass. She looked at him, her face pale as starlight, and tried to smile.

"I love you, Tam," she said.

"Shh. Save your strength."

Tears clogged his throat. He set his hand to her cheek, willing his life, his soul into her.

It should have been him. She should have turned the blade on him, not herself. Anyone but herself. Regret burned him to the heart.

"Jen." Her dad stumbled to her side.

"Quick," Tam said. "The talisman—take it off and put it on Jennet."

"I don't think..." Mr. Carter felt about his neck and chest, but there was no silver chain, no glowing talisman at the ready to save Jennet's life. It had been used up.

Tam blinked furiously, trying to keep his vision clear.

Hands trembling, Jennet's dad tore a strip off his

orange robes and bound the wound, then tied a tourniquet further up her arm. She winced, but didn't say anything.

Above them, the sky was dark, bright, black and bejeweled. The dragon's wings pummeled the air around them.

Roy staggered over, his eyes deep hollows of anxiety. Zeg came and knelt at Jennet's head.

"I stopped the worst of the bleeding," he said. "I'll keep trying."

Tam nodded, trying not to watch the orange fabric around her arm darkening with blood.

Above them, the black dragon circled ever closer, its immense bulk bathed in eerie purple light. The Dark Queen and Bright King stood their ground, wreathed in the light of icy-blue frost, of golden fire.

Tam looked at the weary team, another dart of loss spearing through him as he counted them up.

"Where's Spark?" he asked, afraid of the answer.

Puck joined them, his expression sober. He was riding the fox.

"She is here," the sprite said.

"Where?" Tam glanced around them. No sign of the gamer girl. "We don't have time for your jokes, Puck."

"Wait," Roy said. "She's the fox, right?"

Of course. Kitsune.

"Stuck..." Jennet's voice was a mere whisper.

"You're saying she's trapped as a fox?"

Jennet blinked in affirmation.

Tam finally let go of his brother. He set the Blade of the Elder Fey on the bloody grass and took the fox's head between his hands. There was no sign of humanity in those wild amber eyes.

"Spark," he said. "Spark, you in there?"

The fox wrenched her head away with a low growl.

"Let me," Roy said.

He scooped the animal up and Puck leaped off with a yelp. Roy cradled the fox in his arms.

"Hey, babe," he said. "You know I always wanted to hold you like this. How about a kiss?"

He brought his face close to the fox's and Tam sucked in a breath. Roy was going to lose his nose. The fox bared her teeth, but Roy didn't let go.

"Just one kiss, all right?"

A flash of light, and it was Spark in his arms.

"No way," she said. "I oughta slap you." She made no move to leave his embrace, though.

"Good to have you back," Roy said.

She glanced up. "Just in time for the big show."

The black dragon had come to hover above the circle of standing stones. It fixed its golden gaze on the king and queen.

Monarchs of the fey. You have upset the balance.

As before, the dragon's voice was everywhere and nowhere. It scraped the back of Tam's ears, echoed in his head.

"We had no choice!" The queen stared up, defiant. "Our Realm was shut off from the mortal world. We were dying, *dying*, while you slept, uncaring."

You have no right to meddle between the worlds.

The sapphire dragon came to hover beside the black, tipping its head as if in speech. Tam felt a buzzing in the back of his skull. Slowly, the black dragon blinked. Its long tongue flicked out, forked like a snake's, and touched the tip of one of the standing stones.

Purple light hissed and flared.

"You cannot consign our Realm to oblivion," the king said.

For your actions, we should. Yet there is truth in what you say. Your Realm is indeed weakened.

"Then let us re-open a gate to the mortal world." The Dark Queen's dress swirled about her like smoke. She pointed to where Tam and the rest of the team huddled. "Look—the sacrifice still awaits."

The black dragon turned its eerie, alien gaze upon the humans, and Tam held his breath.

Enough blood has been shed.

Tam got to his feet, struggling against the gritty air, and looked up at the dragon.

"Jennet is badly wounded," he said, his voice catching. "Please heal her. I beg you."

The leader of the Elder Fey regarded him, unblinking. Galaxies swirled in the depths of its eyes. At last it spoke.

Take the Blade and lay it upon her wound.

Tam lifted the thin silver blade. It woke in his hand, humming high and clear. Kneeling, he carefully tilted the flat of the blade toward Jennet's arm. Her dad stripped the bloodied orange cloth away. Deep red gaped, and at the bottom Tam glimpsed the white of bone. He forced his hands steady and pressed the blade against that terrible gash.

"It's working," Roy said.

Beneath the blade, Jennet's muscles were knitting together. Her skin closed, leaving a silver scar bisecting her forearm, and he pulled the blade away.

Sheathe it, ere it hungers for blood again.

Already, Tam felt the blade stirring. He glanced around for the silver scabbard. It lay where Jennet had discarded it, beside the flat stone in the center of the ring. Right between the king and queen.

Quickly

"Do it," Jennet said, her voice weak. A hint of color was returning to her face. "That thing is deadly."

"We got your back," Roy said, rising and giving Spark a hand up.

Tam walked toward the slab of stone, air scraping his lungs. The Dark Queen watched him approach, her eyes pools of midnight.

"Tamlin," she said, her voice full of mystery and promises. "There is still time. Become my Knight. It is not the first time a mortal has chosen to serve me."

She beckoned, and Thomas stepped from the shadows, his guitar slung across his back.

Tam heard Jennet's dad gasp.

"Bard Thomas, tell our bold knight what he will gain when he joins the Dark Court."

"My lady." Thomas sketched her a bow, then turned to Tam. "You will never return to the mortal world again —but the mysteries of the Realm will lie at your feet."

"No," Tam said.

It wasn't a choice he was even interested in. He darted forward, snatched the scabbard, and in one smooth move slid the Blade of the Elder Fey home.

The queen set her hand to his cheek. The tips of her nails pricked his skin. "I will haunt your dreams forever, Bold Tamlin."

He met her perilous, lovely gaze, and the words dried in his mouth.

Then he felt a touch on his shoulder. He turned to see Jennet, her pale hair tangled, a smear of blood on her chin. She had never looked more beautiful.

"You may haunt his dreams," she said, "but I'll be the one living in them."

The queen's eyes narrowed, and she lifted her black thorn.

"Enough." The king set a restraining hand on his sister's arm. "We must each bear a loss this day."

He looked at Jennet, the echo of the queen's want clear in his fathomless gaze.

Tam stepped back, bringing Jennet with him. He lifted the sheathed blade.

"I could draw this again," he said, meaning it. "I bet it would like the taste of faerie blood."

Cease.

Quick as a bolt of azure lightning, the sapphire dragon plunged down and seized the scabbard from Tam's hand.

The Blade is no longer needed. Balance is restored.

"Actually," Roy said, blinking up at the huge black shape, "I think the mortal world still has a problem."

"It's true, sir." Jennet's dad cleared his throat and bowed to the dragon. "The faeries have found a way to infiltrate the human world, using a game interface I helped develop. If the human world is to remain safe, that connection needs to be severed."

He shot a look at Thomas, questions burning in his eyes. The Bard shook his head imperceptibly. The time for answers would come—but not now.

"We *must* have access to the mortal plane," the Dark Queen said, her voice sharp. "Else, I implore you to rip a hole in the fabric of our Realm. I prefer a quick death over a slow decay."

Indeed?

The black dragon closed its eyes. A plume of purplish smoke wafted from its nostrils. When it opened its eyes again and gazed down upon the humans, a shiver scraped Tam's neck. The dragon's gaze pinned them like the light of an impossible, foreign sun.

There have oft been those among mortals who have visited the Realm and safely returned. Keepers of knowledge. Bards and mystics who guard the border between your world and the Realm. It is time to anoint a new guard.

The queen shook her head, her hair like midnight silk. "You cannot—"

Dark Lady, if you wish your Realm to survive, you will bide. No gate will be opened to the mortal world. Yet it is understood you must have sustenance. This crossing point the mortals have spoken of shall remain open, for a select few. Agree to it, or see your world wither.

The Bright King nodded his regal head. "You have my agreement."

Displeasure rolled off the queen in icy waves. The king gripped her arm, and at last she spoke, the words falling from her mouth like bitter stones.

"Very well. It will be as you say."

The leader of the Elder Fey nodded its massive head, and Tam felt a ripple of deep magic run through the Realm.

Mortals. The black dragon's attention returned to them, burning the air. *You are the new Feyguard. Do you agree to protect the boundary between your world and this one, and aid those who stray too far into the Realm?*

"How?" Spark whispered.

"Through the game," Jennet said. "I think."

"What is it saying?" Roy asked. "The Elder Fey want to turn us into some kind of otherworldly border patrol?"

Bard Thomas nodded. "It makes an elegant resolution. The fey folk may interact with the human world, but not unchecked. I believe mortals need magic, as much as the fey folk need mortals." His wise, weary gaze swept over the beta team. "You are privileged with knowledge given to very few. I can think of no better guardians for the human world."

Tam didn't like the solution, but what Thomas said made sense. And he'd realized a while back there was no stopping VirtuMax from releasing Feyland. If the game wasn't totally safe for people to play, at least it wouldn't be an open invitation to the fey folk to run wild in the human world.

He hated to admit it, but deep down he didn't want the Realm of Faerie to wither away. No matter what damage the Dark Queen had done to his life. He flicked his gaze to her impossible beauty, then away before he could get snared in the midnight tangle of her hair.

"Tam?" Jennet said. "What do you think?"

He gathered his attention back to his bedraggled

companions. They were looking at him as if he had all the answers. Funny thing was, he almost did.

He addressed the lightless form of the black dragon. "How do we make sure the faeries don't grab every mortal who plays the game, use their strength, and then we all end up back here with this same scenario?"

Most mortals will be unaware of the Realm's existence.

"How do you know?"

Do you question the wisdom of the Elder Fey? The leader let out a sudden, searing breath.

Tam staggered back but didn't take his gaze from the dragon's hovering form. "It's my world we're talking about. We need some guarantees here."

Few are those susceptible to fey magic. Your world will be safe.

"But—"

"Cease," Thomas said, stepping forward. "The Elder Fey cannot lie. Nor do they twist the truth, as the fey folk do. Believe them when they say the human world will be safe."

"Just not those unlucky souls who get sucked into the Realm."

Jennet touched his elbow. "Remember those old tales. Not everyone who stumbled into a faerie ring or danced under a full moon entered the Realm."

"Aye," Thomas said. "The Elder Fey will close the direct path from the game to the Realm. Now, only a handful of people who play Feyland will find themselves in the Realm of Faerie. Your task will be to watch over them. There will not be many."

Choose.

The word rolled over the Realm, moonlight and sunlight, warmth and frost, magic and despair.

Jennet's touch was warm and steady on his arm. Tam looked at the rest of the team, battered and weary. They had all been changed by this, and there was no going back, no un-knowing that the Realm of Faerie was real.

"Guys?" Tam asked, "what do you think?"

"I'm in," Roy said, some of his old confidence back in his voice.

Jennet's dad glanced at Thomas, then nodded, while Zeg inclined his head in a silent *yes*.

"Completely," Spark said.

Jennet squeezed his arm. "I'm with you. Always."

The words warmed him even more than her touch. Tam took a deep breath and tipped his face up to the leader of the Elder Fey, narrowing his eyes against the eerie light.

"All right," he said. "We agree."

The black dragon brought its wings together with a thunderclap. Its jewel-bright companions glittered in the air around it as a fierce wind swept the circle of standing stones. The purple light flared, so brightly that Tam threw his arm up to shield his eyes.

His stomach twisted. The light turned gold and he

swallowed back the sick sensation of being tumbled out of Feyland.

Tam drew in a ragged breath and lowered his arm, to find himself in his sim-chair at VirtuMax headquarters. A flashlight blared into his face.

"Mr. Linn," a hard voice said. "Not the first time we've caught you breaking and entering. You're under arrest."

JENNET COLLAPSED TO THE GROUND, the trampled grasses rising up to meet her. Her mind swam with images: black dragons etched in purple light, Tam, his mouth set, agreeing to police the boundaries between their world and the Realm, her dad clasping Thomas's shoulders and studying his face, disbelief and joy warring in his expression.

She closed her eyes, her senses humming with the aftermath of the Twilight Kingdom's invasion into the Realm. Maybe it was loss of blood, maybe it was too many clashing magics, but she felt barely connected to her body.

"Jennet?"

She opened her eyes to see Spark leaning over her. Above the brightness of Spark's magenta hair the stars of the Realm shone crisp and clear, mapping constellations she would never know.

"Can you sit up?" Spark asked.

With her help, Jennet levered herself to sitting. The clearing within the standing stones was quiet; no sign of the bitterly beautiful Dark Queen or the radiant Bright King. Puck sat cross-legged in the air, talking to the Bug. Roy and Zeg stood in the shadows, and near the flat stone her dad and Thomas were in deep conversation. The sight made her heart glow.

"Where's Tam?" She glanced around the circle, anxiety rising. Had the Dark Queen managed to steal him away?

"That's weird." Spark's eyebrows knitted together. "He was here a second ag—"

The gamer girl's Kitsune character winked out abruptly.

"Roy!" Jennet called, panic shaking through her. "Zeg, something's going on."

Roy looked up, an odd expression crossing his face. Then his avatar disappeared, too.

"It's okay," Zeg said, though his dark eyes were worried. "I think they're being pulled out—"

Empty air filled the space where he had been. Jennet clenched her hands.

"Dad?"

Her voice barely carried through the still air, but he heard it and hurried over with Thomas.

"What is it, honey?"

"Everyone's disappearing."

He glanced around, clearly surprised that they, Tam's brother, and Puck were the only ones in the circle.

"They must have logged out—and we should, too." He reached and set a hand on Thomas's shoulder. "I miss you, old friend."

Thomas smiled, his eyes brightening. "You know where to find me."

Tam's brother plucked at her sleeve. "I wanna go home!"

"Me, too." Jennet gathered him into a one-armed hug. "Puck—help us out?"

"Fear not." The sprite winked. "The youngling and the changeling will switch places—though the Bug is far better company than that sour creature you call Korrigan." He leaned close, whispering in Jennet's ear. "The boy is fey-touched. Watch over him well."

"I will." She was one of the Feyguard now, after all.

"I bid you farewell, Fair Jennet." Puck tugged a strand of her hair. "Til we meet again."

He spun himself into a series of back flips, laughing high and clear. It was the last thing she saw before golden light swirled over her senses. Dizzy, she tried to hold on to Tam's little brother, but he slipped out of her arms and was gone.

When her head stopped buzzing, Jennet blinked, surrounded by the dimness of the testing center. For some reason, the rest of the team was standing around the doorway. Arguing loudly. She ripped her helmet off and hurried over, her dad right behind her.

In the hallway, two Security guards had Tam by the arms. They waved their flashlights, the beams careening off the walls and ceiling. Jennet's heart thudded. Why were they taking Tam?

She tried to get to him, but her dad firmly pushed her aside and stepped to the front. He slid the lights on and everyone fell silent, blinking in the sudden glare.

"What's going on?" Dad asked, his voice full of authority. He turned to the nearest guard. "Why are you interrupting my beta-testing session?"

"Mr. ah…" The guard squinted at the badge clipped to her dad's shirt. "Mr. Carter. This individual has made unauthorized use—"

"He's a member of my team. Release him at once."

"I don't think so." Coranne Smith stepped from the next room, her thin lips tightened way past their usual sour expression. "What are you all doing here, Mr. Carter? Sabotage? Is this some kind of revenge against VirtuMax for demoting you?"

Jennet's dad folded his arms. "Not at all. In fact, the game is working perfectly. We just had a few final issues to take care of."

"Without me? Has it escaped your attention I'm part of the beta team as well?"

"Yeah but—" Roy began, then stopped when Zeg nudged him in the ribs.

"My apologies for not including you, Coranne," Jennet's dad said. "But we've done nothing illegal. Unusual, perhaps, but not grounds for arrest." He nodded to where Tam stood, held by Security. "Let him go. I'd hate to have to counter-sue the company for harassing one of my team members."

The two guards looked at Coranne. When she said nothing, they released Tam. He quickly slid between Zeg and Roy and put his back to the wall, well out of reach.

"Thank you, gentlemen," Jennet's dad said. "I appreciate your diligence. As you can see, we're working overtime on a crucial project. You may go."

The older guard studied the team members for a moment, then nodded. "All right. You folks have a good evening."

He swept the beam of his light over them, an intimidating move which was a lot less effective with the lights on, then headed down the hall with his partner. Their shoes squeaked faintly on the polished floor.

Coranne Smith narrowed her eyes, pinning Jennet's dad with her gaze. "This isn't over, Mr. Carter. If there is *anything* compromised in the game, I will have you fired immediately."

Roy opened his mouth again, probably to say something about his mom being the CEO. This time, Tam elbowed him.

Jennet's dad smiled with no warmth. "Then I anticipate we'll be working together for years to come."

"We'll see about that," Coranne said. "You're not the only one who can make use of the equipment late at night. Tomorrow there will be a reckoning, Mr. Carter. You may be certain of it."

She stalked forward, and the team parted to make way as she headed for the testing hub. Jennet's dad watched her go, his expression grim.

"I…" Jennet rubbed her palm. "I'm sorry, Dad."

"Let's go." His voice was suddenly tired. "Spark, I know it's late, but can we debrief at your place?"

"No problem." The gamer girl quirked her lips into a wry smile. "I keep odd hours—my people won't think anything of it."

What kind of life did Spark lead, as a celebrity simmer? The slice of it Jennet had seen seemed tame—but then again, Crestview wasn't the hotbed of anything much.

Unless getting sucked into alternate worlds counted, in which case it was action central.

The team trailed down the hall, uncharacteristically quiet.

"Coranne can't do anything to us, can she?" Jennet asked.

"Over what—beta testing like we're supposed to?" Roy shook his head. "Don't worry, none of us will get in trouble. Not even your dad."

He was probably right—he'd shown he could sweet-talk his mom into just about anything. She let out a low breath. After tonight, she didn't care what happened with the beta testing. The hardest work was done.

When the team stepped into the chilly night, she grabbed Tam's hand. After all, her dad had no more arguments for keeping them apart.

"You okay?" she asked, leaning into the warmth of Tam's body.

"Maybe." His eyes were shadowed. "Getting yanked out of game by Security was not my favorite experience."

"The team wouldn't have let them take you."

"I know." His expression remained grim, and she knew what was really worrying him.

"Tam—Puck told me your brother would be returned safely."

"He better be."

Without saying anything, she picked up the pace. The rest of the team hurried too, their breaths misting out in white plumes as they passed beneath the orange splotch of a streetlight.

"Tam... Puck did say your brother was fey-touched now."

Tam closed his eyes briefly, and she saw the burdens he carried etched on his face. His brother. His mother. Life in the Exe.

When he looked at her again, his eyes were bleak.

"I didn't tell you before," he said. "But my house is gone."

"What?" She blinked at him. "What do you mean, gone? Did Korrigan somehow destroy it?"

"No. The drifters down the street attacked us. The place is toast now." He gave a mirthless laugh. "Literally. They fire-bombed it."

"Oh god. That's terrible."

Her mind raced, grabbing possibilities, then discarding them. Even if she could get her dad to offer Tam's family a place in the View, Tam was way too proud to accept what he'd perceive as charity. But maybe, for the short-term, they could work something out.

"Our place is pretty big," she said. "I'll ask my dad—"

"No."

The outright refusal stung. "Why not? You need someplace to go."

"Jennet." He clasped her hand tightly. "Your dad had his view of reality totally wrecked tonight. He's going to have to accept a lot—and having my crazy family staying in his house is not one of them. I'll work something out."

"I'm not letting you sleep on the streets."

He gave her a crooked smile. "I know."

"Hey," Zeg said, drifting over. "About your house, Tam... you could stay in the apartment I built for Auntie

Tina. It's been empty a few months now, and needs some tending."

"I thought that was for your family," Tam said.

Zeg put one big, warm hand on Jennet's shoulder, the other on Tam's. "After tonight, we're all family."

"Say yes," Jennet urged. "Just for a little while."

Tam shook his hair out of his eyes. "If my mom says yes, then ok. Temporarily. Until we can get our place fixed up again."

Under the glow of the streetlights, Jennet caught Zeg's eye. She could tell they were both thinking the same thing—no way were they letting Tam and his family move back into the Exe.

"Heh," Roy said, clearly catching the last bit of their conversation. "Guess I can't call you Exie any more."

Tam shrugged, though his mouth curled up at the corner. "Too bad you're still stuck as a Viewer."

"Don't get too smug," Roy said. "I expect you'll be spending a lot of time up here. Watch out, it might rub off on you."

He nudged Jennet, and she batted his elbow away.

Jennet's dad caught up to them. "The beta testing isn't quite done—though I expect the rest to be uneventful."

"Let's hope," Spark said, her breath misting out in a white plume.

"VirtuMax will be offering some internships this

summer." Jennet's dad cleared his throat. "Any of you who are interested, consider yourself hired."

Spark tipped her head. "Let me check my schedule."

"Count me in," Roy said, his eyes on the gamer girl.

"Thanks," Zeg said, "but I'm pretty busy with the sim-café. Though I'd be up for gaming with the team, now and then."

None of them mentioned what it meant to be the Feyguard, but the knowledge hung in the winter air around them, crystalline and cold.

"What about you, Tam?" Jennet's dad asked.

Jennet squeezed his hand, knowing what his answer would be. Frost twinkled on the lawns like bits of scattered stars, and ahead, the lights of Spark's mansion blazed into the night.

"Maybe," Tam said, squeezing back. "Maybe I will."

<hr />

As soon as the door to Spark's place opened, Tam was inside.

"Bug?" he called, his voice echoing in the huge foyer.

"Tam!"

Footsteps slapped the marble floor. He glimpsed Marny in the hall, smiling widely, and then his little brother launched himself at Tam in a blur of grimy clothes and popsicle-breath. Tam caught him and buried his face in the Bug's hair, inhaling the familiar, beloved smell of sticky eight-year-old. Tears lodged in his throat, and he closed his eyes tight.

A gentle hand touched his shoulder, and without looking he pulled his mom into the embrace.

His family might not have any place permanent to call home, but they were here. Together.

"Let's head to the great room," Spark said. "I'll have the cook bring us tea and desserts."

The rest of the team voiced their agreement, and Tam heard them moving away. All but Jennet. He knew when he opened his eyes she'd be there, smiling at him.

And she was.

EPILOGUE

"Lines around the block at hundreds of retailers across the country prove that VirtuMax's latest is on everyone's must-have list." *The sleekly jacketed newscaster smiled while the camera panned the long line of people waiting in front of the game store.* *"Some of these eager buyers have been camping out for days, determined to be among the first to grab one of the long-awaited FullD systems."*

The door of the featured store opened, sunlight reflecting in a blinding arc from the glass, and the crowd let out a cheer.

Release day. The FullD system was for sale across the globe—and Feyland with it.

Jennet shivered and clicked off the vid feed.

"Now what?" She turned to Tam, sitting on the couch beside her in the game room.

"First, this."

He bent his head and brushed his lips over hers. She wrapped her arms around him and pulled him close, tingles racing like scattered stars through her body. He tasted of coffee and warmth and home—the heart-deep place she'd always yearned to belong.

No fey magic could ever match the rightness, the sweetness of their kisses. But they had work to do. Reluctantly, she untwined her arms.

"Did you know that Spark gave Roy her messager number?" she asked.

"Her real one?" Tam's brows went up. "I guess all of us need to stay in touch."

"Yeah, but I think Roy has a particular kind of touch in mind."

Tam laughed. "I wish him luck with that."

Then he sobered and glanced at the FullD systems humming in the center of the room. Jennet rubbed her thumb over her left palm and took a deep breath. Whatever they faced, they'd be all right.

"Ready?" she asked.

"Yes." Tam stood and pulled her off the plush couch. "Time to gear up. We've got a world to guard."

ACKNOWLEDGMENTS

Thank you to the many people who made this book better: the invaluable feedback of my terrific CP, Peggy, fabulous proof and beta-readers Sean (aka Captain Grammar Pants), Chassily, Theresa McHarney, Carol Piening, and Brynn. Thanks to Arran at Editing720 for quick, professional, and stellar work. Extra-big hugs to my in-house editor, Lawson, and keen-eyed proofreader Ginger.

And thanks in advance to Dom, who, despite my best efforts, always manages to find a couple typos and formatting issues in the print copy. (Look, you got your own paragraph.)

For an absolutely gorgeous cover (again!) huge thanks to Ravven. And for the inspiration to move forward, ongoing gratitude to all the indie and self-publishing advocates out there.

I'd also like to thank the wonderful book bloggers who provided reviews and helped this series find readers: Rebecca McKinnon of The Crooked Word, Mandy the Romance Bookie, Stephanie Asbridge of Reviewing What I'm Reading, Jen Rabey of What's on the Bookshelf (and for being a cool gamer girl), Krista of Breathe in Books, and John of Dreaming in Books. Thank you all!

I also greatly appreciate the readers who have taken the time to contact me, leave reviews, and give me reasons to keep writing. This series wouldn't be here without you.

Resources used include: Katharine M. Briggs, An encyclopedia of fairies: Hobgoblins, brownies, bogies, and other supernatural creatures and Faeries by Froud, Larkin, and Lee.

The song Jennet uses to wake the Elder Fey is *Gartan Mother's Lullaby*, an old Irish melody from Donegal, set to words attributed to Seosamh Mac Cathmhaoil, circa 1904. The song references figures in Celtic mythology, places in Ireland, and words in the Irish language.

Jennet also sings the first verse of the traditional ballad *The Water is Wide*.

Crush It is entirely of the author's devising.

OTHER WORKS

STARS & STEAM

COMETS & CORSETS

THE DARKWOOD CHRONICLES

Deep in the Darkwood, a magical doorway leads to the enchanted and dangerous land of the Dark Elves~

ELFHAME

HAWTHORNE

RAINE

HEART of the FOREST (novella)

WHITE AS FROST

BLACK AS NIGHT

RED AS FLAME

SHORT STORY COLLECTIONS

TALES OF FEYLAND & FAERIE

TALES OF MUSIC & MAGIC

THE FAERIE GIRL & OTHER TALES

THE PERFECT PERFUME & OTHER TALES

COFFEE & CHANGE

MERMAID SONG

ABOUT THE AUTHOR

Growing up, Anthea Sharp spent most of her summers raiding the library shelves and reading, especially fantasy. She now makes her home in the sunny Southern California, where she writes, plays the fiddle, and tries not to game *too* much. Visit her website at antheasharp.com, friend her on Facebook, and be the first to know about new releases and reader perks by subscribing to Anthea's new release newsletter, Sharp Tales, at www.subscribepage.com/AntheaSharp